B.K.

W9-CNU-254

THE PERFECT MATCH

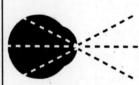

This Large Print Book carries the
Seal of Approval of N.A.V.H.

THE PERFECT MATCH

SUSAN MAY WARREN

THORNDIKE PRESS
A part of Gale, Cengage Learning

GALE
CENGAGE Learning·

Detroit • New York • San Francisco • New Haven, Conn • Waterville, Maine • London

GALE
CENGAGE Learning·

Copyright © 2004 by Susan May Warren.
Scripture quotations are taken from the *Holy Bible,* New Living
Translation, copyright © 1996. Used by permission of Tyndale House
Publishers, Inc. Carol Stream, Illinois 60188. All rights reserved.
Scripture quotations are taken from the Holy Bible, New International
Version®. NIV®. Copyright © 1973, 1978, 1984 by International Bible
Society. Used by permission of Zondervan. All rights reserved.
Thorndike Press, a part of Gale, Cengage Learning.

LP
Warren

ALL RIGHTS RESERVED

This novel is a work of fiction. Names, characters, places, and incidents
either are the product of the author's imagination or are used
fictitiously. Any resemblance to actual events, locales, organizations, or
persons, living or dead, is entirely coincidental and beyond the intent
of either the author or the publisher.

Thorndike Press® Large Print Clean Reads.
The text of this Large Print edition is unabridged.
Other aspects of the book may vary from the original edition.
Set in 16 pt. Plantin.

LIBRARY OF CONGRESS CATALOGING-IN-PUBLICATION DATA

Warren, Susan May, 1966–
 The perfect match : Deep Haven novel / by Susan May Warren.
  pages ; cm. — (Thorndike Press large print clean reads)
 ISBN-13: 978-1-4104-5052-4 (hardcover)
 ISBN-10: 1-4104-5052-X (hardcover)
 1. Volunteer fire fighters—Fiction. 2. Women fire fighters—Fiction.
 3. Stalking victims—Fiction. 4. Fire chiefs—Fiction. 5. Clergy—Fiction.
 6. Arson—Fiction. 7. Large type books. I. Title.
 PS3623.A865P47 2012
 813'.6—dc23   2012020998

Published in 2012 by arrangement with Tyndale House Publishers, Inc.

Printed in the United States of America
1 2 3 4 5 6 7 16 15 14 13 12

To my Lord
and Savior,
Jesus Christ.
Your unfailing love
sends me to my knees
in awe and
gratefulness.

259 6953
Reed Memorial Library
167 E. Main Street
Ravenna, OH 44266

ACKNOWLEDGMENTS

God never fails to surprise me with His abundant provision of encouragers, and no book is ever written without a team. I am overwhelmingly grateful for those who invested time and energy in helping me write, edit, and research *The Perfect Match*. You are all a reminder to me that we serve Him together, and He equips each of us with unique gifts that together produce something that (I hope!) brings Him glory and honor!

My deepest appreciation goes to the following people:

Olaf Growald — Texas firefighter and all-around hero. Wow, you made this book real. Your insights, gentle criticism, and time spent in figuring out how to think like an arsonist breathed life and authenticity into the fire scenes. Any errors in description are simply because I either didn't ask enough questions or didn't listen well enough!

Thank you for your patience and your friendship. You are truly a gift to my writing ministry.

Melissa Anderson — amazing sister and proofer extraordinaire. What a treasure your friendship has become to me. God knew how much I needed you, and I am so grateful for your candor, your diligence, and your encouragement. What a blessing to know that when I need it you're there with a "Sis, you rock!" I love you.

David Lund — cool brother and incredible husband to Nettie-Poo. Your encouragement has blessed me more than you will ever know. Thank you for your enthusiasm, ideas, insights, and especially your spiritual depth that continues to challenge and inspire me. God has great plans for you!

Tracey Bateman and Susan Downs — best writing buddies and iron-on-iron pals. Your laughter and teasing keep it all in perspective. Thank you for helping me unravel my tightly knotted brain at the end of the day and for just loving me despite my quirks (and you know what they are!). You two are gifts of friendship beyond compare.

Steve and Paula Geertsen — best buddies who know how to make me relax! Thank you for all the times you called us up, pizza already ordered, and helped me push away from the computer. Your friendship is salt and light to us, and we are so blessed by your love and encouragement. Thank you for always being there, for believing in me, and for standing by us during this difficult, searching year. We love you!

Tim and Nancy Ramey — inspiration and role models. I wanna be just like you when I grow up! Thank you for this new chapter in our lives and for promoting my books wherever you go. God loves the Warren family a whole lot to let us hook up with you.

Anne Goldsmith — dear friend, and, oh yeah, great editor. You're always right. Really! Thank you for the gentle way you guide me, for your wise insights, and for your incredible smile. Your friendship is a great gift to me. (And I gotta learn that karate chop!)

Lorie Popp — my appreciation for you deepens with each book. I'm so glad that God chose you for my editor. I'm so grateful for your wise touch, for the way you can take a sentence and polish it, and for your sweet friendship. You make the editing process rich!

Julie Chen — I have the best covers (for the original publisher's edition) in history. Without a doubt. Your talents blow me away, and I'm so indebted to you for your creativity. Thank you for all you invest to make the Deep Haven books works of art. Wow.

To David, Sarah, Peter, and Noah. What joy fills my heart when you plop yourselves into my chair and say, "What'cha working on now, Mom?" Thank you for believing in my dreams, for encouraging me, and for every time you say, "No, Mom, don't get up from the computer. I can get my own snack." I am so blessed to be your mother and so delighted with how God is growing you. I pray you will see His great love for you and that it will mold you into people thrilled to be His children.

And, finally, to Andrew. My Perfect Match. Thank you for loving both the Spitfire Susie and the "please-hold-me-now" gal. You will always be enough for me.

My salvation and my honor come from
God alone. He is my refuge, a rock where
no enemy can reach me.

PSALM 62:7

1

Leo Simmons had made good on his mumbled threats.

Pastor Dan Matthews stared at the pager address, and the taste of condemnation swept through him like poison — down his throat, through his blood, into his bones — and pooled in his soul.

Diving into his turnout gear, Dan tossed his fire helmet onto the front seat and gunned his VW Bug toward Leo Simmons's old log house.

Leo might have set the fire, but just as surely as if Dan had struck the match, he had ignited the explosion that brought Leo to this desperate moment.

Dan should have recognized the gathering heat, the greed, the grief, and not a little small-town shame that had fueled this inferno.

Leo's pastor had failed him.

Dan wrestled his guilt as well as the steering wheel while he floored it around Tenth Street East and screeched to a halt behind firefighter Joe Michaels's green pickup. Deathly images ravaged the night as Dan got out, buckling his helmet. He hesitated, transfixed at the flames raging through the bottom floor of the Simmonses' two-story log home. They licked out of the broken windows like the tongues of death; black smoke curled around the porch beams and spewed toxic fumes into the fall night. Despite its status as a historical site, the house sat bordered by newer homes — ramblers and bungalows — on the piece of cleared forest that had once been the old Miller homestead.

A clump of onlookers — some in bathrobes, all wearing expressions of horror — pressed against the envelope of danger, aching for a closer look.

Dan's breath came in short gulps. *Please, Lord, let the family be out!*

An explosion shook the ground as another window blew out. Flames and sparks tore the fabric of the night sky. The howl of the fire as it consumed wood and oxygen set Dan's fine neck hairs on end, reviving the analogy of fire being a living entity, needing oxygen and food to survive. It rattled Dan free and sent him running toward the Deep

14

Haven pumper engine. "Mitch!"

"Get back!" Mitch Davis yelled to the gathering gawkers. Attired in his turnout coat, bunker pants, and helmet, the captain wielded his axe like a billy club. "I said get back!"

His gaze settled on Dan before he turned back to the house and shouted commands at the other volunteers. Although Davis hadn't yet been named fire chief to replace the sudden vacancy left by Kermit Halstrom when he suffered a heart attack, the forest ranger had already moved into the position with some arrogance.

Dan raced to old engine two. Two hose lines snaked out from the truck, and Craig Boberg bent over the hydrant at the end of the block, struggling with the coupling.

The heat blasted from the house like a furnace. As Dan ran to help Joe Michaels, who battled to unhook the fifty-five-foot house ladder from the truck, his eyes began to water. "Is everyone out?"

Despite the fact that Leo had set a fire two years ago that had nearly succeeded in killing Joe's wife, Mona, Joe wore a gut-wrenching, grim look at the tragedy before him. "The first story was engulfed by the time we got here. We can't get in."

Dan's thoughts closed around Leo's family — Cindy, the baby, the boys — and he fought the grip of terror. Through the darkness, the haze of smoke and tears, he saw that the fire hadn't yet consumed the second floor, although the toxic fumes rising through the house may have already asphyxiated Leo's sleeping family.

"The second story!" He seized the end of the ladder. Joe read his mind. He hustled to the far end of the house and propped the ladder against the porch roof. Dan jumped on it nearly before Joe had a chance to secure it.

Dan heard screams as the crowd reacted to his courage.

Or stupidity. He'd left his SCBA gear beside the engine, totally abandoning every scrap of training. Fire-fighting 101: Don't go into a burning house without equipment, namely, a mask, breathing apparatus, and an axe. Safety first. But Dan's well-thought-out actions hadn't netted any outstanding successes over the past fifteen years, and now wasn't the time to ponder the choices.

It would be so much easier if he didn't have to go through life with hindsight flogging his every step. A preacher who spent less time conjuring up past scenarios might have spotted the psychotic signs in Leo's demeanor, taken seriously Leo's morbid self-depreciation and moans of "Cindy would be better off if . . ." Instead of following Leo down to the local pub to listen to his problems, gently hoping to befriend the man, a true man of the cloth would have hauled Leo out, forced coffee down his gullet, and shaken him clear of his downward spiral.

Then again, with the way Dan's words rolled off his congregation of late, he could have beat the man over the head with a hefty King James Bible and still not made an impact. The thought sent a shudder through him when he dived into the burning house to rescue Leo's family.

Jumping onto the roof, he felt profoundly grateful for the steel-toed, insulated boots that let him walk over what seemed like live coals. He had an uneasy sense that little time remained until the place exploded into a torch that would light up half the North Shore. He hoped someone had already dispatched the St. Francis Township fire crew.

But by the time they arrived, the Simmons place would be a carbonized smudge on the landscape. Dan prayed the scars wouldn't include the two boys and their little sister. His eyes burning, he staggered toward the window. Black pressed against the window . . . smoke or simply the fragments of night? He couldn't remember who slept in this room, but he hoped he'd find someone alive.

A second before he cracked his elbow into the glass pane, his firefighting science kicked in. If toxic fumes had gathered in the ceiling, raising the temperature in the room to a combustion point, the sudden inflow of oxygen would ignite a back draft that would blow him clear off the roof.

And kill whoever was inside.

He yanked his arm back. "Mitch!"

Mitch had already climbed halfway up the ladder.

"Your axe!"

Mitch barreled past him and sent the axe in hard — over his head, near the soffits of the house, next to the ceiling. Dan felt the house tremble with the blow. Three more quick blows and the room purged smoke, a stream of black, toxic fumes.

"Now!" Dan yelled.

Mitch sent the end of his axe handle into the top half of the window and cleared it in less than five seconds.

Dan gulped clean air and dived in. The smoke invaded his nose, burned his eyes, suffocating with its grip. He hadn't even worn a handkerchief, and air evaporated in

18

his lungs. Dropping to his knees, he scrabbled around the room, feeling a rocking chair, a dresser, then — oh no, a crib? Crawling up it like a prisoner begging for escape, he climbed over the edge and made his way around the bed.

A soft form. He dug his fingers into the clothing and hauled the baby over the edge, not gently, into his arms. Baby Angelica. He wanted to howl.

"C'mon!" Mitch's voice turned him around as he fell back to his knees, clutched the baby to his chest, and scrambled out. His lungs burned, now begging for air. He passed her over into Mitch's arms as black swam through his brain.

And then hands grabbed his jacket, dragged him over the window frame into the night. Joe called out to him, yanking him to semiconsciousness as someone dangled him over the roof. His hands slapped at air, and he managed to find three ladder rungs before landing on the ground, curling over and coughing out the poison in his body.

"She needs oxygen!" A woman's voice broke through the haze — he couldn't place it. It didn't sound like Anne, their volunteer EMT.

Joe crouched next to him. "Dan, you okay?"

"The . . . boys . . ." He coughed hard, feeling as if his lungs might expel from his chest.

Joe clamped him on the shoulder, squeezed.

Dan turned back to the house. Flames shot from the window of baby Angelica's room. "They're . . . in the back!" Struggling to his feet, he sprinted around the house, pinpointed the room. Black windows, no flames. "Joe, get the ladder!"

Dan rushed back to the front of the house, desperation filling him. Jordan and Jeffrey were only eight and six. The memory of their round eyes on him Sundays as he taught the children's sermon, their smiles in the face of personal sorrow had nurtured his own hope. He gripped the ladder, began to muscle it from the porch.

"No, Dan!" Joe grabbed him, dug his fingers into his turnout coat. "No!"

"Yes, Joe." Dan growled and wrenched free. Somewhere in the back of his mind, he heard common sense shouting as he ran with the ladder and bumped it up next to the back. Still, no flames.

He flew up the rungs. This time he didn't stop to vent the soffits. Adrenaline pumped into his veins, and he swung his elbow high and hard. Pain splintered through his arm while smoke roared out the opening.

He sensed the flashover two seconds before it ignited. The hiccup of time, a sudden gulp of air, as if the flame took a breath, then —

The window exploded out with the force of a land mine. Dan fell off the ladder and landed on the ground in a blinding flash of agony. His breath whooshed out, and blackness crashed over him. *So this is death.*

Somewhere on the back side of consciousness, he heard screams.

"Breathe!" A female voice, this time harsh and angry. He tried to obey, but the pain clamping his left shoulder fought him. "Breathe!" Forcing himself to inhale, he moaned in anguish.

"There you go."

He felt hands on him, feminine and strong, cupping the back of his neck, unbuckling his helmet, easing his head to the ground. "Stay still." The voice gentled, as if tempered by relief. A cool touch on his forehead brushed back his hair. "You're lucky you didn't land clear in Canada."

He wanted to smile but couldn't push past the grief that squeezed his chest. He'd killed those boys. Not only had he failed Leo, he'd failed the man's family.

His throat burned, probably from the smoke he'd inhaled. Somehow he screwed his eyes open. Through a watery haze, he watched the inferno engulf the house, flames four stories high climbing into the night, frothing black smoke. Shingles exploded off the roof; red-hot cinders and ash fell like snow around him. He tried to raise himself on his elbows and earned a fresh burst of torture. His left arm felt like a noodle at his side, and the pain nearly turned him cross-eyed.

Then he saw her, the woman who had dragged him from the house. She had turned to watch the fire, a frown on her fine-boned face. She wore two short, stubby braids and had flipped up the collar on her jean jacket, like he had on his fire coat. Almost absentmindedly, she had her hand curled around his lapel, the other pointing to some unknown sight in the flames.

A short and spunky angel. He had to wonder from where she'd materialized. She seemed to be transfixed by the fire, and something about her profile, her clenched jaw, the way she stared at the blaze with a defined sorrow nearly broke his heart. She shouldn't be here to see this. He had the sudden, overwhelming urge to cover her eyes and shield her from the horror.

She looked at him. Eyes as blue as a northern Minnesota sky speared through him with the power to pin him to the ground. "I gotta get you away from the flames. Brace yourself. This is going to hurt." She stood, clutched his coat around the collar, and tugged.

Okay, she hid serious muscles somewhere inside that lean body. He nearly roared with pain as she propelled him back, away from the shower of ash, the mist of water and smoke. She didn't even grunt.

"Who are you?" he asked in a voice that sounded like he gargled with gravel.

She knelt beside him again, pressed two fingers to his neck, feeling his pulse. "I'll go get you a stretcher," she said, not looking in his eyes.

He reached up and grabbed her wrist. "Wait . . . are you a dream?"

Ellie Karlson had seen men fly out of the sky before, but never had it wrenched her heart out from between her ribs. The way this fireman had looked at her left her feeling raw and way too tender, as if he'd hit a line drive straight to the soft tissue of her heart.

She attributed it to the fact that she'd

23

nearly lost her first firefighter — before her watch even began. At least she'd found out his name — Dan. She'd have to look up his file and figure out how many years he'd been fighting fire. He'd shown the courage of a veteran but the panic of a probie — a first-year rookie.

Ellie stopped her pacing, leaned into the hospital wall, and touched her head to the cool paint. The quiet in the ER ward pressed against her, tinder to every cell in her body that wanted to howl in frustration. Fire she could face. The somber tones of sorrow . . . she could not. The smells of antiseptic and new carpet added to the simmer of the post-fire adrenaline that never left her veins without a fight. She should go back to her hotel, do about a hundred sit-ups, or even hop on her bike for a very early morning ride.

Or maybe she could find a piano and pound out a few rounds of Chopin's Fifth. Something other than this mindless, useless pacing. She noticed a man and a woman sitting huddled against the wall across from the firefighter's room. Maybe praying. Ellie was a woman of action, and praying only seemed to slow her down. Besides, God knew her thoughts, didn't He?

She shot another glance at the man and

remembered seeing him at the fire, helping the less-than-brilliant victim in the next room. Fatigue etched into the lines on his sooty face, layered his burnished brown hair. He leaned forward, resting his elbows on his knees, fiddling with the buckle on his helmet. A woman, whom Ellie assumed was his wife, rested her head against his shoulder, her blonde hair flayed out, her eyes closed. He'd shed his turnout coat onto an adjacent vinyl chair, but even his flannel shirt looked dirty. He was probably some lumberjack down from the north woods.

A nurse, blonde pigtails belying her starched appearance, charged down the hall in their direction, shot a sympathetic look at the couple on the chairs, then entered the man's room. Ellie caught a glimpse of a white-coated doctor blocking her view before the door closed.

She might have to tackle the nurse when the woman exited. Ellie blinked back the sight, right behind her eyes, of fireman Dan flying off the roof, his arms flailing against the backdrop of flame and ash. It still caught her breath in her throat. He'd landed practically at her feet with a gut-tightening *thwunk* and an outcry of pain that echoed through the chambers of her soul.

And then he'd looked at her like she was

some sort of heavenly being — or at least an earthly dream come true. He must have jarred a few brain cells loose. She'd never been anyone's dream. Ever. Their worst nightmare, however, oh yes. She'd been called that more times than she could count. This fireman definitely wasn't the hottest spark in the fire. Fifteen years of scrabbling for respect in the very masculine world of firefighting told Ellie *no one* considered her a dream come true when she stepped over the firehouse threshold.

But she didn't care. She wasn't in town to win the firemen's affection. Respect, obedience, and loyalty, though, yes. And pacing outside this wounded firefighter's hospital room seemed a good way to seed a reputation that said she cared about her men.

Since when had she started lying to herself? The black, scuffed tread she'd worn on the floor wasn't only about gaining a foothold of respect. Something about this firefighter tugged at the soft, hidden places in her heart. Setting aside his smoky gray eyes and his bravado in the face of tragedy told her he wasn't an ordinary soul . . . then again, none of the rank-and-file firemen who deliberately threw themselves between life and death could be called ordinary. Still, something about this jakey's gutsy determination told her he would be a man to count on in a fire.

She had to meet him face-to-face, away from the raging adrenaline and confusion of a conflagration. And, truth be told, she did like hearing his crazy, pain-filled words. Even if they'd die the second she introduced herself.

The door to his room opened. The nurse strode out.

Ellie was hot on her tail. "Is he going to be okay?" Her voice sounded exactly like the person she'd become. Hard. Demanding. Blunt. She wanted to cringe, then decided that she might need to build her reputation in this town on those merits.

The nurse stopped, turned. Her blue eyes considered Ellie with the slightest edging of sympathy. "Who are you?"

"Concerned bystander." Ellie offered a slight smile. It wasn't exactly a lie, but dodging the truth always made her feel grimy.

"The doctor will be out soon. But, yes, I think our pastor will be out in time to preach on Sunday."

Pastor? Ellie's mouth opened, and she knew she looked like an idiot standing there, turning pale, as the nurse walked away. This wide-shouldered, face-death-with-a-roar fireman was a pastor?

27

Of course. She should have guessed it.

In a flash of memory, she saw another man — no, a *boy* — his ponytail flying, careening over the rutted dirt of a fire camp on a pair of roller skis while attached to the bumper of a convertible VW Bug by a water-ski line. His laughter still echoed in the canyons of her heart. *Oh, Seth.*

Why was it that all the heart-stopping, real-life heroes in her life belonged to God? That realization doused the tiny flame of hope that had ignited deep inside.

She resumed her pacing, meeting the gazes of the huddled couple as she stalked by. The hall clock ticked out the next ten minutes in merciless eternal seconds. Ellie nearly flattened the doctor when he emerged, tucking his pen into his jacket. He stopped in front of the couple and shook the lumberjack's hand, a smile on his face.

"He's a lucky one, Joe," the doc said. "Just a few minor burns and a dislocated shoulder."

Ellie nosed up to the group and didn't flinch at the doctor's hard look. "Just checking on him," she said. "Can I see him?"

"Well, I guess —," the doctor started.

Ellie didn't wait. She barged into Dan's room.

Even with his arm in a sling, his right

28

cheek blistered and swollen, and shadows etched under his eyes, he still had the ability to stop her dead in her tracks. Maybe it was that tousled, dark brown hair or perhaps those lazy gray eyes that latched onto her with more than a little interest. Her disobedient heart did a tiny jig when he gave her a lopsided smile.

"So," he said, "are you a dream?"

Oh, she could be in big, big trouble. For a second, she wanted to pull up a chair, dive into his friendship, and delay the inevitable. He seemed to have the unsettling ability to wheedle past her defenses and find her lonely places. She feared Dan the Pastor might have the power to make a girl chuck her life goals, unpack her suitcase, and paint her name on a mailbox. Solid, wise, and just a little bit of a rapscallion. A man who respected her, who thought she might be, indeed, a dream come true.

Except she couldn't be that girl. Not with a bevy of promises pushing against her, keeping her on the run.

Besides, once she told him the truth, the antagonism would begin. She knew too well — the shock, the disapproval, and finally the cold wall that would come with her announcement.

If she hoped to etch a toehold of respect

29

in this backwoods community, it would have to start at this hero's bedside.

"No. I'm a very real and slightly angry reality, fireman. What were you doing on that roof?" She crossed her arms, neatly shielding her heart, and watched his smile vanish.

"Excuse me?"

"You risked your life and the lives of your fellow firemen. Thankfully, no one was behind you, but by not waiting to vent that room, you could have killed my entire crew."

"Your what — wait . . . just who *are* you?" He frowned, and somehow it only added to the wounded-hero effect.

She took a deep breath. "Ellie Karlson. Interim fire chief."

His mouth opened for the shock phase. She debated smiling, but she'd need all her stoic arsenal for phase two. . . .

"No way. You can't be — I mean, a firefighter has to be —"

"A shapely version of a man? A knuckle dragger in high heels?" She arched one eyebrow. "Have hairy fists and dangling nose hair?"

He looked properly chagrined, and she knew she'd hit the bull's-eye. Why did men always think that a woman doing a job that required courage, strength, and stamina had to be built like a tank? Still, now that she'd doused him with the cleansing reality, she should add some painkiller to the wound. Perhaps it would ward off phase three — the big chill.

"I'm not what many people expect. But I assure you, I know what I'm doing." She sat in the chair beside the bed, reached out, and touched his slung arm. "And, for the record, I was impressed by your dedication. We're about saving lives, and you risked your life for that family. Next time, take a partner and your axe and SCBA gear."

He stared at her with a potent mix of horror and disbelief. O-kay, so maybe he'd hit the ground harder than she thought. "It could have been much worse," she offered. "Be thankful you lived through it."

"Too bad the little boys didn't." When he clenched his jaw, she thought she saw tears glaze his eyes.

"But you saved them," she said, confused.

His gaze shot back to her.

"Yes. When you vented the fire, flames ran to the oxygen. The fireball that knocked you off the ladder kept the fire from tracking to the other side of the house. They found the boys and their mother in an upstairs bedroom."

"Are they — ?"

She had the wild desire to run her hand

along that whiskered jaw that seemed one shave away from his respectable position of town pastor.

Suddenly, painfully, he reminded her of a man now dancing through heaven.

Ellie clasped her hands firmly in her lap. "They're in intensive care . . . but . . . well, it doesn't look good." She tried to soften the blow by gentling her voice. She never had adapted well to this aspect of her job.

He nodded, as if he expected the news, and again looked away. "It's all my fault, you know."

She frowned, not clear at his words, noticing how he'd bunched the covers in his right fist. "Yes. But it worked. Not a technique I'd employ, but hindsight is sometimes the best vision, especially in firefighting."

He met her words with his own frown, making her pulse race. *Calm down,* she thought. She'd been surrounded by burly hero types her entire life, starting with her father's fire buddies to her brother's chums to her own fire-crew cronies. This guy wasn't any different than every other jakey. She would just have to get used to those mesmerizing eyes and intriguing smile. Besides, he was probably married . . . but where was his wife? Her gaze flickered down to his hand, now strapped to his chest. No ring.

That could mean nothing. Plenty of firemen took off their rings before a fire. The metal attracted heat. Still, any wife in her right mind would be pacing the corridors with worry, if not standing at the foot of his bed, directing traffic.

She would.

"So, let me get this straight," he said in a voice that sounded slightly . . . angry? "You're Deep Haven's new fire chief?"

Perhaps he hadn't jostled any brain cells in that fall — how could he with his brain packed in an outer case of granite? Hadn't he heard a word she'd said?

"As I live and breathe. I heard the fire on my scanner and hustled over, hoping I could help." She refused to sound apologetic.

He gave her a look — sad, disgusted, horrified — that sucked her back in time and made her feel like the rebellious teenager who'd hitchhiked to Colorado to keep up with her big brother.

It raised her ire like static electricity. Oh, please — they didn't live in the dark ages. Women had been fighting fires on crews for over a hundred years starting with Molly Williams in 1818. Cro-Magnon man needed to enter the twenty-first century.

"Help?" he said in a one-word, caveman grunt.

Maybe she should simplify things, speak slowly, use small words . . . "Listen, bub, I'm here to fight fires and to keep you out of trouble."

Yes, he'd definitely just emerged from the big thaw, for Mr. Tall, Dark, and Neanderthal looked at her with a chauvinistic gleam in his eye and in a low growl tossed aside one hundred years of women's rights.

"Over my dead body."

2

The words were out before he could snatch them back. *Over his dead body?* Where had that come from? Last time he'd spoken those words, he'd been staring down spunky Charlene Richardson, trying desperately to keep his world from crumbling.

"Wait, I didn't mean that," Dan said. "I mean . . . I did . . . but, well . . . *you're* the new fire chief?"

"Do you need to see it in writing?" Her eyes flashed like lightning across a stormy sky.

"Uh . . . maybe that would be helpful."

When she pounced to her feet, Dan felt his chest tighten. With her feet planted and her hands perched on her hips, Ellie suddenly reminded him of everything he'd lost one sunny spring day nearly fifteen years before. What was wrong with him? He was an emancipated male and was all for women working in positions of responsibility, even danger.

Well, *most* women. It seemed particularly unfair that God would again send him someone who looked heartbreakingly cute with axle grease — or soot — on her chin.

"Just gimme a second here to catch up," he said, attempting to calm Ellie's ire with a smile. "I banged my head pretty hard."

"You've got all the time in the world, Pastor."

He swallowed back a choking pain and told himself that Chief Ellie Karlson was *not* the love of his life, nor would she ever rip his heart into a thousand ugly pieces.

"Okay . . . I admit that I'm not scoring many points here," Dan said, trying to ignore the throb of old wounds. "But I'm on the town council and don't remember hiring anyone for that position."

"It's an interim job. Your town manager called our district. I'm filling in until you find your permanent chief."

Oh, boy, wait until Mitch discovered this tidbit of news. There'd be sparks flying in town hall in the morning.

"Pardon my shock, Miss Karlson, but I have this sick feeling that I'm the only one who knows this."

Her mouth opened slightly, and in that instant he saw the slightest flint of fear. It

36

had the effect of a spark on the tinder on his protective urges, an impulse he thought he'd extinguished years ago.

Then she sighed, as if fatigue had brushed over her. When she spoke, gone was the defense, the sarcasm. "Well, then I guess you're the lucky first to find out." Rubbing her forehead with a grimy hand, she sat in the chair again. She looked so utterly fragile in that moment, he again felt the wild impulse to take her hand or pull her into his arms.

"Listen," she said, her voice weary, "I know that having a woman fire chief rubs against the default masculine ego, but I have an MA in management, ten years of experience, and a degree in fire science. I don't expect to fill the shoes of Chief Halstrom, but I promise I'll do my best to make sure you have the latest training and equipment to do your job. You don't have to like me, but I'd appreciate your support."

Not *like* her? Over an hour ago, as she'd brushed the hair back from his face and felt for his pulse, he'd experienced emotions that bordered on boyish, teenage infatuation. But perhaps she was dead-on — he didn't like the idea of a woman at the helm of the fire station. Not that he doubted her abilities — her quick litany told him she knew more about fighting fire than Smokey Bear. But the thought of her wielding an axe or even facing heats that rose to twelve hundred degrees made him wince.

When had it become a crime to want to protect a woman? After all, hadn't God charged men with treating the fairer sex with gentleness? And this woman, with her high cheekbones, tawny brown hair in Pippi Longstocking braids, and small-yet-solid frame seemed indeed fair.

"You're just . . . not what I expected," he said in a low tone. "And something about you running into a fire doesn't sit right with me."

"Yeah, I caught that. But guess what; life isn't what we expect, is it? It twists and turns, and we never know how it will end up until we get there. All we can do is hold on and hope we survive. Hope that some-how what we've done has made a difference along the way."

The slight tremble of her jaw belied the tough-as-an-armadillo demeanor she wanted to convey. He frowned at her words.

"And the difference I'm going to make is to teach you guys how to save lives." Her voice tightened, taking with it the vulner-ability from her expression. Raising her hands, she closed them into tiny fists that betrayed frustration. "I might be a woman, but I've worked hard for this chance. I nearly had to get on my knees and beg for this job, and I'm not going to lose it to a religious he-man who can't see beyond my braids to my brains."

His gray matter worked to find words, but somehow her impassioned expression took the breath right out of his chest.

Her eyes darkened. "You know, for a pastor, I was kind of expecting a 'Wow, you're right. I am a hardheaded lug' or maybe a 'How are you settling into Deep Haven? Would you like some help?' or even 'Thanks for pulling my stupid body out of the flames.' " Her sassy sarcasm had returned, along with a one-hand-on-her-hip pose that screamed, "You slimeball."

"Uh, well . . . I'm not real keen on the hardheaded lug option . . ."

Was she actually glaring at him? It had been a while since a woman did that. Even the choir director at church disguised her glares with a wry grimace.

She blew out another breath. "Okay, maybe I should rewind and do this over. Keep it short and sweet." She stood and extended her hand. "Hello. The name is Chief Karlson. I'm your new boss, and if I ever catch you doing a lamebrain stunt like that again I'll kick you off the force so fast you'll get windburn. Okay?" She raised one soft brown eyebrow and waited for him to shake her hand.

He wanted to shake *her.* "Listen, I didn't mean —"

Three sharp raps on the door, and then it opened, halting Dan's words. He pinned Ellie with a scowl as Joe Michaels and his wife sauntered in. Dan wrinkled his nose against the smell of smoke. "Hey," he said, forcing a smile.

"You look like a piece of toast," Joe said and shook Dan's hand.

Mona curled her fingers around Joe's forearm and held his turnout coat over her other arm. The petite blonde looked nearly as tired as her husband, her hair in tangles, her green eyes etched in worry.

Dan reached out and found her hand. "Thanks for visiting me, Mona. I know you're tired these days."

She rewarded him with a smile. "I'm nearly out of the morning-sickness stage, so I'm feeling much better. Besides, I'll sleep in tomorrow and make Liza bake the muffins." Mona shared her Victorian bookstore and coffee shop with a potter who added spice to the town of Deep Haven. More than once Dan had contemplated asking

Liza out. But truth be told, Liza Beaumont, with her wild bangle earrings and flamboyant style, scared him just a little.

He needed someone who would blend with the rhythm of Grace Church and with Dan's own low-gear speed. He didn't know exactly who, but the standard Proverbs 31 description came to mind, along with the word *docile.*

"Doc says you're going to be okay, but I nearly had a heart attack when you flew off that ladder," Joe said.

"Get in line," Ellie said dryly, her arms folded. Her eyebrow raised in silent reproach.

Joe shot her a brow-furrowed look.

"Joe, Mona, this is Ellie Karlson." For elaboration, Dan couldn't decide between saying "our new boss" or the more revealing "the most recent thorn in my flesh." He opted for, "She pulled me out of the fire."

Joe shook her hand, introducing himself and Mona as local bookstore owners and neatly omitting his status as a best-selling author under the pen name of Reese Clark. With Joe's down-to-earth demeanor and his usual faded jeans, Dan more easily pictured Joe as Mona's handyman than the slick wordsmith featured on the back of Reese's hardcovers.

"Thanks for your help," Joe said to Ellie. "Although I should say that next time you shouldn't be so close to the fire. You could have been hurt." He smiled as if to soften his rebuke. "You don't look familiar to me. Are you new in town?"

Funny, although Dan had known her for the space of ten minutes, he could nearly see Ellie's gears clicking, formulating a response. He wondered what would win — diplomacy or her cutting wit. He had the sudden urge to throw his body in front of Joe before the guy got shredded.

She shocked Dan completely with a wide smile that seemed a thousand times friendlier than anything he'd received. He couldn't deny a confusing spark of jealousy. "Thank you. That's good advice. And . . . uh . . . yes. I just moved here. Got a new job." Her eyes raked over Joe's attire, flickered at Mona, and then landed back on Dan. She grinned. This time he saw a gleam in her eyes that felt downright predatory. He wanted to pull the covers over his head and hide.

"What kind of job?" Joe asked.

Ellie took a deep breath, and that resigned, somber look returned to her face, this time without her defensive battlements. Obviously she reserved her bark and bite for the town pastor. Still, had he expected to win her affection with his "over my dead body" outburst? He suddenly felt like a jerk.

"I'm a firefighter. I heard the alarm on my scanner, and I thought I could help."

Joe quirked an eyebrow.

Dan rolled his eyes. "Joe, this is our new fire chief."

For the space of several seconds, Joe just stared unblinking at Ellie. Then, with a warm smile, the man transformed into Benedict Arnold and said, "Welcome to Deep Haven, Ellie. Glad to have you at the helm."

Dan wanted to strangle the guy with his IV line.

Ellie slowed her Jeep Wrangler as she drove by the steaming, charred remains of the log cabin. With her canvas window open, the night wind carried the pungent smells of burnt wood, melted plastic, and scorched fabric. The two responding fire crews had managed to stop the blaze before it burned to the footings, but nothing easily recognizable remained inside the charred timbers. A few hearty firemen were still layering the house with water, preventing any embers from sparking. Through the broken windows, she watched firemen slogging through

43

the patches of water and steam, turning over singed furniture and other larger pieces with their fire rakes during overhaul inspection. At least they were thorough . . .

And tough. She'd watched this ragtag volunteer crew go at what in Duluth would have been a three-alarm fire with nothing more than two old water hoses and sheer guts. Their courage stomped her recriminations to a fine powder when she remembered how they'd risked their lives to pull a baby, two little boys, and their mother from the clutches of the blaze. If the family survived, Ellie would count it as a miracle. She hadn't even thought to check on the baby girl she'd helped revive. She wondered how a baby with her special condition would fare if she lost her mother.

The sheriff's department had its own group inspecting the scene, and Ellie noticed the coroner's van, obviously here to collect the remains of the lone casualty. Although he'd been burned beyond recognition, she'd managed to pick up a few particulars from Joe, Mona, and Dan before leaving the hospital — particulars like the man's criminal history of arson and Dan's gut suspicion that the blaze was premeditated.

The night had turned lavender as the sun

forced its way into the morning. Ellie felt like she'd pedaled about thirty miles, all uphill. Her muscles strummed with fatigue, and her brain was trying to push its way through her frontal lobe. Soot and dirt covered her jeans and probably her face, and her hair had unraveled out of her braids. She had no doubt she looked like an unkempt campfire girl. Obviously now was not the time to introduce herself to the local law. She needed a groomed, starched appearance and a demeanor that screamed "Chief." Not that she felt particularly comfortable being typecast as that, but until they learned to respect her years of training, her knowledge, and her fire savvy, the external trappings of "capable" would have to do.

She'd fought enough fire-station machismo to know that she'd have to keep her chin up and her skin thick to earn her status. No emotions. No fears. Especially no tears. If she wanted her firefighters to obey when she told them what and where to attack, she had to be tougher, stronger, quicker, and braver than the men she served. No one needed to know that inside she felt like she had the first day she showed up at the Colorado fire camp, a naïve teenager, wondering what she'd signed up for.

Dan's words rang in her head: *I have this sick feeling that I'm the only one who knows this.* Perhaps now, while the cinders cooked and the need for decent leadership heated the air, was the perfect time to alert the local law to her arrival. If this little town was stereotypical, news of her appearance would be among the top headlines in the morning paper anyway.

Pulling in across the street, she gulped a breath for courage and climbed out of the Jeep.

The smell of ash and the breath of water moistened the air. She strolled up to a man dressed in a gray police uniform and a black down jacket. He stood watching the medical examiner team-bagging the victim, a twisted look on his face.

"Excuse me," she said quietly, standing slightly behind him. "Are you the chief of police?"

He turned, his dark eyes more concerned than threatening. "Can I help you?"

Ellie forced her hand out, complete with a smile. "Ellie Karlson. I'm the interim fire chief."

She had his full attention now, along with a disheartening scowl.

"I hope Romey mentioned me." She recalled at least three conversations with the Deep Haven mayor, and in the last one she could nearly *hear* him telling her he'd informed the city police. "I just arrived tonight."

The man recovered well, took her hand, gave it a solid shake. "Sam Watson, chief of police. And, yes, I guess Romey did mention that he was sending someone my way." His gaze traveled over her quickly, and when he met her eyes again, a smile hinted on his face. "You weren't the someone I was expecting, but I'm glad to have you aboard."

Then he turned to the steamy shell of the Simmons home. "Your timing is uncanny. Did you see the fire?"

Ellie scrambled to unglue her tongue from her mouth. No gasps? No sneers? No "over my dead body" comments? "Yes. I heard it on my scanner. I went with one of the firemen to the hospital."

The chief nodded. "I heard Dan was injured. How's he doing?"

She stepped up next to him and buried her hands in her jeans-jacket pockets. Early morning on the North Shore in September carried with it the anxious breath of winter. She shivered. "Had a dislocated shoulder. They set it and I think he's going to be fine." Well, his *body* would recover. She wasn't so sure about his mind. Why had he

47

attacked her? So far, three out of four Deep Haveners had welcomed her with kindness. Did she emit some sort of odorous pheromone that caused the town pastor to rear up on his hind legs like a grizzly and come out slashing?

"Dan seems to think the fire was set by the victim. He evidently has a history of arson?"

The chief scowled, his lips tight. "Spent two years in county lockup for arson. Got out a month ago on parole."

"Has he had a hard time fitting back into life?"

Sam nodded slowly. "I thought he'd been pulling out of it, however. Smoky Joe's BBQ gave him a job, and I saw him in church last week." He sighed. "Guess we don't see these things coming, huh?"

Ellie frowned. "Thing is, the typical arsonist has a fascination with fire. A sort of love-hate relationship. A suicide burn doesn't fit the profile."

"Well, Leo didn't fit the standard profile. He was sloppy, and we caught him nearly red-handed, running from the fire he'd set."

"Strange. Most arsonists enjoy watching their handiwork — even have a sense of disappointment or grief when the fire is extinguished. Running isn't usually their standard reaction. How was this fire set?"

"He doused some garbage outside the house with gasoline and set it ablaze."

"Sounds like a crime of passion more than the work of an arsonist."

Chief Sam watched with a grim set of his jaw as the ME toted Leo's body to the van. "Maybe the fire was accidental."

Ellie let herself feel the pain in his voice. An accidental fiery death of a man convicted of arson. The scenario felt . . . convenient. And she couldn't escape the irony. If it had been accidental, fate had surely enacted its revenge.

That thought felt like a blow right to the sternum. She didn't want to imagine how fate might repay *her* mistakes.

Thankfully, her life and Leo's weren't in the hands of fate. Which, in Leo's case, pushed this inferno into the realm of suspicion.

"I'm going to swing by tomorrow in the light of day and nose around, see what I can find. Fires usually leave some sort of signature." Ellie turned again toward the chief, hand outstretched. "Thanks —"

"Hey, you!" The strident voice held fatigue and not a small amount of fire-induced hoarseness. Ellie whirled and saw one of the firemen striding toward her. Being over six feet, he held a fire axe like a toothpick, and his soot-streaked face added menace to his appearance. The look he gave her felt invasive, even predatory. "Don't I know you?" The way he said it made her glad that he didn't.

She drew herself up. "I don't think so. Your name is?"

"Mitch Davis. Captain." He frowned at her, as if disbelieving her words. "You were at the fire."

Ellie nodded slowly, pretty sure his words leaned toward accusation.

His face darkened further, defying the impossible. "I don't know what you were thinkin', but don't ever run into a fire scene again. You could have been killed. And the last thing we need is spectators —"

"Mitch, this is —," Chief Sam started.

"— getting in the way of our job."

"— the new fire chief."

Mitch stared at Chief Sam like he'd been backhanded. He blinked. And then Ellie's worst expectation materialized in his expression. His face screwed up in disbelief and maybe horror.

"What?"

Even the police chief took a step back.

Ellie nearly stuck out her hand in a peace-making gesture but then guessed she might lose it to the fire axe. "Fire chief. Interim." Fury gathered at the way this man had reduced her to sentence fragments. Ellie blew out a breath, raised her chin. "I know it comes as a bit of a shock, but, yes, I'm here to fill in until you find your permanent replacement."

If looks could kill, she'd be a smoking pile right where she stood. Then, lifting his axe in a movement that sent ice through Ellie's veins, he pointed it at her. "We'll see about that." Flicking a death look at Chief Sam, Mitch turned and stalked back to the scene.

She forced herself to exhale. "That went well."

Chief Sam looked at her, and a slow smile slid up his face. "I think you're going to fit in just fine here, Miss Karlson."

Later, as she slowly motored past the tragedy traced by steam in the wee light of morning, the police chief's kind words cushioned her fatigued brain. Round two with the town law had gone significantly better than the warm-up event with the town's religious representative. Perhaps she should have gone with her instincts and tried to befriend Dan first, then eased into her announcement with grace and finesse.

Except the pastor hadn't been the older but kinder chief of police. He'd been a devastatingly handsome fireman who boldly announced she was a dream. Wow, did that feel good. But she'd do well to remember that despite her deepest, most hidden wishes, she couldn't afford to let her heart off its leash. Even for friendship. The minute she started investing emotionally into her firemen, beyond professional comradery, was the minute she compromised everything for which she'd slaved. Over the years she'd had her share of offers . . . from marriage to a few proposals that would have made even her father blush. But she'd handled them with the icy demeanor of a woman who knew that the second she let herself fall into a fireman's arms was the second she put his life in danger. Instead of concentrating on his job, he'd channel his energies into protecting her. She'd attended enough funerals to know she didn't want to be at the receiving end of a folded flag.

One black dress was enough.

Even her oratory to the town preacher about making a difference could return to haunt her. It sounded a bit too desperate. And, from her limited experience, desperate information was nothing but bait to a man of the cloth. The last thing she needed was Dan donning his pastor garb and peeking inside her soul. Not that she'd let him anywhere near her. His growled threat still rang in her ears. *Over his dead body?* How did a man with the sensitivity of a bullfrog ever get to be a pastor? She'd wanted to slug him. The man sounded like an echo from her past . . . something she'd spent over a decade learning how to dodge.

"Seth, *you* think I'm making a difference, right?" she said into the sky, into the expanse beyond the darkness where the stars still flickered despite the onslaught of morning. Angry tears edged her eyes and she clenched her jaw. Fatigue and two ugly emotional battles had obviously pushed grief to the surface.

She'd simply let Preacher Dan get under her skin. Something about him seemed a little too smug, too invasive. Too he-man. Next time, she'd double her defenses when he walked into her airspace.

She turned onto Main Street, cruised past dark and forlorn houses angled along the shoreline, and finally pulled up next to the Gull's Roost Hotel. Its wavy, sunken porch hinted at past battles with the lake, and the whitewashed building spoke of anything but elegance and comfort. But the moment Ellie saw the place, complete with a front porch that overlooked Lake Superior and promised a spectacular sunrise, she knew

53

she'd found her home. Temporarily, at least. And pending a serious fire inspection. But for now it was cheap, close to the fire station, and allowed her only friend to bunk with her.

Franklin. She hoped the basset hound hadn't woken, discovered her absence, and howled out his frustration.

Climbing out of the Jeep, she headed into the lobby. The desk clerk had set out a Ring for Service sign, so Ellie tiptoed up the stairs, grimacing at a loose floorboard that groaned under her clandestine arrival.

She had the first room on the left — the "honeymoon suite." She eased the door open, locked it behind her, and headed to the bathroom. Thankful that the old hotel had at least updated the bathroom amenities, she stood in the shower, adjusting the spray on the nozzle to all three settings before she felt the stress finally begin to peel off.

After wrapping herself in an old terry robe, she turned off the lights and sat on the corduroy sofa by the window overlooking the lake. Franklin had opened one saggy eye the moment she walked into the room. Now he stood, stretched, and moseyed over to her feet, where he flopped in a fresh heap and sighed. She smiled and rubbed him behind his ears. "I couldn't agree more."

The sun now tipped the waves with fingers of rose gold. A flock of gulls slept on the outcropping that rimmed the bay. The smell of lake water and autumn scented the air, despite the hint of a bakery preparing its morning offerings. "Am I making a difference, Seth?" she repeated softly into the silence.

But she heard no answer in the hollow of her soul.

3

Dan stood in the hallway, dressed in the flimsy gown and bathrobe the hospital provided, staring into the intensive care unit. Tubes, monitors, and IV lines dwarfed the tiny forms of Jordan and Jeffrey Simmons. He watched their chests rising and falling with the life-support systems, and the center of his throat felt raw and thick.

Sighing, he shuffled up to the nurses' station. Sandra, one of his favorite church members, sat at the desk, a pen shoved above her ear, working on the computer. "Hey, there," he said softly.

She looked up and smiled. "What are you doing out of bed?"

"Can't sleep."

"Are you in pain?"

He didn't quite know how to answer that question. His shoulder ached as if someone had taken a sledgehammer to it, but that pain couldn't touch the gaping wound in his heart. It almost eased his inner agony every time his shoulder spasmed. "Where's Angelica?"

Sandra nodded, as if understanding his artful dodging. "Down the hall. In pediatrics."

Dan pushed his IV pole ahead of him as he strode down the hall to the pediatric wing. *Please let her be okay.* The four small rooms that made up the pediatric corner of the rural hospital smelled strongly of cleanser, cotton, and medicines. The wall had been papered in bears up to the chair rail, and the nurse for this section, Kelly Peterson, wore a smock in a similar pattern. She looked up from her desk. "Hey ya, Pastor. Are you looking for the Simmons baby?"

He nodded, not quite sure how to read Kelly's sad expression. Generally, most people wore a sorrowful, accepting look when discussing Angelica. Dan often felt a strange need to sling his arm over the baby's mother's shoulder to bolster her brave smile. But now, perhaps Nurse Peterson's sad expression had to do with Angelica's dire condition.

He steeled himself as he approached her room. An IV line and the monitor cables draping into the crib seemed odd accessories to the pastel flannel pads and blanket. Angelica lay on her back, eyes closed, a tube taped to her open mouth. Her long lashes and gentle breathing belied the trauma she'd suffered.

"How is she?" Dan asked Kelly, who'd followed him into the room.

"Better. She's down to 70 percent oxygen, and we're just waiting to see if any infection sets in. So far, she's fared better than we hoped and she continues to improve."

He reached into her crib, touched her tiny, velvety hand. The fingers didn't close nor did she even twitch.

"We have her sedated so she won't dislodge her oxygen tube."

"She doesn't have much movement as it is." Although nearly sixteen months old, the baby seemed like rubber, her muscles soft and refusing to propel her into movement. Cindy Simmons had handled the slow development of her Down syndrome child with great courage. She believed that God had gifted her daughter to her, especially since Angelica had been born a few months after Leo's incarceration. Dan had learned more about faith watching Cindy than he had studying for any of his sermons.

"I'm sorry, little girl," he said softly. Tears blurred his eyes, and he swallowed before they spilled down his cheeks. "I promise to make sure you're okay." Even if I failed your father. He gulped a deep breath. "I'll do right by your family, little one." He turned to Nurse Kelly. "Will you keep me posted on her condition?"

She gave him a grim smile and nodded.

He returned to his room and spent the next four hours in restless slumber. Dr. Simpson arrived sometime after Dan's tasteless breakfast and declared him fit for discharge. Thankfully, Joe showed up during Dan's exam with appropriate attire shoved into a paper bag. Dan wrestled himself into his shirt, left one arm dangling, and was grateful his friend thought of bringing track pants instead of something with a zipper.

Dan felt like he'd been run over by a cement mixer. Still, he wanted to hit something hard when Sandra appeared with a wheelchair.

"I've got legs."

"So you do," Sandra answered politely. "Use them to walk over here and plop yourself in this chair."

"Not a chance." He stood and made to dash for the door, but Joe stopped him.

"You want your walking papers, you gotta take the ride," Sandra said, smiling as if she was taking pleasure in seeing him humiliated.

"C'mon, Dan. I'll drive." Joe gave him a sassy grin.

"Thanks, but one dislocation is enough." Dan levered himself into the chair and slouched as Sandra steered him out of the room and down the hall. He didn't look up until he reached the front doors.

"Now, don't forget your appointment with Dr. Simpson on Tuesday," Sandra said before she wheeled the chair away.

Dan thanked the nurse and pushed open the door. Less than twenty-four hours in the hospital and he felt like a prisoner on parole. Free at last. A fresh autumn breeze and a sky filled with sunshine and cirrus clouds greeted him like a friend.

His thoughts turned to his to-do list, which could knock him to his knees. He had another wall to build on his house, his sermon to review, and about five telephone calls to make, not including the call to social services about Cindy Simmons. She had been airlifted to a Duluth hospital with burns over 40 percent of her body. Evidently they'd found her in the hallway of the burning cabin, probably scrabbling to find the telephone. Even if Angelica and the boys pulled through, they'd have to have temporary homes until Cindy recovered.

"Do you want to head home?" Joe held the hospital bag full of Dan's turnout coat, his bunker pants, and steel boots. "How about stopping at the Footstep for a cup of java? We have a new mix in — it's from Thailand. And Mona's trying out a recipe for scones." He grimaced in playful humor. "I have to confess that the last batch was pretty iffy. I told her to paint them and put them in Liza's store as Lake Superior rocks." Joe laughed at his own joke.

"No, thanks," Dan said, "although the offer is *so* tempting." He made a face that said otherwise. "Actually, I have to get up to the house. Need to put up the south wall."

"Not with that shoulder, pal. I heard the doc. No movement for at least five days. You'll have to wait."

"I can't. I need the place roofed in by winter." Two years ago Dan had acquired a choice piece of property overlooking the lake and just this summer, after trading in his SUV for a cheaper 1974 VW Bug, broke ground for a two-bedroom cabin. Admittedly, the project felt a bit like scaling Mount McKinley on his hands and knees, but he'd laid the foundation and had the two longest walls framed and standing. If

61

he could put the trusses up and nail down the roof before winter, he'd tarp it over and work on the interior while the January wind howled.

Joe tossed Dan's bag of gear into the back of his pickup. "Tell you what. You sit tight for a few days, let that shoulder heal, and I promise to spend the next three Saturdays as your framing slave."

Dan laughed, earning a spur of pain in his shoulder. Maybe he should accept Joe's offer. "I thought you're in the middle of a new book. I don't want to cut into your creativity." He rolled his eyes and lilted his voice as he said it.

Joe glared at him. "Watch it, Dan. I may know how to weave a few words together, but don't forget who scored on you during last week's hockey game."

"Lucky shot. It bounced off the pipes. Besides, goalie isn't my regular post."

"That was obvious." Joe fired up the truck and backed out. "I don't suppose you'll be up for tonight's game? We're going to be two short, what with Leo . . ." His voice trailed off into a grim silence.

Dan blew out a breath of remorse that lumped in the deepest part of his soul. Why hadn't he seen Leo's desperation? He'd followed Leo to the Lucky Seven only two weeks ago, sat next to him, and drank a Coke while the man washed down three whiskey shots and half a bottle of beer. Dan gently combated Leo's sour mood with snatches of Scripture or testimony from his own journey through sorrow. He thought his words had found fertile soil, even through Leo's liquor fog. At least Leo had showed up for their weekly pickup hockey game stone sober and hadn't headed back to the pub after the match. Moreover, he hadn't spotted Leo's gray pickup parked at the town watering hole during Dan's irregular drive-bys during the week. And hadn't Cindy reported that Leo had landed a job at Smoky Joe's BBQ restaurant?

Dan had rejoiced in small victories too early, it seemed. He should have followed his gut instinct and visited the man. Perhaps he'd relied too heavily on the gentle nudging of the Holy Spirit instead of raining down a dose of good old-fashioned fire and brimstone on Leo's self-destructive behavior.

He should have made sure Leo stayed clean, his thoughts on reality instead of locked in the guilt of the past.

Then again, sometimes reality felt like a hard chop to the knees.

"No, I'm going to make myself a Denver

omelet and work on my sermon," Dan said quietly. Maybe some time in the Word would give him both perspective and comfort. Lately he sometimes felt as if he'd be more effective slapping a puck around or fighting fires or even sweeping floors in the local pub than preaching the Word of God. He should spend his Friday praying for help — maybe a new spiritual insight into the health of the souls in his congregation. Why couldn't he be more like Oswald Chambers or even C. S. Lewis — inspiration pouring from every sentence?

Maybe he needed a helpmate. That thought had nagged him more than once over the past year. Weren't women sensitive to the needs of a congregation? Suddenly the image of Ellie Karlson, local interim fire chief and porcupine, flashed through his mind. Oh yeah, she was a regular June Cleaver.

He still had to take a deep breath whenever Ellie's sooty face, filled with worry and framed against the orange glow, leaped into his mind. Something about her made his stomach churn, or perhaps it was his chest. He couldn't believe he'd actually called her his dream. He'd wanted to dive under his hospital bed about ten seconds into their conversation. Dream. Right. So she had an incredible heart-attack smile and freckles across her nose that stirred his heart. She certainly wasn't dream-girl material. Especially for him. He needed a woman sold out for God. A woman passionate about serving her Savior, with a heart for ministry. He needed a woman who wouldn't need adventure to keep her happy.

A woman for whom he was enough.

Oops. Perhaps Charlene had left a deeper scar than he realized. That agonizing reality should have been obvious the second he'd threatened Ellie like the town ogre.

First Leo and now Ellie. His abysmal pastoral skills had reached new depths.

"What are you preaching on this week?" Joe turned his pickup toward the church and Dan's adjoining two-bedroom parsonage.

"I'm focusing on John fourteen verses five through fourteen about having faith in Jesus and doing great things in the name of God." Dan tried to ignore the sharp twist of those words in his soul. Had he ever done great things for God? "I've been reading *Fox's Book of Martyrs,* and the things those saints suffered for the sake of Christ would send you to your knees."

Joe nodded. "I met a man on a flight to Alaska who was a missionary in China. His stories still give me nightmares. Sometimes I wonder if I know what it means to sacrifice for the sake of the gospel. I wonder if I've even gotten dirty reaching out to the lost, let alone suffered." He sighed and shot Dan a wry look. "All my close friends are Christians, and I can't drive more than fifty miles without finding a church. I go round and round the Matthew 28 great commission, and I have to ask what exactly does God want of me here, now, in Deep Haven, Minnesota?"

Dan looked out the window, Joe's words skimming the open wounds in his heart. They pulled into the parking lot of Grace Church. The compact building, with its pine-paneled sanctuary and groomed, carpeted rooms seemed like home. Comfortable. Easy. The church groundskeeper had raked the lawn, and a delivery of fresh flowers sat in front of the door, the altar bouquet ready for Sunday's service. Neat. Pretty.

"Good question, Joe," Dan murmured quietly. "What, exactly?"

"Over your dead body? Fine with me!" The wind snatched Ellie's voice and quickly devoured it as she pedaled down the Gunflint Trail toward Deep Haven late Friday afternoon. It was probably a good thing that no one could hear her. It wouldn't win her any points in the town for someone to hear her waging loud, emotional arguments with thin air. Any psychologist worth her salt would agree, however, that a good old-fashioned verbal brawl brought catharsis.

Even if it was only with a memory.

Although, as the wind filled her ears, Ellie couldn't decide if she was fighting with the man she'd seen last night in the hospital or a younger, more tempestuous smoke jumper who had done his dead-level best to make her quit her job as a forest firefighter.

Whomever she fought with, she was going to win. She'd worked too hard, too long to let a man, living or dead, get in the way of her goals.

Ellie applied the brakes and brought her mountain bike to a stop along the road. Still a good three miles out of town, her perch on the steep highway overlooked Deep Haven like a king on a hill overlooking his kingdom. The endless blue of Lake Superior, the largest of the Great Lakes, started at the far horizon and ended in rolling white waves against a bouldered shoreline. Her mother had used the adjectives *cozy, quaint,* and *safe* when she'd written about Deep Haven after her vacation last summer. Since then some unexplained urge to explore the town tucked in the woods had spoken to a dark and quiet place inside Ellie.

When the Duluth Fire Department received the inquiry for the interim fire chief, she'd jumped on the opportunity faster than a bulldog on a sirloin. She'd had to spend more than a few hours in extra training and place her neck on the chopping block, but for the next three months, the job of fire chief rested in her hands. She alone had command over the fleet of volunteer firefighters, and if she did her job right and well, three months could stretch into a nice long future.

Finally, then, she might stop roaming. She'd turn in her road maps, invest in furniture, and maybe even land a piece of real estate. She'd done hard time to earn this job, and she deserved the shot at it. Five years in school, then a decade filling in at fire stations around Minnesota, trying to etch a niche for herself. She'd worked everything from forest fires to urban chemical blazes, and she knew how to organize a five-alarm attack, how to sift through the ashes, and when to call the investigators. She hoped landing this contract would allow her to stand still long enough to catch her breath, snatch the pieces of happiness that seemed just out of her reach, and somehow make sense of the patchwork of sorrows that defined the fabric of her life. Starting with Seth's death.

Now that she'd had five hours of sleep, a decent breakfast, and had pedaled away her fatigue into a sunny afternoon, sanity took hold. The questions that had plagued her at dawn were only the desperate cry of her alter ego, the eighteen-year-old who had followed her brother across two states to impress him.

Or had it been to impress God? That thought flickered through her brain, then died. It didn't matter. She refused to weave through the past to uncover her motives. She'd had a sure footing in the kingdom of heaven since a small child, and just because her church-attendance chart over the past few years looked sporadic didn't mean that she had forgotten her maker or her salvation. She read her Bible when she could, spent many a Sunday curled up on her sofa, exhausted, listening to praise music and reading through the Psalms.

Still, she had to admit, she felt like she'd hit a glass ceiling with God. She wanted the peace Seth had seemed to exude like a fragrance and spent most of her time trying to figure out the magic words or perhaps the right moves to break through to that level of spirituality. Lately, however, she'd begun to believe that a deep relationship with the Almighty of the universe might be reserved for the special, the *good* people in life. People like Seth.

People like Dan.

The pedal up the hill had been grueling — sweat had dried on her temples, run down her spine. But now, with the wind tangling her hair and the fresh lake balming her face, the ride back down seemed adequate reward. She worked her brakes as she coasted into town. Taking a right at Fourth Street she deliberately cruised past the Simmons place. In the glare of day, the remains looked ghastly, the smell of cinder and ash still thickening the air. Water filled muddy holes in the trampled lawn, and yellow police tape outlined the property. A neighbor, dressed in a pair of faded jeans and an old sweatshirt, raked leaves and the debris into a pile. She waved to Ellie.

Ellie smiled and returned the greeting. She would stop by later, wearing her steel-bottom boots and armed with a rake, and do a walk-through. Dan's worry that the home had been deliberately torched by the owner would have bearing on the insurance claim, and it fell under her new jurisdiction to follow up on that gut feeling.

Cutting down McGill Street, she braked at the bottom of the hill. Friday afternoon had brought in the outlanders, and cars lined Main Street. She saw families feeding seagulls, a man jogging along the beach, a couple sitting on the porch of their Victorian home. Walking her bike onto the sidewalk, she noticed the house wasn't a private residence but a bookstore and . . . a pottery shop? The smell of fresh coffee and something delicious in the air turned her up the walk. She leaned her bike against the steps.

Franklin would have to wait for his afternoon jog along the beach. It wasn't as if he lived to chase gulls. The old dog had about as much energy as her ninety-year-old grandmother, and Grandma Audrey might even have the animal licked in a fifty-yard dash.

A bell jangled as Ellie opened the door, and she found herself in the gleaming, quaint entrance of two little stores. To her right, through an arch, a bookstore complete with overstuffed green and blue sofas and a coffee bar called to her like a sweet fragrance. To her left, a craft shop beckoned. Pottery, quilts, and artwork from the area filled a room that looked as large as her mother's family room. Ellie stood there a moment, not quite sure which haven to

71

enter first.

"Hi, there," said a woman coming out of a door at the end of the hallway. "Welcome to the Footstep of Heaven." Her dark eyes twinkled, and she flipped back her long black braid tied with a piece of leather. Around her neck looped a beaded, turquoise-and-red necklace, similar to the jewelry Ellie had seen crafted by the Navajos in Arizona. The piece fit with the woman's faux suede turquoise jacket and her flare-legged black jeans.

"Hello," Ellie responded, wondering suddenly if she'd taken a turn into some hippie hangout.

"C'mon in." She moved past Ellie and into the crafty side of the store. Like a child after the Pied Piper, Ellie felt her legs moving to follow. "Anything in particular I can help you find?" She sat down at a metal table painted in various shades of red, turquoise, and white.

Ellie shook her head, not quite sure what had brought her into the store. She didn't collect anything except a few picturesque postcards, and she certainly didn't want anything that might break in the bottom of a duffel bag. Still, the quaint designs of the mugs, plates, and bowls tugged at the simple side of her. She picked up a mug.

Deep enough for a serious cup of hot cocoa — Ellie's drink of choice — it fit her hand well, with a notch for her thumb at the top of the handle. "These are beautiful. Are you the potter?"

"I am. Liza Beaumont." Liza folded her hands on the table and beamed one of the warmest smiles Ellie had ever encountered. Something about the woman felt . . . friendly. Perhaps it was the fact that she worked with her hands, something Ellie appreciated from her piano-playing years. Or maybe it was the fact that the woman didn't seem to fit into the flannel-and-denim stereotype of Deep Haven. Nevertheless, Ellie found herself wandering around the store, picking up pieces, admiring them. She stopped at a collection of photographs depicting various views of Deep Haven and the surrounding forest. "Are you also a photographer?"

Liza groaned. "Ack. No. I also sell on consignment. Those are by a friend of mine who travels through here occasionally. He did a wonderful series on the town lighthouse if you want to see them."

"I saw the lighthouse. I'm staying next door at the Gull's Roost Hotel."

"Oh, I love that place. Have you eaten their blackberry waffles? You'll think you've died and gone to heaven."

Ellie smiled. Well, she wasn't quite ready for that yet, but . . . "I did have a donut from the little stand across the street."

"World's Best? Oh, that's a dangerous place. I think I've gained ten pounds on their fried cinnamon rolls alone."

Ellie eyed the woman, built like a soda straw, and highly doubted her words. "I had a long john. I don't think I'll need to eat for a week."

"Well, Deep Haven doesn't lack for yummy places to eat." Liza ticked off a number of restaurants while Ellie inspected the photographs and a collection of painted rocks. "By the way," Liza said suddenly, "would you like some coffee? On the house?"

Ellie turned, warmed by Liza's offer. Why not? She certainly needed all the friends she could find if she hoped to survive public opinion. "Sure. Thanks."

"Cream? Sugar?"

"Black, please."

Liza made a face, then smiled. A moment later she returned with a hot cup that smelled like vanilla. "The specialty of the day . . . Macadamia Nut Crème." Liza motioned her over to a wrought-iron chair. "So, are you here on vacation?"

Ellie sipped her coffee, weighing her answer. In the light of day, not surrounded by a couple of macho firefighters, the truth felt less like she was sticking her head out for the executioner. "No. I'm the new interim fire chief." She watched Liza for a stunned reaction. Maybe a grimace or even a frown that would reveal her prejudices.

Liza wrinkled her nose as a smirk edged up her face. "That is about the best news I've heard all year."

Ellie stared at her.

Liza laughed. "Oh, I'm so sick of Mitch Davis strutting his stuff around town. He thinks that since he was the captain of the volunteer force, he'd automatically be named chief. The man's ego is blinding, and if I have to listen to him wax eloquent from Mona's side of the shop one more minute I might have to stick a pot over his head."

Okay, Liza had just charmed her way into Ellie's heart. Ellie took another sip of coffee. "This stuff is good, by the way. I'm used to drinking the half-petrified sludge from the bottom of the firehouse pots. I'll have to make a habit of dropping by."

"Did you check out the bookstore?"

Ellie shook her head. "I'm not much of a reader."

Liza put her hand over her mouth in mock

horror. "Another mutant like me!"

Ellie frowned but couldn't help but smile. "Mutant?"

"Oh, I'm surrounded by a regular army of readers. I secretly think they believe that people aren't really human unless they read." She folded her hands and nodded with a solemn look. "Mutants."

Ellie laughed. "Well, here's to finding another mutant." She raised her mug.

Liza grabbed a can of Lipton ice tea and raised it. "Here's to our new fire chief. Long may she reign!"

Okay, yes, Liza was definitely a keeper. Ellie let out a giggle like she hadn't since her teenage years. "Thanks, Liza."

"So have you met our very handsome firefighters yet?" Liza waggled her dark eyebrows.

Ellie's smile faded. "A few. I showed up at the fire last night. Saw them in action."

"Oh yeah, the Simmons place." Liza shook her head. "What a tragedy. And just when Leo seemed to have his past behind him. Joe said it might have been suicide?"

Ellie shrugged, unwilling to make accusations. In her position, even speculation could render trouble. "I'll need to do a cursory investigation before I know whether to call the state fire marshal."

76

"What a nightmare for Cindy and her kids. Joe tells me they're in intensive care."

Ellie stared into her coffee. "Yeah, they looked in rough shape when we brought them in."

"So you were at the hospital?"

Ellie nodded.

Liza went silent, her eyebrows drawn together. "Wait, you're not the woman who had it out with our pastor, are you?"

Ellie sighed. Small towns. They could spread gossip faster than a firestorm.

Liza slapped the table. "This is great. Okay, tell me everything." She leaned forward, eyes twinkling, as if they were lifelong friends. "According to Mona, she and Joe walked into a heated conversation that was one spark shy of exploding. What did he do?"

Ellie took a deep breath. "Nothing actually. Poor guy, I sorta . . . got offended by something he said." She paused. "He reminds me of someone who used to be against my firefighting. I guess I took Dan's comments personally." She looked up at Liza and decided to invest in her friendship. "Actually, he reminds me of someone I cared about."

Liza's eyes widened. "Pastor Dan reminds you of an old boyfriend?"

Ellie laughed. "No! Seth was my brother."

Liza nodded, as if she might have been a psychologist before her life as a potter. "I see. So . . . not a boyfriend . . ." She steepled her fingers. "Pastor Dan is single, you know."

"No, thank you. The last thing I'm going to do in Deep Haven is fall in love — especially with a firefighter. And aside from the fact that the man works for me, he's the town pastor. It would feel like stealing a nun from her vows."

Liza chuckled. "It's not like that. Dan is just a regular guy. He's not a priest or anything." Her eyes darkened suddenly. "Um . . . I'm sorry. I didn't mean to take anything for granted. Dan's also a Christian. So he's . . . well, he's not really available unless —"

"I'm a Christian too, Liza." Ellie smiled at the warmth in Liza's expression. "I have been for years. I just . . . well, I just haven't attended church for a while." She shrugged, trying to avoid the indictment spearing her soul. "The job. It keeps me busy."

Liza had a look that told Ellie she saw right through her. "I can imagine. Well, I hope that you find the Deep Haven fellowship . . . embracing. I attend Grace Church. And Dan is my pastor, which would of

78

course give someone, like a single girl, a good opportunity to meet him in a less-than-threatening way. Outside, say, the *regulations* of the firehouse." Liza grinned in a way that made Ellie smile and shake her head.

"Thanks for the suggestion, but seriously, Liza, I'm not here for love. I've met the pastor up close and personal, and I got the gist of his feelings about me." Dan's threat rang in her ears. "I'm here to do a job, and no one, *especially* Dan, is going to stand in my way."

4

Saturday morning. Showdown in the Deep Haven fire station parking lot.

The late-morning sunshine had scraped away the chill of the day, but it did nothing to warm Dan's bone-cold unease. Tension gathered in the air like static electricity as half the town arrived for a semiformal town meeting to listen to Romey Phillips introduce the new fire chief. A scant wind, carrying with it the smells of autumn and the freshness of the lake, scattered leaves into the air. Men and women clumped in conversation, dressed in all varieties of flannel, fleece, and sweatshirts, some drinking coffee, others devouring fresh donuts from World's Best. Dan counted all twenty-one members of the fire department and noted the vast majority wore expressions of grim curiosity.

"Women and firefighting go together like women and the military," Mitch Davis groused to Doug Miller, comrade-in-arms. "It ain't safe. Besides, the men spend most of their time digging the ladies out of trouble. Makes for problems, if you ask me." Mitch looked very Rambo-like today in an old army jacket and long scraggly hair, his beefy hands curled around a cup of black coffee. His dark eyes cruised past Dan as if hoping the pastor caught his remark.

Dan refrained from jumping on Mitch's comment. He might share the man's general hesitation to plunge women into a fire, but Ellie Karlson wasn't just any woman. She had enough grit to stare down a fire and douse it to a whimper, and she certainly could toe up to Mitch Davis and his gang of troublemakers. But it would take all of three seconds for Davis to ignite Ellie's ire and set off an explosion that would rock the foundation of this little town. Sides would be drawn, and in less than a week Dan would face a firestorm sweeping through the fir-lined avenues of Deep Haven. It wouldn't be long before his board of elders called him up to establish some sort of theological precedent against women working in jobs of danger.

Not to mention the fight he'd have with his natural, *God-given,* protective tendencies.

No, he didn't worry about Ellie having enough grit. At the moment, it had him scared to the bones.

"Beauty of a morning," Joe Michaels commented as he handed Dan an elephant ear in a grease-dotted napkin. He indicated with his mug of coffee Dan's left shoulder, his arm still slung to his body. The arm of his jacket hung limp and armless. "How's the shoulder?"

"Sore." Dan adjusted his sling, as if testing out his conclusion. "Yep, achy and tight."

"Give it a few days." Joe sipped his coffee. "I got thrown from a horse once down in Mexico and popped my left shoulder out. Wanted to die on the spot. But a couple weeks later I was back in the saddle with the rest of the gauchos."

"Is there anything you haven't done?" Dan asked. Joe's adventures, transcribed in his fictional Jonah series books, had become something of folklore around Deep Haven. Dan had a hard time getting past the easygoing Joe to picture him hauling in fish in Alaska or herding reindeer in Siberia. The man had lived a rich life before moving to Deep Haven. Of course, Joe would argue — especially around his wife and brother — that his rich life had begun when he moved to the tourist town and signed on as Mona's handyman.

"Yep," Joe said, his gaze roaming over Dan's shoulder. "I've never picked a fight with the fire chief on her first day on the job."

"Hey, she started that. I simply told her —" Oh, right. The last thing you need is to betray your near-death declarations to a woman who trampled them to slush or the fact that she sucked you back in time to face your broken heart.

Joe shot him half a smile. "Told her what?"

"Nothing." Dan finished off his pastry. "We weren't fighting. She has a way of turning my words around that just —"

"Gets under your skin?"

Dan glared at him. "Wipe that smirk off your face, Michaels. No. The woman is defensive and hotheaded at best."

"Well, the hospital room definitely felt hot when we walked in." Joe continued to grin like the cat who'd caught the canary.

Dan narrowed his eyes. "Not hot . . . cold. Miss Porcupine has the bedside manner of an icicle, and all you saw was me trying to be friendly. She didn't like it, that's all."

"Friendly. Okay. I agree that she might need some friends." He shot a pointed look at Mitch and his huddle of hotshots. "So, now that you're not strapped to a hospital bed, are you ready for round two?"

"Not on your life. I'm going to stay out of her way and hope I don't lose my job —"

"Or get burned?" Joe had an annoying twinkle in his blue eyes.

"Stop, Joe. Seriously. She's not looking to make friends in this town. She made that abundantly clear."

But as Dan watched the subject of their conversation climb out of a yellow Jeep, straighten her jacket, grab a clipboard, and stride toward the center of the parking lot, he couldn't help but remember that fleeting look of vulnerability that had risen in her eyes when she spoke about making a difference in Deep Haven. In that moment, she'd looked like she needed a friend. He imagined it couldn't be easy to prove herself in the firefighting world of swarthy and swagger.

Nevertheless, today she'd donned her default don't-mess-with-me expression, stoic and gritty and utterly masking any unspoken fears about her job. She'd pulled her hair back into a tight braid, and her eyes glinted, without humor, as she surveyed the group. She wore a black jacket and matching pants that he supposed were designed to drive any hint of femininity from her aura.

It didn't work. She looked like a million and a half bucks, and for a second Dan wanted to scoop her up and run for the hills. A soft place inside him hated both the opposition that simmered against her and the fact that he had somehow lined up on the side of her aggressors.

Mayor Romey Phillips had also arrived, dressed casually for a Saturday in jeans and a down vest. He met Ellie with a sound handshake and a smile. A small man with a quick brain under his hairless head, Romey had helmed the town council for longer than Dan had been serving this community. If anyone had a heart for Deep Haven residents, it was Romey. Perhaps they should also trust his choice for interim chief.

"Ladies and gentlemen," Romey started, raising his hands.

Dan and Joe moved to the front of the crowd. Ellie stood slightly back, her chin raised, her eyes dark. Dan caught her gaze and offered a smile. The smallest hint of a frown crossed her face before she looked away. Dan felt a stab of disappointment. Obviously she wasn't going to make it easy for him to apologize.

Apologize? He hadn't done anything

wrong, had he? He clenched his jaw and listened to Romey introduce Ellie, listing her credentials and her interim status. She would be among those considered, of course, for the permanent position, and Deep Haven was ever so grateful to have her direct their department on such short notice.

When Ellie thanked him and stepped up to address the crowd, she had steel in her expression. Dan braced himself for her listen-up-and-listen-well speech.

"Thank you for your attendance today," she said loudly with warmth. The crowd shifted slightly. Dan frowned. "I know this has come as a shock to many of you, and I thank you for your support." She smiled then, a white, bright smile that said, *I'm here to serve.* "I've had the pleasure, by the way, of working with one of your crew before. Paramedic Steven Lund worked with me in Duluth a number of years ago." She waved to a tall man leaning against a black Suburban. Lund smiled back with what seemed like genuine affection. "Steven knows some of my training techniques, and he'll be assist—"

"We've already been trained," yelled Mitch. He'd discarded his coffee and now stood, arms folded, looking like a soldier of

86

misfortune in his fatigues and muscles.

Ellie didn't flinch. "I've seen you in action, Mr. —"

"Davis," he supplied with a growl.

"Thank you. Like I said, I saw you attack the Simmons fire, and while I merit you on your determination to get to the heat and save lives, your methods were haphazard. My job is to form you into an efficient unit that can attack a blaze from many fronts. I plan to teach the forensics of firefighting, the different methods and chemicals used for various types of blazes, and I hope to hone you into a team."

"We are a team. We don't need a new leader." This from Ernie Wilkes, one of Mitch's forest-ranger cronies. Dan squelched the urge to run over and bang both their heads together.

Ellie nodded, as if she expected this response. "I've been training and fighting fires for over a decade so I know how fire crews work. They're a special kind of family, and I don't want to break that up." The breeze off the lake played with the loose tendrils of her hair, softening her hard look. "If you'd permit me, I'd like to introduce you to some of the newest techniques." She pulled a light green, rectangular object from her pocket, roughly the size of a claymore mine, and for a second Dan wondered if she was going to lob it into the huddle of opposers trying to turn her to rubble with their smoldering glares. She held it aloft. "For example, do you know what this is?"

Nothing but silence accompanied the weight-shifting postures of the crowd.

"It's a super PAL," she answered. "Otherwise known as a Personal Alert Safety System or PASS monitor. The newest models turn on automatically and detect motion. Firefighters, if you're felled, your PAL emits a noise that helps us find you, and it just might save your life."

Joe nudged Dan and nodded. Dan ignored him.

Ellie angled a smile at Mitch and Doug that didn't seem as warm as it did authoritative. "I'm glad to have your cooperation, men."

Dan smiled as he recognized the tone of voice. Next she'd pull out her sarcasm and the bloodshed would begin. Dan had to give her points, however, for toeing up to Mitch and his pack with patience and grace. She had half the man's girth and, at best, could look him square in the Adam's apple. Still, she refused to be knocked to her knees by his snarl.

Dan had to wonder — what had *he* done

to ignite her wrath? Certainly he hadn't been as offensive as Mitch, had he? Had he turned into an offensive jerk in the hospital, symbolically throwing his body in front of a woman who didn't want to be saved? He shuddered to think that he hadn't learned anything from the past. Or were all men destined to pound their chests in male machismo when they saw a woman in danger?

Perhaps the best way to protect her wasn't to tackle her ambitions but to befriend her, watch her flank, and keep the real enemies — namely Mitch, Ernie, and Doug — from sabotaging her future.

Dan watched Mitch fume as she read off her list of current volunteers, all present, and took the names of three wannabe firemen. Dan noticed that Guthrie Jones stepped forward into this group, and he wondered if it had to do with the fact that his older sister Cindy Simmons was now fighting for her life in a Duluth hospital. When Judy Franks and Marnie Blouder introduced themselves as dispatchers, Ellie's smile immediately warmed.

Ellie spent the rest of the morning arranging the firefighters into crew groups, extracting experience and information, and passing out training schedules. She also issued them pagers to be worn 24/7.

When Joe tested his pager, Dan nearly jumped out of his skin. "That'll wake the dead."

"Or me in the dead of night, I suppose," Joe said. "Poor Mona. She hasn't slept a decent night through since she got pregnant." Joe pocketed the beeper. "I never knew pregnancy was so tiring." His eyes held a twinkle.

"I think the fun is just starting, pal," Dan commented as he tried out his own pager. "What does Gabe think, by the way?" Gabriel Michaels, Joe's younger brother, lived in a home for the mentally challenged not far from Deep Haven.

"He's thrilled. Can't wait to be an uncle."

Dan noticed that in all Joe's exuberant musings about their developing baby, he carefully left out his bone-deep fear that the baby might carry a gene for Down syndrome — Gabe's condition. Until Joe was willing to bring it up, however, Dan steered around it. Still, he couldn't help but wonder how this fear might seep into the Michaels' joy.

"She certainly seems capable," Joe said, looking at their new fire chief. Dan followed Joe's gaze and watched Ellie as she helped Guthrie figure out his pager.

"Yes, she does," Dan said with a low moan.

Ellie threw a piece of driftwood into the Lake Superior surf. "C'mon, Franklin, go get it." The basset hound stared up at her, baggy eyes blinking. He looked in the direction of the stick, back at Ellie, then with a huff, flopped down and closed his eyes. "Oh, super, I can't even get *you* to obey me."

Shoving her hands in her pockets, she closed her eyes and let the wind brush the hair from her face. Cool and crisp, the wind carried with it the slightest hint of rain. Good. She noticed that the fire alert in the Boundary Waters Canoe Area had been notched up to high. They could use a good shower.

The sun hovered just above the shoreline, a brilliant flame painting the wave tips red. Around her, gulls eyed her as if she might be a benefactor, their heads bobbing as they called out their complaints. "Shoo," Ellie said, balancing her supper — a turkey croissant she'd picked up from the Loon Café — on her knees. She had no doubts that the greedy birds would dart in and snatch it the second she relaxed her guard.

She'd better toughen up her defenses if

she hoped to eke out a smidgen of respect from the men she'd met today. She'd been mildly disappointed to discover that the Deep Haven Fire Department didn't host even one woman. The two ladies who showed up to run the emergency dispatch felt like a cool drip in a hot spring.

She mentally categorized her crew — John Benson, Doug Miller, and Craig Boberg formed the backbone of the company. With ten years or more experience each, she'd be able to trust their gut instincts and would lean on them for leadership. She'd put probies Guthrie Jones, Lionel Parks, and Simon Sturgis through their paces, but with her slim crew, they'd have to man hydrants, drag hose, and fill in the gaps until they were ready to face a fire. A group of other lumberjack types formed the bulk of the crew, headed by Mitch Davis and Ernie Wilkes, who hated her guts if she read their body language correctly. That left Joe Michaels, Bruce Schultz, and Dan to win over. Joe seemed friendly enough with his wide smile and twinkling eyes. And Bruce Schultz had shaken her hand with a solid grip that told her he wasn't afraid to let a woman lead. But what about Dan?

His words from their dismal meeting at the hospital still rang in her mind: *Over my dead body.* Dan wouldn't seriously try and derail her job here, would he?

She shouldn't let the preacher frighten her. Twice she'd caught him looking at her, grimacing. It didn't help that he looked like a hero fresh off the pages of some sweet romance novel, with his dark hair raked by the wind and a slight stubble of whiskers on his chin. It nearly rocked her from her stoic emotional footing. She could admit that for a second, against the backdrop of adrenaline and fear, Pastor Dan had chipped a piece out of her heart. She'd be better off to forget him. It wasn't like they'd be taking strolls in the sunset. In fact, such strolls might unravel all her hard work. She could just imagine the ribbing they'd get from the firemen . . . ribbing she couldn't afford in the heat of a fire. She'd have to maintain a professional distance if she hoped to etch respect in the eyes of her fire crew.

She finished her sandwich, glaring triumphantly at the seagulls, then wrapped her arms around her bent legs, staring into the waves. The wind played with her hair, now down and tangling. In track pants and a U of MN-Duluth sweatshirt, she felt nearly normal, free of the tightly strung fire-chief persona. Briefly she wondered why she worked so hard for a job she dreaded.

The sound of crunching rocks made her look up. She scowled as the man of her most recent thoughts tromped his way toward her. And wouldn't you know it, he wore a U of MN hockey jersey over his sweatshirt, dredging up a spray of bittersweet memories.

"What are you doing here?"

"I thought you and I should have a talk." Dan sat down beside her, obviously not at all ruffled by the lack of invitation. "You skipped out on me at the hospital."

"Oh, I'm sorry. Weren't you finished threatening me and telling me what a fool I am? I guess you rallied your pals. I had a regular fan club down at the firehouse today. Thanks."

"Wow." Dan's eyes widened. "Okay, first of all, I didn't 'rally' anyone. Mitch and Ernie have a genetic predisposition toward apelike behavior. It takes very little to whip them into a frenzy. And as for the other night, I was tired and most likely under the influence of heavy painkillers. I didn't mean what I said." His voice turned dangerously soft. "I'm sorry."

She looked away, afraid that her emotions might be written in her expression. How dare he make her feel like the villain. Her throat threatened to close. "You're not for-given."

He drew in a long breath, then picked up a stick and began to draw in the rocks. The wind reaped his freshly showered scent and sent it back to her, picking at her sour mood.

She felt like a heel. "Okay. Fine. I forgive you."

"Can we be friends?" He held out his hand, and that, along with his smile, demolished her last barriers of annoyance.

"Just friends, okay? No more dream girl declarations or he-man threats."

Was it her imagination, or did he color slightly? It looked devastatingly cute with his tough hockey shirt and wind-whipped hair. "You got it." His grip felt soft, wide, and strong. She let go almost immediately.

"So what do you want to talk about — besides my abhorrent profession?" She looked away before those way-too-piercing eyes drilled into her soul.

He laughed, and the sound of it, full and sweet, tugged a smile out of her.

"How's your shoulder?" She gestured to the sling. "I guess you won't be swinging a stick anytime soon, huh?"

He blinked at her, his gaze clouding.

"The hockey jersey. I just assumed —"

"Oh, right." He looked at himself, as if

95

stunned by his attire. "I'm a wing. Deep Haven Hotshots." He shrugged, but his eyes lit up. "And I'll be fine for practice."

"Hotshots? As in forest firefighters?" She sunk her head into her hands. "I should have guessed. I'll bet half my fire crew is on the hockey team, right?"

He shrugged. "We do have snow and ice for eight long months. Not a lot to do around here —"

"So, in other words, if we get a call I just need to phone the hockey rink?"

"Or the church. Most of those guys . . . well, with the exception of a few, are regular attendees. Like I said, not much to do around here." He smiled and spiked an eyebrow. "Hey, you don't sing, do you?"

She made a face. "Only in the shower, and even then Franklin howls."

Her dog had decided to check out the comfort status of Dan's tennis shoes. Dan rubbed the dog behind one of his floppy ears. "Franklin. As in . . . Ben?"

Why that question spiraled right to the soft tissue of her heart, she didn't know, but she felt warm to her toes. "Good guess. I thought it appropriate to name him after the first firefighter."

"I used to have a dog. Petey. Cocker spaniel and black Lab mix. Great dog."

Franklin opened an eye at Dan's monologue and rolled over. "He was hit by a car a couple years ago. Never could bring myself to replace him. I guess I'm a one-dog fella."

"Gets lonely that way, I'll bet." Oh, where did that come from? She wanted to wince, but suddenly she had to know. Why wasn't he married? He was the town pastor — didn't he have to take an oath that he'd get married straight out of seminary or something? Or . . . maybe he'd taken a different kind of oath, one that would ensure that her reputation was indeed safe as they sat on shore, talking into the twilight. She suddenly felt a tad ill at even noticing his white smile, his dark, run-your-hands-through-me hair, and his gentleness with her dog.

"Oh, I keep busy," he answered without a twinkle, as if her question — no, her *probing* — went right over his head. Good. She shouldn't be — *wasn't!* — interested anyway. "So, you're from Duluth?" he asked.

"Yep. Born and raised in a little house on the hill. Woke up each morning to the foghorn. I used to love watching the boats motor into Canal Park. It seemed like such an exotic life. Forlorn, perhaps, but exotic."

"And . . . you like exotic?" His eyes had darkened and his tone deflated, as if weighted by sadness.

97

"I guess so. Maybe. It's better than for-lorn." She chuckled, and he responded with a one-sided smile that didn't quite reach his eyes. "What's it like — being a pastor? I suppose you hear a lot of sob stories."

The sun had sunk beneath the western rim of the lake, leaving a trail of maroon in its wake. Dan threw a rock into the waves. "Now and then. I'm a pretty good listener if you ever need an ear."

Oh no . . . that was the last thing she needed — to let the man go searching around her soul, only to discover her scarred heart. "Thanks. But . . . well, I have Frank-lin."

"Yeah, he looks like the listening type." Dan glanced her way, and there was friend-ship in his eyes.

It dragged the truth out of her before she knew it. "Well, he doesn't preach at me, and that helps."

When Dan winced, it was clear she'd hurt him. "I'll try not to preach."

She felt like an insensitive clod. "That didn't come out right. I'm sorry. I just . . . well, let me just say it aloud. I'm a Chris-tian. But I work hard, and that means I don't always make it to church. So don't come around and start leaving blank at-tendance records on my desk. Got it?"

He narrowed his eyes slightly, and it gave him a way-too-dangerous, threaten-her-emotional-boundaries-type look. "Uh-huh."

The air suddenly felt thick, and she fought the urge to get up and run. Fast.

He considered her for a long, painful moment before he spoke. "You know, being a pastor is a challenging job. I have to admit I struggle for words sometimes. I'm never quite sure if I'm making a difference, to tell the truth. It's not like fighting a fire. When you're done, you know if you've won or lost — if the fire has bested you, or if you've escaped. Sometimes you escape with burns, but you always learn something. It's not like that in ministry."

In the gathering darkness, his dark profile seemed young, his face fierce and passionate. "The man who died in the fire last week was one of my parishioners. I failed him, Ellie. Instead of confronting the man about his downward spiral, I let him struggle. I sidled up beside him and lobbed him spiritual truths when I should have waged a frontal attack. Stopped his head-on collision with despair . . . I don't want that to happen again."

"Dan, you can't save everyone," Ellie said, dodging the uncanny feeling that he had a finer point to his story, one that should make her squirm. Still, with his magically tender and even vulnerable voice, he'd moved her emotions from defensive to empathetic. The guy had a way of making her feel . . . soft. Aware of the gentler side of herself, the one she tried to ignore or even hide.

"No, Ellie; in fact I can't save anyone. But I can point them to their Savior, the only one who can save. And in this particular case, I blew it." He tightened his jaw. "And I don't want to make a habit of that." While he looked at her, the passion in his eyes made her mouth run dry. Suddenly he wasn't Dan the pastor, but a young smoke jumper with blond hair, loading his parachute. "I know I don't know you well, but I don't want you to get hurt."

"I'm not so easily hurt, you know," she said, but her voice caught. "I do know what I'm doing."

"Do you? I hope so."

She tried to answer, but nothing came out of her knotted throat. Seeking escape in watching the seagulls riding the waves, she rubbed her hands on her arms and wondered why she couldn't unlock the dark chambers of her heart. He did say he wanted to be her friend. But some wounds were too deep for casual inspection.

"Listen, I didn't come to Deep Haven to defend my profession to you or anyone else," she finally said, knowing her voice sounded choked and way too vulnerable. "I have a job to do. And I'm good at it. If you want to stand in my way, you're going to get trampled."

"I'm not going to stand in your way."

"Good."

"But I am going to watch your back. And if you start to get into trouble, I'm going to be there to pull you out."

"Oh, like when you went after the Simmons kids? You nearly got killed. And thanks, but I don't need another death on my head." She cringed at her sudden outburst, but the words were already out.

"You're not going to let me forget that, are you?"

He looked so wretched, so sick at heart, it chipped away at her anger. "Not if it will save your life," she said, then managed a slight smile. "Listen, I'm here to watch your back, Pastor. And it would do you well to remember that."

His expression changed, and those smoky eyes turned dark, intense. "And what if it's *your* life that needs saving, Ellie? Who are you going to trust then?"

5

The church bell echoed against the pine and birch that embraced the city, its sound accentuating the beauty of the sun-drenched Sunday. Ellie paused her sleuthing through the soggy remains of the Simmons home and stared through the charred window frame, watching the family across the street hustle out of their house. It raised a spur of memory:

"Ellie, hurry; we're already late!" Her mother's voice would trumpet through their bungalow, followed by the smell of burning toast and the sound of her brother's raucous laughter.

"Forget it, Ma. She can't find the right tube socks to match her dress!"

The image faded on the sound of Seth's laughter and left a burning trail of sorrow in its wake. Grief had the ability to pop up at the most unexpected times and grab her by the throat. She swallowed hard and turned back to her work, trying to ignore the residue of guilt. Just because she wasn't a regular church attendee didn't mean that she should feel like a delinquent teenager.

She and God were on speaking terms, even if it did seem to be a rare conversation these days. Despite her attempts, she'd given up hoping she'd ever find that magical relationship with God that Seth had raved about. Perhaps that kind of connection with the Almighty of the universe was reserved for the *real* saints, with the majority of the world destined to stand on the fringes.

Ellie sighed, defeat rushing over her. Although her post as interim chief was less than twenty-four hours old, she felt like she'd been on the job for a decade, complete with fatigue and war wounds. After her way-too-revealing conversation with the pastor last night — one that had left her with an unsettling sense of longing and anger — she needed to focus on exactly why she'd moved to Deep Haven.

It certainly wasn't to cultivate friends . . . well, not that she was inherently against the idea, but certainly not the type of "friends" who made her feel like fixing her hair and painting on makeup. And wouldn't that portray the steely image she needed? The firehouse was a hotbed for rumors. The last thing she needed was someone even musing about her spending time with a firefighter on her crew under a lavender sunset. Suddenly her career would be in shreds. If not her career, her reputation.

Spending time alone sifting through the burned remains of the Simmons home would give her focus, help her hone in on her objective. And she could say she had spent the morning in useful activity.

There it went again, the unexpected spurt of guilt.

She tried to focus on her work. The first step in determining the cause of a fire was pinpointing its origin. The Simmons home groaned, and the hairs on Ellie's neck rose. Walking through a fire-gutted house, relying on the strength of damaged foundation posts seemed slightly shy of smart, but she knew the risks when she signed on.

Starting at the door, armed with her camera and a short pike pole to help her negotiate over furniture and melted plastics, she traced the fire path from the least damaged to the deepest charred rooms, trying not to disturb any evidence that might reveal arson. From the entryway, which opened into the family room, she tracked the smoke line, the etching of where smoke and heat blazed down from the ceiling. She noted that the overhead lightbulb had melted in the direction of the family room, where the heat concentrated. Stopping at a light switch, she pried it off the wall. The wires were still intact so the fire here had licked along the lath-and-plaster wall, leaving the wiring unscathed. The fire hadn't invaded the electrical system. Overhead, the ceiling had dripped water into pools of watery embers.

She wore her steel-toed, Kevlar-bottom rubber boots today, her turnouts, and a helmet; she realized that she'd forgotten, in the past year of management classes, how heavy her gear could be. In a fire, with the bunker pants and SCBA breathing gear, she often likened herself to a turtle trying to crawl through a black maze.

As she marched down the hall, the odors of burned plastics, wood, and fiber stung her nose, bit at her eyes. She stepped inside the decimated kitchen and treaded carefully over glass splinters, the remains of an overhead light. She shone her flashlight on what had been a brass lamp, its arms now warped and tangled from the heat. The aluminum casing for the lightbulbs hung in frozen drips, hinting at the intense heat of the blaze. The top half of the room —

wallpaper, cupboards, and wall clock — had been chewed up by flames and melted almost beyond recognition. The pattern, however, indicated that the fire had moved like a wave across the kitchen, seeking oxygen and a fresh fuel supply.

She approached the blackened window frame, examined the spray pattern of the glass shards. Splinters littered the floor as well as the ground outside. Obviously a casualty of the fire rather than an arsonist's attempted entry.

As she moved across the adjoining room — a pantry? — her feet slapped through puddles and dug through debris — plaster, wood, insulation — torn open as the fire-fighters had overhauled the house, search-ing for smoldering heat. The door to the room hung only by its lower hinge, and the deeper surface burning at the top told her it had smoldered before fiery breath had blown it open, freeing the fire to consume the house.

She peered into the room — a bathroom. And, from its condition, the possible source. Only the porcelain toilet, badly blackened, and the tub remained. On the far wall, noth-ing but spaghetti-thin shards remained of the studs, betraying the fire's desperate search for oxygen as it gulped air from the cracked window. From her vantage point she could look right through to the family room and beyond that to the street. To her right, on what remained of the bathroom wall, the wallpaper, or perhaps paint, curled down from the walls like chocolate curls. Just above a deformed mess beside the toilet, Ellie made out a slight fire cone, the *V* of the fire. Below it, the tiny vanity, mirror, and what she guessed had been various cleansers and shampoos had melded into a pile, and next to it was a deformed mound of hardened black plastic.

When Ellie stepped closer, the floor groaned. She stilled and heard her father's voice: *Don't ever go into a fire without your buddy.* He'd been on the force long enough for his warning to resonate with wisdom. She had obviously discarded common sense this morning in favor of accelerating her career. She'd not only left her PAL but also her UHF radio on the seat of her Jeep. Not that she'd have anyone to call if she fell through the bathroom floor and broke her legs in the basement.

That thought stopped her heart cold in her chest.

Slowly she set down the pike tool and hoisted her camera. Taking a series of shots of the bathroom, she then crouched and carefully tugged at the melted plastic blob, which she surmised had been a garbage receptacle. The thing had hardened, and whatever was inside had been encased in its mass. A river of congealed plastic led to the vanity rubble.

Ellie sifted through it with gentleness. Whatever had started the fire had generated enough heat to melt plastic and chew through the wooden vanity without slowing to account for the different combustion temperatures. It had fed on the ample fuel under the sink in flammable cleaning supplies, breathing the scant oxygen from the open window, until it filled the room with enough gas to blow out the door and flashing over the kitchen, hunting breath and fuel. Still, if it had blown out through the kitchen, certainly the family would have heard the explosion.

But the lack of alligator scaling, the high-heat scars left on the surface of wood, suggested a different story. Ellie guessed that the blaze had simply gobbled through the wall to the family room, exploding across the ceiling, gulping the air, and killing the victim instantly with toxic carbon monoxide. That would account for the carpet still intact in the corners and the fairly insignificant burning of the sofa and the recliner, despite the man's condition.

Had Leo Simmons been a smoker? Perhaps he'd dropped his cigarette in the garbage, thinking it was extinguished. A cigarette would smolder among the tissue, building heat, melting the plastic until it finally ignited. But paper produced smoke — more smoke than wood and other fuels. Enough smoke to sneak out under a bathroom door and trigger the smoke alarm. No, this fire was fast and hungry. It ignited suddenly, reduced the litter basket to liquid, then almost immediately discovered the fuel under the sink. Within three minutes, the room would have been a fireball, more flame than smoke, and by the time the blaze gnawed through the wall and flashed over the family room, the smoke alarm would have been useless.

The burn patterns suggested an accelerant. An arsonist or a very fatal mistake?

A suicide arsonist would set the fire to smoldering, do his deadly deed, and wait for the blaze to cover up the results. He certainly wouldn't set a fire, then retire for five short minutes in the family room to watch the Minnesota Twins lose a pre-playoff game, especially with his family sleeping upstairs.

Whoever had set the blaze had done so

moments before he escaped . . . before his act could be discovered.

She'd have to interview the neighbors, see if they could recall who might have visited Leo Simmons Thursday night shortly before his house burst into flames.

Meanwhile, she had enough suspicions to call in the fire marshal from Duluth. A fire investigator with a computer system, canine units, and forensic techniques would help her track down the person who'd nearly killed an entire family.

And perhaps, then, she wouldn't be seen as the invader in Deep Haven but a protector.

Ellie backed out of the bathroom, stepped carefully through the kitchen, and started down the hallway. The wind had picked up, scattering leaves and other debris across the family room. She hesitated near the door, thinking of Leo and his shock as flames rolled across the ceiling, devouring the oxygen and burning his lungs.

The house moaned and she felt it shudder, as if heaving a sigh. She had a split-second warning before the crack sounded. Throwing her arms up, she closed her eyes as the world caved in on top of her.

Dan stood in the vestibule, shaking hands

with his parishioners. He couldn't count how many times he'd summarized the event surrounding his injury and outlined his hopeful prognosis. He ought to place a sign over his head or take out an ad in the *Superior Times*.

Even so, it touched his heart that so many people cared. Edith Draper had promised to send over a casserole — a hearty Minnesotan cream-of-mushroom-soup, tater tot, and pulverized meat affair, as if his injured shoulder had somehow impaired his taste buds. But he could hold out hope that the meal might include the woman's rice pudding. Most of the congregation took him for the usual underfed, measly cook bachelor. He didn't have the heart to tell them that he'd spent every summer during college in the sweaty kitchens of some of Minneapolis's finest restaurants. Perhaps he should be hunting the want ads for line-cook positions.

Bruce Schultz stepped up, pumped his hand, thanked him for the sermon, and teased him about missing hockey practice. "Don't tell me you can't shoot with one arm."

Joe, right behind Bruce, gave the man a light punch.

Mona looked more rested this morning

and had developed a motherly glow. She still hadn't donned maternity clothes, however, and Dan wondered when she'd announce her pregnancy to the congregation. As he chatted with the Michaelses, Dan noticed Liza lining up behind them, a saucy smile on her lips. She had her arms folded, but those dark eyes definitely simmered with trouble. When she stepped up to him, he braced himself.

The woman had a way of stripping down casual conversation to the bare essentials. "I met her, Dan."

He worked to keep up.

"I'll have you know, she's not going to let you run her out of town."

Who — ?

"The new fire chief." She answered his nonverbal question, obviously posed in his frown.

"I'm not trying to run her out of town." His gaze darted past Liza, and he smiled at Doc Simpson. "Besides, we smoothed things over last night."

"Oh?" Liza's black eyebrows arched.

He winced. "That didn't come out quite right. Let's just say that she and I came to an agreement."

"Like you staying out of her way? letting her do her job?"

"Like me doing mine." He tracked back to Ellie's face when he'd accused her of trying to run a one-woman show, not needing any help. She'd gone stark white, as if she'd been punched. And then abruptly she stood, wrenched her pooch to his feet, and coldly bid Dan good night. Okay, so it hadn't exactly ended *well*. He'd hit upon a soft spot — or a dark fear. It had kept him sitting on the beach long after she'd retired to her hotel.

Something haunted Ellie — enough to make her want to keep Dan outside her private walls lest he get a good glimpse of it.

Obviously, the woman hadn't unlocked her secrets for Liza either. "Well, I did try and tell her that you were a pretty good fella —" Liza's warm smile appeared, and somehow it loosened the breath in his chest — "and . . . single."

"Liza, you didn't."

She smirked. "I thought, you know, since I did such a good job with Joe and Mona, I'd move on to higher obstacles."

He scowled at her.

She laughed, unfazed. "Pastor, you should know that no one is immune to my matchmaking."

Her grin was so infectious his scowl

turned to a chuckle. "It won't work, Liza, but thanks for the good intentions. I'm afraid I'm simply not the marrying kind. Almost took the plunge once but —"

"Don't tell me you came to your senses."

Well, that about summed it up. Reality had hit him hard and square in the chest, leaving a wound so deep he wondered if he'd yet recovered. "Maybe I just know that the right girl for me isn't out there. I'm happy single . . ." He moved past her and reached out to Doc Simpson, praying Liza would keep moving.

"Yeah, sure. We all are," Liza said, then walked away.

Dan tried not to let her words grate at him as he finished greeting his parishioners. He was happily single. Or maybe he simply wasn't ready to surrender his heart again for a woman to trample. He'd barely survived the first time. Besides, his wife would have to be committed to life as a pastor's wife. Serving. Letting him keep doctor's hours, putting up with other people needing his time and attention. It seemed like a job better suited for a single man. No wonder the apostle Paul had urged those heading into ministry to remain single.

He was saying good-bye to Ruth Schultz when he spotted a man, his long dark hair tied in a ponytail and dressed in a tweed jacket, black jeans, and hiking boots standing with his back to him near the vestibule. "Noah?"

The man turned. "Hey ya, Preach." A wide smile graced Noah Standing Bear's face as he extended his arm and took two long steps toward Dan. "Glad to see you."

Dan always felt slightly dwarfed by this man, despite his own six-foot stature. Noah was over six feet tall with the girth of a small grizzly. But his demeanor was pure lamb. A former gang member, Noah worked as a youth pastor in Minneapolis and ran a summer camp on the Gunflint Trail for delinquent inner-city kids. "What are you doing here?"

Noah took a deep breath, as if holding back a flood of emotions, but his eyes betrayed his secret in a bright glow. "Anne and I are getting married."

"Yes!" Dan high-fived him. "Not that I had any doubts, but still, she has a mind of her own, and I'm glad to see you get a ring on her finger."

"You and me both." Noah looked like the man who hung the moon, all grins and puffed-out chest. Or maybe it was simply his stocky build and standard demeanor. If anyone exuded the joy of salvation, it was

Noah Standing Bear. The guy had stories that sent Dan's chin to the floor in alarm, his heart soaring with the redemptive work of Christ. "Anne and I are getting married in the city, but we want to have a small party here at the church. Do you suppose we could work that out?"

"Are you kidding? When?"

"We're getting married the weekend before Thanksgiving."

"That is the best news I've heard all year. Where is Anne?"

"She left a couple weeks ago with Katie, one of my staffers."

"I know Katie." Dan easily pictured the redhead, a cute ball of Irish spunk and courage. The woman had a way of leading kids to Christ that was simple and understandable. Sometimes Dan wished he could take notes.

"Katie and Anne's sister are in the wedding, and they had to have fittings for their bridesmaid dresses and iron out a few details."

"So you've been engaged all summer?" Dan frowned at him. "You didn't tell me."

Noah shook his head. "Sorry, Dan. We didn't tell anyone except a few of the staffers. We didn't want the kids watching us and forgetting why they were there."

"Right." It didn't take much for street kids who lived soap-opera lives to turn a godly courtship into R-rated gossip. "Well, the church would love to host you. I'll put it on our calendar. Let me know what I can do to help."

"Thanks, Dan. Anne will be thrilled." He curled his program in his hand. "I gotta run. I'm heading down to Minneapolis this afternoon."

Dan walked with him into the parking lot. Noah unstrapped his helmet from his motorcycle and worked it on. "Joe told me about your injury . . . and your new fire chief." This time the shine in his eyes had nothing to do with his own love life. "Heard she made quite an impact on you."

Dan grimaced. "No. Just trying to do my job."

"Oh, really?" Noah pulled the bike off its kickstand. "And what's that?"

Dan let the image of Ellie sitting on the beach, the wind teasing her hair, those blue eyes hiding too many secrets pass over him. He sighed. "Keeping people out of trouble."

"Hmm," said Noah, his smile dimming. "I guess I didn't know that was your job description." He jump-started the bike, then sat and revved the engine. "Well, just so long as you leave something for God to do!"

he said over the roar. Then he smiled,
flicked a salute, and motored off.

6

Ellie blinked, her eyes tearing as they adjusted to the fog of debris now settling on the floor. She had landed on her elbows, and they felt like they'd been shattered. Her eyes nearly crossed with the pain that pulsed up her arms. She took a breath. No sharp burning in her chest. Hopefully she hadn't cracked any ribs. Something heavy lay on her lower legs.

Groaning, she twisted and discovered that the overhead beam to the second floor had given way. Crashing against the staircase, it had scattered the banister beams like bowling pins, raining them down upon her as it fell. The beam then broke and pinned her neatly to the floor.

She felt for her flashlight, found it, and shone some light on the situation. Two very menacing-looking nails had missed her leg by a fraction of an inch. She could be bleeding out on this carbonized, water soaked floor if it weren't for providential protection.

Again, God had spared her life despite her foolishness. She had to be setting new records. *Thank You, Lord.*

Turning back on her stomach, she reached out for a handhold, something solid.

She hadn't fallen through the floor, but pinned the way she was in the hallway, nothing but boards and litter filled her grasp. She pulled on a floorboard, but it splintered into black ash in her hands. The smell of ash seeped into her nostrils, and her legs felt like smoldering cinders.

Tasting the sharp edge of panic, she bit it back even as frustration balled in her throat. With a roar she lunged against her pinnings. The sound echoed back at her, lifting the fine hairs on her neck. Fighting tears, Ellie buried her face in the pocket of her folded arms. Why did she let her stubborn pride push her to the edge of safe and sane?

The sudden wave of memories, filled with the smell of smoke and the taste of frustration, took her breath away:

Seth stood in her way as she entered the fire camp, his feet planted, his eyes hard. "Turn around and go home," he'd said in a tight voice.

"No!" She'd flung her backpack over her

shoulder, faked, and sprang around him. He nearly raced her to the administration tent where the firefighters checked in.

"Does Dad know you're here?"

His question felt like a slap. "Yes. Well . . . okay, no. But it doesn't matter. I'm nineteen and old enough to figure out how I want to spend my summer."

"Yes, on the beach or camping with your friends or maybe working at McDonald's." Seth seized her arm. She turned, and his expression looked more like panic than fury. "You can't stay here."

"I can, and I will." She'd wrenched her arm out of his grip and walked away, his warning stinging her ears.

"Over my dead body."

Ellie closed her eyes, listening to his voice fade in favor of the birds chirping and the sounds of the neighbors returning from Sunday services. Lunch would be on the table soon, and the little girls would be told to change out of their dresses. Meanwhile, across the street, the town fire chief would die of starvation and her stubborn pride.

Ellie groaned. It wasn't like anyone was going to come looking for her. She had no friends in this town, especially after the way she'd treated Dan.

She winced, remembering his words: *And*

who is going to watch out for you?

At the time she'd thought them invasive. Presumptuous. Chauvinistic.

Now they'd become painfully prophetic.

She knew better than to tromp around a fire scene without a partner. That's what deputy chiefs were for . . . except she didn't have one of those. The closest thing she had to an assistant was Franklin . . . or perhaps Mitch Davis, the volunteer captain.

Oh, joy.

He'd certainly have a good time with this one. He and Dan could hold each other up while they laughed at her. She wanted to curl into a ball and hide.

Then again, maybe this was a fitting demise to her dismal start. She barely had her head above water with this job, and this morning she had let her ambitions run away with her brain.

Maybe she could quit while she still had the pieces of her pride. Olaf Growald, the Duluth chief, would welcome her back without a word. She had been a good deputy.

What good would scraping out a spot for a female chief accomplish, anyway? The question hit her like a sledgehammer. Sure, she'd fought like a badger to earn her place, but now at the top of the heap, could she really make a difference in the landscape of Deep Haven life? And would it even begin to erase time or redeem the sacrifices made to get her here?

The empty places in her heart stung with the memory of raucous, infectious laughter and the smile of a boy who seemed to radiate the sun.

She had to make a difference. She owed it to Seth.

And she'd accomplish nothing if she starved to death trapped under a pile of debris.

Ellie lifted her head, spied her pike pole. Stretching, she barely nicked it with her gloved hand. Maybe she could —

"Ellie?"

The voice of salvation — or maybe doom — came from the doorway. Ellie pushed back her helmet, craned her neck, squinted at the dark outline in the doorway.

Tall, broad shoulders, tousled dark brown hair . . . she sighed. "Hi ya, Pastor."

Dan peered into the gutted house at Ellie's dark, sooty face, and horror slid over him in a wave. "Are you okay?" He strode into the house, picking his way over charred timbers. "What happened?"

She wiggled, but she wasn't going anywhere with a layer of wood piled atop her, most of it resting on the now splintered staircase. Weakness washed over him when he saw how close she'd come to being crushed.

"I came to do some preliminary investigation —"

"Alone?" He picked up two pieces of banister wood, piled them at the foot of the stairs. He had no doubt the entire house could cave in on their heads if he dislodged the wrong ceiling joist.

"Yeah, alone. You can quit laughing at me now."

Laughing? With his heart lodged in his throat? "I fail to see the humor in this, Ellie. You could have been killed." He continued to work to free her. "Is anything broken? Maybe I should call the guys. We can get a stretch —"

"No. I'm fine. Just . . . just get me out of here." She wiggled again, and the entire pile began to groan.

"Stay still! I'll dig you out; just stay still." What she had obviously failed to see, apparently because of her position, was another ridgepole, burnt to a thread, above her. With the loss of the joist next to it, all the weight could shift and bury them. "Just . . . lie there."

He moved another banister rail, but she wasn't having any of his orders. Grunting, she twisted against her shackles. Dan heard the pile shift again. "Ellie, please trust me, will ya? I promise I'll get you out of here." His crisp tone cut into her efforts and she froze. "You're going to bring the roof down on us."

He stepped over her, examining the timber that trapped her.

"What are you doing here?" Her voice sounded tight, as if she were holding in her fear.

"I was headed up to my cabin. Saw your Jeep." He didn't add that he'd sat at the stop sign long enough to pile up traffic before he'd turned her way. Something about her bold yellow vehicle sitting alone outside the house had triggered a sharp — and rightful — concern.

More than one timber had fallen, and the one pinning Ellie was still connected to an adjoining timber that looked like it might decide to follow. "Uh, Ellie, here's what we're going to do. I'm going to lift this end of the beam as best I can. You wriggle out."

He crouched, gripped the end, lifted.

She moved like a soldier, fighting against the claw of the joist. "No good. I can't figure it out. My legs are free but I can't budge. I think my bunker pants are caught."

"So wriggle out of them."

She shot him a dark look.

"You *are* wearing something underneath them, right?"

She nodded but had managed to color an interesting crimson. "Um . . . okay, long johns."

He smirked. "That's appropriate attire for this neck of the woods. C'mon, shed those bunker pants."

She made a face at him but somehow managed to pull off her turnout coat, then drop the suspenders from her waist. She squirmed out of the pants like a lizard shedding its skin, and a second later stood in the doorway in her stockinged feet, free and, by the way she wouldn't meet his eyes, dying on the spot.

He lowered the joist. "Let's get out of here."

"What about my pants?"

He walked over, grabbed her by the arm, and pulled her out onto the porch. The afternoon sun glinted off the gathering storm in her blue eyes. "You in your pajamas and alive is a thousand times better than a fully dressed casualty. We'll get the city to shore up the house; then you can go in after your . . . um . . . pants."

She looked so utterly ridiculous, however, standing in her turnout coat, which effectively managed to cover most of her backside, her face grimy and her helmet levered back on her head like it might be her father's, he couldn't help but laugh. Now safely outside the hover of danger, he saw the humor.

She punched him square on the shoulder.

"Hey, is that how you treat your knight in shining armor?" He rubbed his shoulder but couldn't work up a frown.

"You're not my knight. You're just . . . oh!" She turned away, her fists clenched. Poor woman. She looked like she might haul off and slug him again . . . or perhaps cry. Her jaw tight, her eyes didn't meet his and he thought he saw actual fumes spiraling from her ears.

Lifting her helmet, he leaned down to her eye level and tried to pull a smile out of her. "Sorry, Chief. I hope I didn't offend you by, you know, rescuing you or anything."

She looked up at him, her face red. He fought the urge to duck. What was it about this woman that refused to appreciate the ironic humor in this situation? Especially after her declarations of independence the night before. He wasn't even going to attempt a lecture on safety. He liked all his teeth in his mouth, thank you.

Ellie finally worked out words. "Well, now, I suppose all the guys at the station will have a good one on me." Again, the clenched jaw, and this time did he spy tears?

"Wait. You think I'll turn you into the town laughingstock?" The last thing he wanted to do was listen to Mitch run her down. Dan would go to his grave with this episode if that's what it took to protect her.

She swiped away an errant tear in lightning speed. "Tell them what you want. I don't care."

"Yeah, well, I'm not going to tell them anything, Ellie. I promise. That's what friends do. Pull each other out of scrapes and keep their secrets."

The gaze she turned on him was so searching he felt it spear right through him to the soft tissue of his heart. He could barely breathe, let alone speak.

Finally, she smiled. Tentative and just enough to make him believe the sun might rise again in the morning. "You're my friend?"

"I thought we ironed that out last night on the beach."

She looked down at her stockinged feet. "And you're not going to tell the guys that

I'm running around town in my jammies?"

He scratched his chin, as if mulling it over. She whacked him again on the shoulder and nearly toppled him off the porch. But there was a genuine light-up-the-world smile on her face.

"Well, it'll cost ya," he said.

She narrowed her eyes, the smile dimming. "What?"

"Dinner."

"I can't . . . um . . . well, I'm not the greatest cook."

"Oh, c'mon. You're a fire chief. You're supposed to be able to make five-alarm chili. I thought it was part of the job."

She winced with one eye closed.

He laughed. "Calm down, Miss Good Housekeeping. I was planning on doing the cooking — or maybe picking up some sub sandwiches. But I have a cute place up the trail I'd love to show you."

"Can I change out of my jammies?"

"Ellie, you can wear anything but your badge."

Her smile disappeared. The light in her eyes blinked out, and her playful expression faded with a twitch. "Then I guess I'm going to have to say no."

He felt a chill shudder through him. He'd meant it as a joke . . . well, okay, not a complete joke. It would be nice to get to know the woman without the internal armor that came with her job. But if he had to chip away at it, he'd take her fully armed and outfitted for battle too.

"I was just kidding, Ellie," he said, but he nearly heard the lock turning in her emotional barricade. She turned away from him, hopped off the porch, strode across the yard, and hopped into her Jeep. He watched her in silence, his heart sinking.

But he didn't miss the quick swipe of her hand across her face as she gunned the engine and tore past him.

Ellie stomped her brakes before some ambitious cop pulled her over . . . in her long johns, tears running down her face. She could just imagine what the local law would think . . . or worse, what the town gossip page would write.

Local fire chief breaks sound barrier. Ellie Karlson, Deep Haven's new fire chief, was arrested Sunday afternoon, wet to the bone and dressed in thermal underwear, for breaking every speed limit in Deep Haven. She gave no account for her excessive speed. . . .

Except, of course, if it were true gossip, it would describe one tall, dark, and curious pastor, his timely appearance, and his lifesaving rescue. Hopefully it wouldn't mention that his north-woods charm had nearly turned her to mush. To think she'd actually considered, for more than a minute, having dinner with him. She wanted to keep driving right off the pier. Did she think she'd finally found a man who might, just possibly, see beyond her badge to a woman full of fear as well as courage? a woman who could be both feminine and fierce?

Thankfully, he'd snapped her to her senses with that "no badge" comment. How dare he? Obviously Pastor Dan was threatened by the thin piece of tin, and for the second time today she could thank God for stepping in to save her.

She crawled down Main Street, forcing a smile, trying not to focus on the families walking along the shore or feeding the gulls. Sundays had always been filled with games, big dinners, and laughter in the Karlson home. How long had it been since she'd spent the day in rest? enjoying relationships?

Nearly fifteen years. She gritted her teeth and forced back the wave of melancholy. Getting knocked down had obviously jarred loose her emotional baggage. Maybe a good shower, lunch, and a walk with Franklin would help her pin it back in place.

She waited until the street emptied, then

dashed out of her car, taking the steps to the hotel two at a time. Passing an elderly couple rocking on the porch, she kept her head down, barreled through the hotel lobby, and ran up the stairs.

Franklin looked up from his place on the center of her bed as she slammed the door behind her. His big brown eyes blinked.

"Don't ask," she said, peeling off the coat, throwing her helmet on the chair, and stepping into the shower.

The hot spray sloughed off her frustration. She braced her hands on the shower walls, let the water course over the back of her head and down her spine.

Would Dan keep his word? She winced, rewinding her dire predicament, his laughter and his promise. He'd seemed . . . sincere. So much so it had nearly toppled her off her professional bedrock. Friends. *Right.* The second she gave in to that impulse was the second he'd be pushing her to hang up her fire axe.

She'd do well to remember that she'd had her pick of men over the years, and none of them — not one — had been able to see past the job. No, she'd made her choices, and she wasn't going to trash fifteen years of sacrifice for a moonlight walk and a husband to cozy up with when the night got cold. Or when life got tough.

She needed a man to protect her like she needed a lump on the head.

But hadn't Dan just sprung her out of a very long and embarrassing imprisonment?

She shouldn't have let his voice, so filled with concern, rock her. Long ago she had decided that the standard marriage, family, and homemaker life wouldn't fit into her life goals. Then why, with a *whoosh,* did the image of Dan's hand in hers fill her brain? It hadn't helped that he'd led her, with firm gentleness, out of harm's way.

Maybe she wanted protecting more than she wanted to admit.

Or maybe Pastor Dan simply had a way of finding all the unprotected corners of her heart and zeroing in for the kill. She'd have to give him wide berth if she expected to escape his very subtle, charming blitzkriegs. She had a job to land, a reputation to prove.

Turning off the water, she hopped out, dried off, then unearthed a pair of track pants and her new Deep Haven sweatshirt. After slicking her hair back in a tight braid, she woke up her lazy dog, pulled him off the bed, and headed for the door in her jogging shoes.

Miss Good Housekeeping, indeed. She slammed the door. Come Monday morning

he was going to discover she didn't have a
domestic bone in her body.

7

"You made her mad," Joe Michaels said as he jogged around the high school track.

"You think?" Dan ran beside him, sweat beading on his temples, his chest heaving. After a day of training, he felt worn to the bones, fatigue a heavy blanket on his shoulders. He was in worse shape than he thought. "How many times around?"

"Four. You'd think we were on the high school track team or something."

"This is not how I'd hoped to spend my Saturday." Dan thought of his cabin, still waiting for the back wall to be constructed. "How many times did we go over the different classes of fires?"

Joe shook his head. "I'm just trying to recover from the stress of hauling that dummy down the ladder. I think she put boulders in the arms."

Dan glanced at Ellie, who was proving a point by running fifty paces ahead of the pack. She'd made no friends today, talking to seasoned firefighters like they were probies. Between the beginning firefighter instruction about the tetrahedron of a fire, the different types of fire and standard techniques for extinguishing each, and the organization of FAST — Firefighter Assist and Search Team — Dan wondered if she thought any of them had working gray matter. Half the guys had left after lunch, announcing that she'd used up her allotted time. The remaining bunch, twelve of them who had decided they liked their work — or maybe their feisty chief — had run rescue scenarios all afternoon.

Only a light, autumn-scented breeze and the fact that he'd have another chance to see Ellie made the day bearable for Dan.

Who would have thought, a week after his colossal foot-in-the-mouth comment, that she'd still treat him like two-day-old roadkill? She hadn't even met his gaze, even when their hands had touched while retrieving water from the cooler. The porcupine returneth.

He finished his lap in tight silence. Joe and he veered off the track, gripping their knees, breathing hard. She had already finished and walked between her "men," checking on them, drinking her water. She had her hair back in a ponytail and had donned a baseball cap to shade her eyes. With her workout clothes and springy step, she looked about sixteen. If it wasn't for the fact that she'd made a point of humiliating them all by folding a forty-five-pound hose then hauling it the length of the football field, he would almost think she was here to cheer them on — a firefighter groupie.

"How are you doing, Joe?"

Slave driver stood against the sun, her outline putting Joe and Dan in shadow. "How's Mona?"

Joe straightened, wiping his brow. "Feeling good finally. Thanks for asking."

She smiled as if she hadn't, only an hour ago, berated him for "killing" his victim by dropping the dummy forty feet on its head. "Liza told me you picked out names."

Dan shot Joe a look. "You have names?"

"Maybe." Joe ducked his head. "Mona has a small list she's compiling."

Dan looked from Ellie to Joe and back. Since when did she know more about Joe's life than his best friend did? Dan tried not to feel affronted.

Joe turned to Ellie. "Are you done torturing your firefighters, or is there more fun on the agenda?"

Ellie gave him a narrowed-eyes look, one

that came with a smile that voided any malice. Why did Joe always get away with sassy comments? Fire Chief Ellie would flatten Dan with a scowl if he even hinted at being tired. Dan shook his head, turned away, watched the other firefighters gathering their duffel bags. Mitch Davis and two other firefighters, looking burly and not at all winded, stood in a clump, probably trying to decide whether to shower before heading out to Billy G's Pub and Bowl.

"No, I think that'll be enough training today, Joe. Thanks for sticking in there," Ellie said.

"I gotta get home, then. Mona's probably back and looking to fill my ear about her doctor's appointment. She's bracing herself for weight gain, and my job is to talk her down from the ledge."

Was that a giggle from Ellie? Dan nearly glared at Joe, who took off toward his bag of gear.

Which left Dan standing with Ellie. She glanced at him. Her smile dimmed. "Uh . . . thanks, Dan, for your hard work today. How's your shoulder?"

It throbbed and felt like someone had used it for batting practice. "Oh, fine. Thanks. I know how to bounce."

Ah, a faint smile from the fire chief. It

almost felt like the real thing. "You'll be a great addition to the FAST team. Thanks for taking the position." She turned to leave, but he reached out, hooked her arm.

"Ellie, how are you?"

She looked pointedly at his hand on her arm. He removed it but stood close enough to keep his question between them. "I'm fine." She didn't look at him.

"Fine? As in 'I just made it through my first week by the skin of my teeth,' or fine like 'Wow, I'm thrilled with my new job. What a cinch'?"

She stared at him hard, as if debating which answer to give. Then with a loud sigh she shrugged. "Considering half my crew abandoned me at lunchtime and the other half thinks I'm Attila the Hun, well, I think things are about as terrific as they can be."

"I'm still here. And I'm pretty sure you're not a Hun. At least you're a lot less hairy."

One side of her mouth hitched up. "I shaved my beard off this morning."

Dan touched his chin. "Me too."

She really smiled now, and it felt like a fresh breeze. "Donning your pastor motif, huh?"

"Yeah, well, gotta please the masses. Can't show up at the pulpit looking like a hooligan."

139

She laughed. "Somehow I can't picture you as the hooligan type."

He blinked at her. "Oh, really?" He knew his smile had dimmed, but his brain traveled back to only a week ago when she'd thought he was the local brute squad leader. "I'm glad to hear that."

A gentle, comfortable silence passed between them. She stuck her hands in her jacket pockets while the wind played with the caramel-colored strands of hair it had dislodged during the day. She wasn't wearing makeup today — something he hadn't missed, but now he noticed how much younger she looked without it. Standing here with the sun grinning down at them, he almost felt fresh out of high school, his entire world before him.

"Hey," he said through a bevy of swelling feelings, "why don't you come to church tomorrow? Joe and Mona attend. And Liza." He had his eyes on her reaction, hoping she'd say yes, but out of his peripheral vision he saw Joe digging through his duffel and grabbing his cell phone.

Ellie rubbed her arms as if cold, and a faraway look entered her eyes. "Yeah. Maybe. What time?"

Joe flipped open his cell phone and immediately his face darkened. Something was wrong.

"Ten-thirty service. Adult education is at nine-fifteen."

She made a mock painful face. "I don't have any church clothes."

Oh, how he wanted to say something about her long johns. Some quip that might make her laugh or even forgive him for his offensive comment, but Joe's expression had him off balance. "Wear your jeans. We're a casual church."

"Really?"

Joe now stood board still, his face twisted. Then, as if perceiving Dan's gaze, Joe turned, stared at him. Joe was ashen.

"Yes. Excuse me, Ellie, will you?" Dan hurried toward Joe, who listened into his cell phone, nodding, his eyes locked on his pastor. Dan felt a streak of fear at the torment in Joe's expression.

"I'll be right over. It's going to be okay, honey." Joe closed his telephone, looked at it. He swallowed in an audible attempt to force back emotions.

"What's up, Joe?" Dan noticed that the man was shaking.

Joe closed his eyes. In a voice so low it sounded more like a groan, he said, "Mona lost the baby."

■ ■ ■ ■

Ellie watched the two men walk away. Something about Joe's posture made her heart sink. Dan had his hand over his friend's shoulder, pastorlike. As they'd been chatting — or was it teasing each other? — she'd seen his subtle shift from playful fireman to town minister. Concern filled his eyes, he frowned, and then his attention had snapped to his friend in need. All that focused worry had tugged at a forlorn place in her heart. She wondered suddenly what it would be like to be on the receiving end of such compassion.

She shrugged it away and jogged over to Bruce Schultz and Craig Boberg, who were tossing their gear into large duffel bags. "Thanks a lot, guys. I appreciate your dedication today."

Bruce gave her a warm smile. "You surprised me, Chief. I didn't know all that about hazardous materials. Don't get many of those up here."

His words blessed her. She'd spent most of the week preparing her lecture on Hazmat procedures. In the big city, it was part of basic firefighter training, but she'd suspected that on the North Shore of Minnesota, the biggest hazardous-material event was cleaning up Main Street after the annual Moose Days Festival.

"Thanks, Bruce. Hey, I'm putting together a new schedule. I'd like to staff the station 24/7 with an on-site captain and an EMT. I noticed on your experience that you'd taken an Introduction to Fire Officer course. I don't suppose you'd consider taking a test to become captain? I need another capable body."

Bruce tucked his helmet under his arm. "I'll think about it. How often are we on?"

"I think you'll be on once every four days. I'd sure appreciate it."

She left him and marched up to Mitch Davis and his group. Ernie Wilkes had stripped down to his jeans and was pouring water over his head. She averted her eyes. "I'm putting together a duty schedule," she said to Mitch and went on to explain new staffing. "I'll add you into the roster, okay?"

But Mitch wasn't listening to her. His gaze went over her shoulder, and a smile twitched his face. Two college-aged girls had jogged onto the track and were slowly making progress around the quarter-mile loop. Their eyes were fixed on the clumps of firefighters, beauty-queen smiles on their faces. Ellie rolled her eyes . . . firehouse groupies.

She turned to deflect them when Mitch strode past her and fell into step with them.

So she'd add him to the schedule. It would only increase his hero status. She shook her head and bid the other firefighters farewell. She heard a few making plans to meet at Pierre's Pizza down the street, others at the bowling alley. No one mentioned a word to her. She tried not to let that ping in an empty place inside.

Hauling two of the rescue dummies to her Jeep, she opened the door and plopped them in. By the time she returned to the field to collect the hoses, the crew had dispersed . . . including Mitch and his two fans.

She took a deep breath and sat on the grass. Franklin had jumped off the front seat of her car and now found his way into her lap. She rubbed his ears, twisting them gently between her fingers as she ran over the week's events.

She'd served one entire week as chief. No calls — well, except for a cat wedged under someone's latticework. She'd managed to get the animal out with her pike pole without having to call out the squad.

Ellie had to admit, *nowhere* did she know of a fire chief required to make house calls. She'd envisioned putting together training schedules, coordinating EMT services, working the budget, overseeing the maintenance of machinery, and commanding incidents. At least that was what she'd trained for.

Instead, she'd spent half her time cleaning the firehouse until it shone, checking equipment, poring over files, assembling her crew into squads, and meeting with city officials. The other half of her time she'd been glued to the telephone, trying to prod the fire marshal to send up a fire investigator. In the end, she'd had to trek out to the Simmons place — this time armed with Steve Lund, her paramedic and friend — and gather evidence from the bathroom herself. She'd boxed it up, along with photographs and two witness reports, and sent it to Minneapolis. How they'd uncover the truth two hundred miles away baffled her, but she'd done her job and closed the case until they called her back.

If she were honest, the high point of her week had been the daring cat rescue. It had been ages, two years at least, since she'd donned her turnout coat for a real blaze. Even though all she faced were a couple of nasty front claws and a worried elderly woman, the adrenaline had run through her veins like a shot of caffeine.

She missed the action.

Today, training with her men, she'd felt challenged, alive, passionate about saving lives. Today she felt like a real chief.

And then Dan had to make her laugh. That, too, felt good. He'd mocked her in a gentle way, rekindling all those budding feelings of friendship from their encounter on the beach. And the fact that he hadn't mentioned her mishap last Sunday had touched her. So maybe he was a man of his word. A man she could count on . . . at least in a fire.

Could she count on his friendship too? Maybe she should hang up her shield long enough to find out. He seemed to respect her authority, and he hadn't groaned once today, although she knew his shoulder had to be turning him inside out. He'd been the first to pounce off the grass, the first to invest in her discussion of Hazmat procedures, and although she avoided meeting his eyes, she saw him slug at least two other men who were whispering.

She didn't want to speculate on the topic of their low-murmured conversations.

Yes, Dan had regained some of the ground he'd lost with his "take off your badge" statement. The next time he pushed his way into her life, if he did it gently, she might let him linger.

Not too close, but close enough to ease the loneliness.

As she leaned back in the grass, watching the wind push around the cumulus in a beautiful azure sky, she decided that maybe indeed it had been a good week. Not a cinch, but certainly well within her grasp.

Perhaps she'd finally discovered the future that Seth had given his life for her to find.

Dan paced the waiting room, going from one side of the brown carpet to the other. Occasionally he'd stop, lean against the window, and watch the shadows stripe the parking lot. The sound of his soda can tab as he flicked it kept him bound to reality, to the sound of the telephone ringing, the smell of medicine. Deep inside, however, he wanted to crawl away and sob.

What could he say to his best friend, who right now was in one of those curtained-off rooms down the hall, holding his wife's hand as she gave birth to their stillborn child? The news felt like a line drive to Dan's chest, so all he could do was pace, hoping he could dredge up some comforting words from the well of pain in his soul.

He closed his eyes and groaned. "Help me, Lord." His inadequacy made him want to scream. Here, the moment when his dearest friends needed him the most, he was about to fail them. He didn't have glorious words that would lift them beyond sorrow. He had only his own grief, his own questions. His own snarled emotions clogging his chest.

Scripture ran through his head — words from the Lord that might offer solace. "Take heart, because I have overcome the world." Or "We know that God causes everything to work together for the good of those who love God and are called according to His purpose for them." Or even, "I know the plans I have for you. . . . They are plans for good and not for disaster." But they seemed somehow inadequate, despite their truth. How did he console a woman who hadn't been able to hold her firstborn child, hadn't named it, hadn't felt its tiny fingers curl around hers? How did he tell Mona that everything would be all right when deep in his gut he himself wondered?

Sometimes he didn't understand God. Why did He allow us to hope and love, only to yank it away? It was in these bleak moments that Dan had to grab a death hold on his faith. On his belief in a good and loving God. Was it Isaiah who said, "If you do not stand firm in your faith, you will not stand at all"?

And yet, despite Dan's head knowledge of a sovereign God, he knew what it felt like to have life swirl down the drain and wonder why God had pulled the plug.

Why, in all the pivotal moments of life did he feel as though his words, his training, vanished? He wanted to do something vivid and substantial, to say powerful things that changed lives. He wanted to be like Stephen, who in the face of his accusers preached a sermon and died a death of boldness. Or have the ministry of Paul, passionate and wise for the sake of Christ, all the way to Rome. But no, all Dan could do was crush his Coke can and fumble with half-remembered verses.

How he longed, just once, to be used by God in a mighty way. To change a life.

Memories of Leo flogged Dan as he stared out the window. Why hadn't Dan told the man exactly how he felt watching him trash his future and discard his family? For that matter, why hadn't Dan run after Charlene when she had given him back his ring? told her that he was wrong, that yes, he could still love a woman who wanted to risk her life day in and day out?

Except, could he? His knee-jerk reaction to Ellie's profession told him he hadn't advanced too far from his stance fifteen years ago. How he wished he could snatch back those words and his brilliantly offensive request that she discard her identity to be worthy of him.

He felt like a cad. Part of him had wanted to jump in his car, race after her, perhaps toss rocks at her window, then hit his knees until she forgave him. Instead he'd stood bound in the clamp of mixed emotions, watching her drive away.

His love wasn't enough to stop his fiancée from leaving him for a life of adventure. Why did he think he'd fare any better fifteen years later?

Still, he wanted another shot at Ellie's friendship. After today's defection by half the fire crew, she had to be nursing some wounds. Despite her don't-mess-with-me demeanor, she needed someone on her side, if not to support her, then to watch her back.

He'd heard enough slander from Mitch to know any misstep on her part and he'd run Ellie out of town with the dogs. But to be her friend, Dan would have to wait. Hope for sometime when her defenses weren't at DEFCON 5, when her soot-streaked face wasn't turning his brain to mush.

And when his dearest friends didn't have

tragedy breathing down their necks.

Turning, he threw the soda can into the receptacle, then wandered to the reception desk. Roxie, one of the night nurses, had just come on duty. He asked about Mona.

"I'll see if she's ready for visitors," Roxie said.

Dan didn't know the Native American woman well, but he recognized compassion in her eyes. There were few people in Deep Haven who didn't know Mona. Her loss would have rocked her friends and family had they known about the baby.

So why hadn't she told them? Dan had mulled that over more than once. Although he and Liza knew — and obviously Ellie from her question about names — Mona had made a point of keeping her joy to herself.

Was it her fear of this very thing? Dan knew about Gabe, Joe's younger brother, and Gabe's Down syndrome, but Joe and Mona wouldn't delay their announcement because of fear, would they?

He braced his hand on the counter, suddenly sure of his deduction. He endured another wave of grief as he realized that their worst fears had probably materialized.

Roxie set down the receiver. "Yes, you can go back. The doctor is finished."

151

Dan trudged down the hall, walking the green mile back to Mona's room. He could hear voices, and as he drew closer, he heard Joe telling Mona that he was proud of her, that she'd done well. Dan didn't know much about miscarriages, but he suspected it wasn't a painless event. He slowly pulled their curtain back.

Mona lay on the bed, a thick cotton blanket up to her chest. She wore a hospital gown, and sweat pasted her blonde hair to her temples. Fatigue hung under her eyes in bags, but she attempted a quivering smile. Dan's heart lurched when her eyes filled with new tears. The redolence of death saturated the room.

Joe's jerky smile portrayed his attempt at composure, but his red, puffy eyes betrayed a man on the bitter edge of anguish.

No words came to Dan. How could they? *Please, oh, Lord, help me minister to them.*

Dan took Mona's hand. His throat felt so thick he could barely push out words. "I'm so sorry," he whispered.

Then, not knowing what else to do, he dropped to his knees beside her bed, rested his forehead against her hand, and wept.

8

The call came in well after midnight Thursday morning, judging by the texture of the moon pushing against the curtains of her firehouse office. Ellie bolted upright, her pulse notched to high and her feet hitting the cold cement floor before dispatcher Judy Franks had finished relaying the call.

Car accident on Route 61 north of town. Ellie keyed up the radio microphone and told Judy to page squad three. She'd divided the twenty-some volunteers into three groups, each taking turns serving as primary in a twenty-four-hour call period. At some point, she hoped to have a captain for each squad manning the firehouse, along with an EMT-trained firefighter.

Until then, it was only Ellie and Doug Miller doing a twenty-four-hour tour. They rushed out to the garage, jumped into their turnout gear, and dived into the rescue rig. Franklin, bless him, had followed her to the edge of the firehouse and stood watching as they opened the door and pulled out into the deserted street.

Doug sat quietly beside her, not saying a word about having her at the wheel. Of all her men, he was the quietest. She could count the words the burly wrestler-type had spoken to her on one hand.

Moonlight illuminated the pavement, and the darkened houses seemed like eerie watchmen as the rescue unit screamed past them, siren blaring, just in case they encountered motorists.

Half a mile out of town, she switched off the siren, feeling stupid. Nothing but the shadows of birch and pine trees cluttered the road. She didn't look at Doug, who stared out the window as if on an afternoon drive. Gripping the wheel, she floored the rig, thankful for the fact she didn't have to dodge minivans and SUVs like she'd had to as she'd careened down Duluth's streets.

Over the chatter box she heard a few of her squad members calling in and Judy reporting the accident's location. Ellie mentally calculated the response time, knowing they were eating away precious seconds of the "golden hour," the envelope of time when a person's recovery is most optimistic.

She saw the crash as she finished a turn in the road. Headlights peeled back the night around a large oak, where a Ford Bronco lay on its side, passenger side down. Ten feet away, an elderly woman in a parka, her nightgown flapping in the lake breeze, waved them over as Ellie pulled onto the shoulder.

Whoever had been driving had done a good job of trying to kill themselves. The SUV had jumped the ditch, bounced off a beech tree, and landed with its roof propped against a thick oak.

Ellie winced at the slash in the beech's trunk. Throwing on the five-hundred-watt lights, she hopped out of the vehicle. The instant bath of light gave the scene a blunt, jarring reality.

Ellie didn't miss the odor of fuel saturating the air.

"I tried to get her out, but the door wouldn't move," said the elderly woman as she tramped up to them.

"Thank you, Francine," said Doug, while Ellie moved to the side of the unit. "We'll take care of it from here."

Ellie grabbed her class B fire extinguisher and shoved it into Doug's arms. "Watch my back. I'm going to see if I can find that leak."

With her flashlight, Ellie scanned the area

for power lines, letting out a breath of relief when she saw that the SUV had missed the pole.

Doug was right behind her as she crept up to the Bronco. Ellie heard the crunch of glass under her boots and moaning from inside the vehicle. "Hang in there," she called. "We'll get you out."

Angling her flashlight, she scanned the undercarriage of the SUV, locating the fuel line. Sure enough, fuel leaked out of a puncture between the front wheels. Reaching into her pocket, she pulled out a golf tee. "If this thing goes up, douse it good."

She heard the sound of a motor in the background, a car barreling up the highway. Moving with care, she worked the golf tee into the puncture until it sealed the fuel drip. Even so, fumes emanated from the saturated ground. She prayed the electrical systems from the car wouldn't set it off.

Ellie could barely reach the door. "We need to immobilize the vehicle." The worst thing she could do is cause the Bronco to fall forward onto its tires by climbing on it, inflicting more damage to the victim inside.

"I'll get her," Doug said instead, setting down the extinguisher. Standing on the tire, he began to hoist himself to the hood.

The Bronco rocked and Ellie jumped

back, afraid it would land on her. "Get down, Doug!" She yanked on his coat. The man fell back and landed hard on the gasoline-spattered ground.

An expletive flew from his mouth. "What's wrong with you?"

She rounded on him. "Where did you go to rescue school?" Not waiting for an answer, she ran to the rescue vehicle and retrieved the Hi-Lift jack. Doug had found his feet — and his snarl — by the time she returned. She ignored him and shoved the jack under the frame of the doorjamb. As she began hiking it up, she heard a car pull up behind the rescue unit.

Sweat beaded between her shoulders as she worked. In a moment, the car rested tightly against the tree. "Now we climb on," she said loud enough for Doug to hear.

She gripped the tire and felt hands behind her, pushing. She turned and looked into Dan's eyes. The concern in them spiraled right through to her bones. She hadn't seen him since Sunday when she'd heard him preach. But that day he'd looked haggard and pained. He'd spoken on John 14, somewhere near the end, about finding peace. "Do not let your hearts be troubled and do not be afraid." That verse had resonated deep inside her and picked at the scabs she'd so carefully tended. Her legs had hustled her out of the sanctuary before Dan could turn those probing eyes on her and see how he'd opened old wounds.

She knew enough about being troubled and afraid to fill a lifetime of sermon illustrations.

"Hi," she said but didn't let her eyes linger for his mind-scattering smile. In a second she was crouching on top of the driver's-side door.

The window had been shattered; jagged glass draped the window frame. "Hello in there," she called softly.

Someone moaned in reply. Shining a light into the window, Ellie made out a woman. Curled in the fetal position, she was holding her forearm as if trying to keep it immobile. Her face twisted in the light, and as she met Ellie's gaze, her expression radiated shock. Ellie surmised the victim had banged her head into the window, evident by the glass embedded in an ugly spidery wound that dripped blood into her dark hair, down her thin face, and off her jaw. She looked about Ellie's age.

"Hang on," Ellie said in an even, calming tone. "We're coming in after you."

She looked down at Dan, still standing at the ready beside the vehicle. Doug moved to greet Joe Michaels, Guthrie Jones, and Lionel Parks — most of squad three who'd arrived. Ernie was still unaccounted for.

Ellie reached in, tugged on the unlocking mechanism in the door. She heard it click, but when she tried the door, it gave only enough to slip a finger between the frame. "Dan, get me a pry bar, will ya?"

While she removed the glass from the window, careful not to let it rain down on the victim, Dan ran to the rig and returned in a second with two pry bars. He mounted the SUV behind her and dug the bar into the door beside hers. "On the count of three."

Together they seesawed the door open, the metal screaming. She wasn't unaware of Dan sitting right behind her, his strong arms around her while they worked in tandem. Guthrie, a probie with a wide, round face and eager eyes, stood below, watching like a first grader. Although he'd already passed his beginning firefighter course, his status was indirect assistance only. Joe stood at the ready with a C-collar and backboard.

The door screeched open another six inches. "Guthrie, we need the door chain." A second later the eager lad, his eyes afire, returned and helped her drape the chain around the door, securing it to itself with the slip hook. She tossed it to Dan, who jumped down and secured the line over the hood and around the steering column under the carriage near the front bottom wheel. Anchoring it tight, he attached the hand winch.

Ellie met Dan's eyes, recognized in them the intensity of the first night they'd met when he'd told her she was some sort of dream come true, and felt her heart twitch. He had the look of a man who knew what he wanted and wasn't going to let tragedy stand in his way.

In a second they'd winched the door open. Ellie lay on her stomach and maneuvered her way inside, bracing herself on the steering wheel. "Can you move, ma'am?" she asked.

The inside of the car reeked of blood and beer, and terror radiated from the woman. She looked like she'd been out for a hot evening in her leather jacket, black jeans, and styled long dark hair, now matted and sticky with blood. Her face had taken a beating, and a bruise cupped her eye.

The woman nodded, but her wide eyes indicated otherwise.

Pushing herself out, Ellie motioned for the C-collar. When she moved back inside, she felt Dan holding down her legs, again reading her mind. Her hands free, she snapped the collar on the woman. "Were you wearing your seat belt?" she asked.

The woman barely shook her head.

Ellie held it still. "Okay. Don't move." She debated taking off the roof to lever the woman onto a backboard but decided speed prevailed over precaution. The woman's pulse felt erratic and fast, and her color reminded Ellie of putty.

Hooking her arms under the woman's arms, she hollered up to Dan, "Haul me up!"

Strong hands on her jacket and waist told her that someone had propped up a ladder. When she negotiated herself and the victim out of the window, she saw Joe ready with the backboard lying on the side of the car. With care, she laid the woman on top of it. "Hang in there, ma'am," she said to the woman, who still hadn't released Ellie's arm from her white-knuckle grip.

Quickly they secured the victim and lowered her to the ground. Ellie made quick work of splinting her arm, fixing on a non-rebreather mask, and taking the woman's vitals. By the time the ambulance had arrived, the woman was packaged and ready for transport.

Guthrie stood ten feet back, his eyes full of hero worship when Ellie closed the ambulance doors. Joe and Dan were layering the fuel-soaked area with foam, creating a barrier between the fuel and oxygen. Doug and his pal Ernie, who had finally arrived twenty-plus minutes into the incident, stood glaring at her from the clasp of light. No doubt Doug had embellished their incident to epic proportions.

She unhooked the winch, watching Chief Sam and one of his deputies taking a statement from Francine. Tucking the apparatus back into its compartment, she didn't hear Dan steal up behind her.

"Good job getting Bonnie out."

"You know her?" Ellie turned and jumped at the effect of Pastor Dan Matthews, up close and personal, looking devastatingly handsome in his turnout coat and hint of dark whiskers. The guy hadn't stopped to comb his hair, of course, and it curled defiantly from under his pushed-back helmet. He braced one hand on the SUV door, leaning into their conversation.

"Yeah. She and her husband own the General Trading Store — that big log department store on the harbor. Just recently separated." He shook his head. "They came to me for counseling a few weeks ago.

We had one session and they didn't return, although Bonnie tried to schedule another." His face twisted, as if he took their absence as a personal failure. "I wanted to help her, but I have rules against counseling alone with a woman. Poor Bonnie. She's had it rough. From what I hear, her sister Emilee was killed in an auto accident a few years ago, and Bonnie's felt pretty alone."

"Looks like she's trying some different methods of counseling." Ellie remembered the redolence of beer swilling the vehicle.

He nodded, a grim look on his face. "Well, I was impressed with your quick thinking. You knew just what to do."

She smiled at that. "Well, thanks. It's nice to know I'm earning my keep."

"Was there any doubt?"

She opened her mouth, incredulous. "Remember, and I quote, 'over my dead body'?"

He winced, closing one eye and then the other. It was so endearing and filled with exaggerated pain she laughed. "Okay," he admitted, "so maybe I had a teensy bit of doubt. But my stupidity had more to do with me than you, believe me."

Oh? She wanted to follow that statement right down to his secrets. "Hmm. You know how to pique a girl's interests, Mr. Do-Right."

"Do I now?" His gaze had turned decidedly mischievous. "Well, I don't suppose I could tempt you into a cup of coffee down at the Loon Café? It's open all night, and I know Becky could rustle us up some eggs."

Ellie checked her watch — 4 A.M. She should be running home, climbing under the covers, snuggling with Franklin. But something about Pastor Dan's smile felt like an embrace, and she couldn't disentangle herself from his charm. "Okay."

"I can't believe it's closed." Dan shook his head and angled Ellie a look of exasperation. Framed in the glow of early dawn, it softened all her features and dropped her age about ten more years. He felt decidedly delinquent, as if he'd been out all night cruising on a hot date.

But Ellie didn't look like that kind of girl. With her Laura Ingalls braids, her jean jacket, and clasped hands on her lap, she looked sweet and pure.

He wanted to slap himself. He shouldn't be thinking about kissing her. Not only would she fire him on the spot, but Ellie Karlson was the last woman he should consider for a wife. He gave a half chuckle, just thinking about her trying to lead the women's Bible study. . . . She'd probably make them do laps around the church if they didn't memorize their verses.

"What's so funny?" When she looked at him with those breath-stealing blue eyes, all his humor disappeared. Perhaps he was in more danger than he realized.

"Uh, nothing." He sighed. "Well, I didn't know the Loon was closed on weeknights."

"Not much of a nightlife, huh?"

Was she teasing him? She did have the most beautiful smile, and she employed it now, rendering him . . . "Uh . . . no . . . I, ah . . ."

She laughed. "I'm kidding you, Pastor! Loosen up."

"Right." Sweat trickled between his shoulder blades. "I guess I don't know what to do. I wanted coffee."

"And eggs. In fact, I think you promised." She yawned, but her eyes twinkled behind her hand.

"I don't remember promising."

"Well, if you're not going to feed me, then I'm going back to the ranch. Franklin is waiting." She had a tweak to her smile, however, and for some reason he couldn't get past the idea that she wanted to be here with him. That somehow he'd made a giant, don't-pass-go leap from fiend to friend.

He suddenly felt very, very warm. "Hey, I have an idea. Let's go . . . well, okay, I don't know if you'll like it, but I'd like to show you something."

She narrowed one eye. "The same something you wanted to show me a week ago without my badge?"

He shook his head. "I meant it when I said I was sorry."

"It's okay, Dan. I'm not wearing my badge today."

"Not like you don't have to. I mean, it's up to you, but I don't have a problem —"

He liked it when she laughed. It filled his car with the texture of happiness.

"Well, I was a little . . . touchy that day," Ellie admitted. "It's not every day that the fire chief needs to be rescued. My pride may have been a bit bruised."

He smiled. How he appreciated a woman who could see herself from the outside and admit her weaknesses. "And now?"

"After your stellar incident report on how well your fire chief managed tonight at the crash site, I think my ego will fully recover."

"Ah, the stellar incident report." He tapped his fingers on the steering wheel. "So this is an attempt at extortion. You'll go with me in exchange for flattery?"

"Absolutely." She smiled and sucked him right into her world. Grinning like a man cleared of all charges, he fired up his VW Bug and drove through the streets. Ellie watched the houses tick by without comment.

"Have you found a place to live yet?" he asked.

She shook her head. "I moved some of my gear over to the firehouse. I'm sleeping there most nights anyway. I know I should find someplace to rent before I go broke, though."

"You know they say that the hotel could fall over with a big wind."

She chuckled. "That or burn to the ground. I don't even want to think about how many fire hazards I saw. I'll have to meet with the manager and have him implement some changes before I book another week there. At least I'm next to the fire escape."

"So you're sleeping at the firehouse? with the guys?" He didn't mean for that tinny, disapproving tone to emerge — he hoped she wouldn't guess it was more personal than moral.

She scowled at him. "No. Not *with the guys* as you so delicately put it."

"Sorry."

She whacked him playfully, and he was relieved to see a smile on her face. "I'm in my office with the door locked; they're upstairs in the bunk room. It's almost like having my own apartment."

"Then you don't walk around in your long johns?"

She glowered at him. "No. I reserve that for my trips into town. The grocery store, the library, the bookstore. I have a rep now. The Jammie Girl."

Pure glee rippled through him at her self-teasing. "Well, Jammie Girl, have you ever played any stick?" He pulled into the high school parking lot and drove around back to the ice arena.

"Stick?"

"Yeah. Hockey. Do you know how to skate?"

This time when she looked at him, he saw pure challenge in her fiery blue eyes. "My brother was a goalie for his high school team. He got good because he practiced against me."

"Then let's shoot some stick, Jammie Girl."

9

"Are you sure you don't want more pads? This ice is hard." Dan circled Ellie as she pushed herself to a sitting position on the ice. She was going to have a bruise on her hip the next time she looked in the mirror, but she forced a smile.

"Nope. Not if you don't check me again."

He looked sufficiently offended. "I didn't check you. That was a pure and simple arms-circling, feet-scrambling *oompah* right onto your . . . um . . . padding." He skated by and hooked her under the arms, helping right her, then glided away, just as she got her footing.

Bummer. She wouldn't have minded terribly if he'd helped her a smidgen longer. She rather liked the sensation of his strong hands holding her up.

"Okay, yes. I'll admit it's been a while since I skated, but these are men's skates — nearly two sizes too big for me, I might add

— and you . . . you *looked* in my general direction and sent me sprawling."

"Two-minute penalty for looking," he announced to the unseen crowd. Then he grinned and she nearly fell again.

Dressed in a practice jersey — he let her wear his game jersey — he looked about seventeen years old, complete with tousled hair, teasing gray eyes, and a whiskered smile that spoke anything but mature or responsible. And when he skated by, he brandished his secret weapon — a part-masculine, clean-soap, mysterious, and very heady Dan fragrance that left her head spinning.

If she ever wanted to enjoy a man's friendship, it was now. She felt safe laughing at his jokes and poking fun in return. Natural. Like they'd been friends for years.

"Tell you what," he said, skating close now, "I won't use my hockey stick. Just my blades. You have the advantage."

"You're on, pal. What's the score?"

"Oh, a bazillion to one?" He smiled triumphantly and pumped his hands in the air, doing a hoo-yah victory chant.

She rolled her eyes. "I have at least two."

"Oh, sorry. A bazillion to *two.*"

She had to like a guy who didn't let her win. No, he wasn't trouncing her like he said — she'd managed to deflect more than one of his shots — but she'd seen enough of his slick moves on the ice to comprehend that he could skate circles around her. Still, he played a game that made her feel matched, not defeated.

She tapped her stick on the ice. "Face-off."

He skated close, his hands behind his back. "Ready?"

"Drop it."

The puck landed between them and she slapped it away, racing after it across the ice. The skates were loose and wobbly on her feet, but she felt as if she could fly. Dan skated right behind her, gliding like a prince, looking like he was born on the ice. She reached out with her stick, hooked the puck, and maneuvered it behind the net. Dan lunged for it with his foot, but she whacked him hard on the shin.

"Hey!"

"You're wearing shin pads!" she yelled and snapped the puck toward the goal. It bounced off the pipes.

Dan leaped after it, giving it a good kick. It sailed past the blue line and slowed to a stop ten feet in front of her goal. Scrambling after it, she heard Dan beside her, his skates cutting the ice, and reached out her stick,

171

trying to wave him off.

He laughed and skated around her, letting her scoop up the puck and send it sailing back to his end of the rink. By the time she caught up to it, her pulse felt in overdrive, her adrenaline surging through her veins.

Dan skated all around her, in and out, kicking at the puck. She dodged him, her high school years on the rink returning to her in a rush. The crisp smell of ice, the wind filling her ears, the frozen breath of the air cool on her hot cheeks seemed an intoxicating potion. She was twirling, twisting, and . . . and suddenly it wasn't Dan laughing, dodging at her — it was Seth. Tall, blond, wide-shouldered Seth.

"C'mon, sis, don't let me get it!"

"Not on your life, pal!" she said and knocked the puck away from him, changing directions, weaving like a pro. She flew down the ice, then over the red line.

"Go; go!" Seth yelled, his breath over her shoulder.

She reeled back, shot — score!

"Way to go!"

Dan's voice filled her ears, and she was back in the present. Dan punched the air, just as thrilled that she'd scored on him as when he pitched it in. He grinned, his eyes alight. "You *do* know how to skate. I'm totally impressed."

She felt a blush creep up her face. "Thanks. Actually, my brother taught me."

"Sounds like quite a guy." Dan had a trickle of sweat coursing down his face. "Does he still play?"

And just like that, the fun died. Grief sucked out her breath, and her buoyant moment popped. She didn't even try to fight it. "No. He . . . ah . . ." Tears filled her eyes. She turned away, skating quickly now, heading for the exit.

Why did sorrow ambush her whenever she felt poised on the edge of happiness?

Because she didn't deserve it. No one should have a right to feel happy when another person died in their place. No one. Especially not a kid sister who should have walked away from danger when she'd had the chance. Before her brother was forced to save her life . . . and lose his.

She stepped out of the rink, blurry eyed.

Dan was a step behind her. "Ellie, what is it?"

She shook her head and kept walking.

"Ellie?" Dan grabbed her arm, then gently pressed her to turn. She wouldn't look at him. He cupped her chin and raised her face. "What's the matter?"

Clenching her teeth, Ellie fought to keep

her emotions from crashing over her. "Seth was killed in a forest fire when I was nineteen."

His groan was a ripple of pain that came from his chest and found its way to her heart. The empathy and kindness in it pushed her pain to her throat and obliterated her last layer of defense. A wrenching sob tore out of her, one that even she had never heard, and nearly doubled her over. She clamped her hand to her mouth and began to shake.

"Ellie," Dan whispered and put his arms around her. Without a muscle to resist, she tucked her head and leaned against him. He was wide and gentle and held her without reservation, his strong arms around her. Her body shook with the power of her loss, and even so, in the spasm of grief, within the envelope of his embrace, she had the faintest sense of discovery. Of something whole and fresh and alive seeping into the hollow expanse inside her.

Torn between wanting it and fearing it, she simply dug her fist into his hockey jersey, closed her eyes, and let the tears flow.

Ellie Karlson, sobbing in his arms.

As usual, being near the lady turned him to putty.

One second she was wiping the ice with him, gritting her teeth and growling like a wolf; the next she opened her heart and let him inside her private anguish.

If he thought about it long enough, he knew the paradox would tie him in knots. So he simply held on, brushed her hair, and rested his cheek on the top of her head. He didn't try to shush her; somehow that didn't seem right. But he could stand here in the dark and silent arena, the breath of ice misting the air, and hold her until she didn't need him anymore.

He hoped it was a good, long time.

Too soon, he heard her exhale a shuddering breath, and then, with a sigh, she backed away. He loosened his hold slightly but left his hands on her shoulders so he could lean down and meet her eyes. "You okay?"

She nodded and tried a smile. Failed.

He ran a hand down the side of her cheek. "I'm sorry about your brother. I can tell you loved him."

This time the smile took, and she nodded again.

"And however he died . . . I know he'd be proud of you if he saw how you skated today." He tugged on her braid as he said it.

Something glowed in her eyes. "Tougher

than you thought, huh?" Her voice wobbled.

"Oh no, Jammie Girl. I always knew you were tough. And fast. But now I know you can check me into the boards without an inkling of guilt."

She wrinkled her freckled nose at him. "And don't you ever forget it."

He felt delight shoot through him. "Never." Taking a deep breath and hoping it might clear this sudden muddle of his brain, he checked his watch. "It's nearly 6 a.m. Want to see if the Loon Café is open?"

She yawned and stretched, raising her hockey stick above her head. "I guess I could go for a stack of pancakes. It'll be better than cold oatmeal."

He made a face, and she laughed appropriately. Leading her over to a bench, he bent to unlace her skates. For a moment, she didn't move. Didn't breathe. He looked up. "What's the matter?"

She'd gone pale. "It's just . . . no one has ever done that for me."

"Done what?" He continued to tug on her skate.

"That. Undo my skate. Make me feel . . ."

Cherished? Special? Dan wanted to finish for her.

"Protected."

Okay, he'd settle for that. He wanted to

quip something like, "It's about time" or "What's so wrong about that?" But he'd learned his lesson the hard way twice, and this time he reacted with Ellie savvy. "Don't let it go to your head, Chief."

The color returned to her face in a nice glow and told him he'd scored points. "I won't." She let him finish her skate and produced the other one for his assistance.

The sun had sprinkled the parking lot with dots of rose gold, turning the scattering of oak leaves into bronze, the maple into copper. Ellie walked beside him, and when he held out his elbow, she looped her arm through his.

The smallest of smiles played on her lips, despite the red that still rimmed her eyes. He hadn't realized how short she was. Despite her strong, compact body, she could probably fit under his arm well. He suddenly longed to find out.

But her hand on his arm was enough. Friends. He opened the car door. As she moved around the car, the wind caught the strands that had escaped from her braids, and she stopped to push them away. A small gesture, but in it he saw Ellie Karlson, fire chief, pushing away the things in life that stood in her way.

He must have had that revelation written

in his expression. She stopped, stared at him with an odd half smile. "What?"

"Nothing," he said. How was he supposed to tell her that she'd etched a tiny place inside his heart this morning? That being her friend was a thousand times better than he'd expected — and he'd expected a lot. That somehow, inexplicably, she seemed to fit into his life, and he hoped she wouldn't push him away too. But those thoughts were too fresh, too vulnerable to speak aloud. He shrugged. "You play good hockey."

"Yeah," she said slowly, her gaze locked on his. "You do too."

Ellie flew down the hill, the wind singing in her ears, bent low over the handlebars of her mountain bike. Dan, right behind, had finally quit yelling at her to slow down and had accepted the challenge of keeping up.

She couldn't remember when her heart felt like it could take flight, but that ethereal feeling surrounded her whenever Dan called her up and asked her to "hang out" with him, as if they weren't really dating.

Well, she couldn't really call what they were doing dating. Dan had kept a respectable "friends only" distance since last week when she'd had a near breakdown at the hockey rink. But something about the way he looked at her, with pure sunshine in his eyes, made it *feel* like a date.

What was she thinking? She'd been the one to draw the line in the sand. Hadn't she sketched out their "just friends" destiny on the beach? And she'd reaffirmed it in the car after breakfast at the Loon Café, informing him — well, okay, *hinting* — that she'd never dated a fireman and didn't plan to. At least that's what she had intended with her, "Thanks, Dan. This was . . . unexpected. And . . . fun. You're a good friend."

If she were to take a close look, she'd admit that he hadn't crossed any invisible lines. Every time they were together, from service calls to training, he didn't even breathe that they'd spent more time together than apart, even calling her Chief Karlson or simply a curt Chief. But they'd had pizza twice, once sitting in a secluded enclave of beach, gone jogging once, and hiked up a river last Sunday afternoon. Two nights ago he'd cooked her an omelette that still made her mouth water, and then they'd watched a movie at the firehouse. Of course, he'd been on a twenty-four-hour shift at the time.

She could hardly write off those episodes as *pure* friendship, could she?

She should. Ellie knew she had no business dreaming about anything more with this man or with any other. She had a job, a focus, a purpose in life. Seth's sacrifice demanded that much.

But as she overlooked Deep Haven, barreling down the Gunflint Trail, Dan's friendship felt easy and on the sweet edge of enthralling.

Her workload felt easy also. She'd endured her first couple of weeks working in the house with the fire captains and rescue workers on staff and had even appointed a deputy chief to back her up on days when she went . . . oh, say . . . biking with Dan.

She shook her head free of her thoughts and cast a look back at Dan. He pedaled just a whisker behind her, wearing a look of sheer determination, his face into the wind, his hair blowing against his bike helmet, his biceps defined as he gripped the handlebars. He flashed her a grin. "Right on your tail, Flash."

She laughed, then bent over the bars and guided her bike like a pro as they sailed into Deep Haven city limits. Turning on Fourth Street, she deliberately led them past the Simmons house.

Dan pedaled easily beside her. "They're going to tear the place down in a few days."

"I still haven't received the forensic report," she said, slowing to look at the desolate site. "But the medical examiner's report detailed cause of death as carbon monoxide poisoning. Toxic smoke from the flashover."

Dan flinched, and his expression reminded her that Leo had been his friend. "We'll figure it out, Dan. If it's arson, I'll get to the bottom of it."

He nodded, but something deep in his eyes told her he wasn't listening. She'd come to call it his "pastor moments," when thoughts of his congregation filled his mind. His face took on a texture of worry, even pain, and she hadn't quite figured out how to respond. It reminded her of Seth, and she couldn't deny the ever-so-subtle fear that nipped at her.

Such looks could drive men to do dangerous things.

"Let's head down to the Footstep," she suggested, trying to pull Dan out of the grip of his job. "I want to talk to Liza."

He nodded and kicked off without a word. The Footstep of Heaven Bookstore and Coffee Shop had been decorated in a harvest theme. Pumpkins, gourds, and pinecones lined the front porch, and sprays of drying chrysanthemums arrayed in baskets center-pieced the maroon tablecloths on the porch tables. Someone had affixed a scarecrow to the door, dressed appropriately in a flannel shirt, bandanna, and cutoff shorts. He looked like a straw version of Joe.

Ellie leaned her bike against the porch and followed Dan into the store. While Dan veered to the right into the bookstore, Ellie hesitated, then headed into Liza's section. A college-age girl, with long red hair and dressed in bell-bottom jeans and a tie-dyed shirt, sat at Liza's painted metal table. "Hello. Can I help you?"

Ellie stood, mesmerized for a moment by the artistry of a designer who had combined Scripture into a stunning landscape appliquéd quilt hanging on the wall. "Uh, yeah. I'm looking for the owner."

"Oh, Liza's out back. Working." The girl folded her hands and smiled.

"This is beautiful," Ellie said, touching the quilt. The verse on it read "You will know the truth, and the truth will set you free."

"Thank you," the girl said. "I made it."

"What verse is it?"

The young lady walked over to the quilt and ran her fingers over it. "John 8:32. I love this verse. I don't think people really understand it."

Ellie picked up a mug, ran her finger over the etched handle. "Oh?"

"Yeah. I think if people really had an understanding of the truth — the depth of God's love, the freedom He gives from sin and despair — it would radically change their lives. They'd live in true freedom. In true joy." The young woman had a smile tipping her lips, and her eyes were rich and green and shining. "Are you a believer?"

Ellie nodded, but her heart twisted. Obviously she was missing something, because the truth had never felt freeing to her. Not joyous, but confining.

Her face must have betrayed the bitter truth because the crafter smiled warmly. "It's a hard concept. That's why I surrounded the quilt with sunshine and light. As if it were God's light pouring through believers when they truly embrace the concept." She pointed to a dove near the edge. "This is the Christian, soaring in the embrace of all that glory."

"It's incredible. I never thought about it that way."

"My name is Katie." She held out her hand, and Ellie found herself drawn into the circle of Katie's smile. "I work here part-time when Liza's creating. Are you new in town?"

"Sorta." Ellie put the mug back on the shelf. "I'm filling in for the fire chief."

"Wow. That's . . ."

"Dangerous?"

Katie laughed. "No. Daring. Bold. Different. Welcome to Deep Haven." She glanced over Ellie's shoulder. "Hi, Dan."

"Hey, Katie." Dan walked into the room, and Ellie watched as he gave Katie a one-armed hug. They exchanged an insider look that suddenly had Ellie's stomach tightening. "When did you get back?"

"A couple days ago. Are you coming down to the wedding?" Katie asked him.

"Are you kidding? I've been waiting for this day for over a year." Dan didn't let the woman go, and for some reason this only irritated Ellie. In fact, his bright smile and warmth toward Katie told Ellie only one thing.

Dan treated all the ladies in his congregation with the same kindness that he'd been showing her all week. She wasn't anyone special in his life. Just another sinner with a need to be enfolded into the congregation of Deep Haven. Just friends, nothing more.

She felt raw and hollow, and the air in the room turned thick and muggy. "I'm going to go find Liza," she said in a small voice. Dan didn't seem to notice the way she nearly fled from the room.

She felt like a teenage idiot. Obviously

Dan had read her correctly that first day.
Just friends.

She was the one who hadn't been obeying.

10

She wasn't in the congregation. Dan stood at the pulpit preaching a sermon and scanning each face for Ellie Karlson.

If he'd done something to offend her, he didn't know what and he felt sick about it. After their bicycle ride yesterday, she'd disappeared into Liza's studio behind the house. When he finally realized she'd left without him, he'd raced to the station, only to find her Jeep gone, along with her dog.

It wasn't parked outside the hotel either. With a heavy heart, he'd pedaled home, changed clothes, and driven up to his building site to pound out his frustration on sixteen-penny framing nails. The slick of sweat, a layer of sawdust, and the fatigue that embedded his muscles had felt like a sufficient barrier between his wounded heart and reality.

Ellie had gotten under his skin. Her laughter, her go-to-the-goal attitude, her belief in his sincerity combined into a potent mix he couldn't ignore. She made him feel as if anything he touched turned to gold. The fact that she'd cracked open her steel exterior to let him glimpse her passion, laughter, tease, and grit made him feel like superman.

And then, just like that, the walls went up, the door to their friendship slammed shut, locked.

She hadn't returned one of his calls to her cell phone.

And now, as he preached on John 15, he wondered if indeed he'd been cut off, like the vine that bears no fruit.

" 'I am the true vine, and my Father is the gardener. He cuts off every branch that doesn't produce fruit, and He prunes the branches that do bear fruit so they will produce even more. You have already been pruned for greater fruitfulness by the message I have given you.' "

Dan set down his Bible, then braced his hands on the pulpit. "This passage is difficult at best, but for now I want to skip over the pruning and start with verse five of John 15: 'Those who remain in Me, and I in them, will produce much fruit. For apart from Me you can do nothing.'

"Some of us may feel cut off by God. As

if He's severed that relationship, cast us into a blaze. But I think Christ is not talking here about the potential to be severed from our salvation but rather our usefulness in the kingdom of heaven. It is clear that all of us have times when we are on fire for God. When whatever we do or say is filled with riches and truth, when we know without a doubt that God is channeling His love through us."

Dan smiled. "At least I hope that it's true. But even if it isn't, and for those who are going through a dark time — a time when you wonder if your Christian faith, your efforts for the kingdom matter — take heart; you may be being pruned." He reread verses one and two. "Pruning is the cutting back, the refining, the reshaping. By what? The message. When we are experiencing a time of dryness, our answer isn't to try and sprout on our own but to dig deep and let God's love, God's truth heal those wounds and help us become stronger. How? Through God's Word."

He lifted his Bible. "Invest in this book. Saturate your roots with Scripture. Psalms is a great place to start. Remind yourself of God's love, His power, His righteousness. Move on to Matthew and take a fresh look at Jesus and how He reaches out to us in creative and thorough ways. This is the 'remaining' that Jesus commands in verse five. Jesus wants us to cling to Him during those dark, fruitless times." Dan's gaze found Mona and Joe, sitting in the third row, their hands clasped.

His throat burned as he continued. "Hold tight to Christ during your dry, infertile times, whether it be a pruning or pure tragedy. And through your connection to the Vine, God will fertilize your faith and bring you to fruitfulness." Dan willed his words to resonate in his own barren heart, where the parched ground needed the touch of living water.

"This is our hope in Christ. That whatever befalls us, if we remain in Him, He will bear fruit in us. Nothing is without purpose, without hope, with God as the gardener."

Dan blew out a breath and forced a smile. "Next week we'll be talking about verse eight, bringing God glory and why our fruitfulness matters to Him — and to us — eternally."

He bowed his head in prayer, then led the congregation in the benediction. When they stood, he saw someone rise in the back. Why he hadn't seen her before — maybe because she'd been hiding behind Bruce Schultz — seemed outrageous. Ellie looked stunning today in a simple black skirt and white peasant blouse, her hair up, revealing her slender neck.

She'd attract the attention of every man in town. He tried not to let that fact bother him as he marched up the aisle toward the vestibule to greet his departing congregation.

Nor the fact that she ducked out of the last row without a word to him.

The call interrupted a tuna-fish-on-rye sandwich and jolted Ellie from page thirty-two of a riveting story about a paramedic running from the death of his sister. Non-reader Liza had passed her the book after snatching it off Mona's inspirational fiction section. For the first time in years, turning pages didn't seem like a chore. Perhaps she should spend more time trying to dig up good books rather than reading *Firehouse Magazine.*

At the sound of the alarm, she tossed her sandwich onto the paper plate, turned the book facedown, and ran for her gear. Craig Boberg and Bruce Schultz appeared from their corner of the house, and in less than a minute Ellie had manned the rescue truck, Craig at the helm of the pumper truck.

She keyed up the two-way radio mike.

"Deep Haven Station responding. We're 10-17. Please repeat address."

Judy repeated the call. Structure fire four miles north up the Gunflint Trail at a lodge called the Garden. Ellie turned on the siren. Lunchtime on Tuesday wasn't a great time to peel through traffic, even in sleepy Deep Haven. Maneuvering the engine, she instructed Judy to page all the squads and to send the water tanker. A fire doubled every five minutes, and a structure fire, especially that far away, could be an inferno by the time they arrived. Unless they were near a lake, they'd be short on water until they found a way to pump it in.

Ellie had memorized every street, logging road, and state service road within her territory, and with the new GPS that she'd installed into the unit, she found the address without a problem. When she exited the highway, churned up dust on a dirt road, then passed under a wooden archway with a hanging decorative sign, she deduced, her heart sinking deep in her chest, that the place was some sort of resort. No telling how many vacationers were in their rooms lounging, or worse, asleep. She spied three two-story log buildings tucked between snap-brittle pine and parched birch — kindling to the blaze burning deep inside the main structure. As Ellie turned into the circle drive, she made out trace amounts of smoke puffing from behind the roof.

Before the dust settled behind the pumper, Dan and Joe showed up out of nowhere and seized the extra turnouts, boots, and SCBA gear. Ellie gave the guys silent kudos for their response time — quicker even than the station's. They must have been hanging out together, a fact that gave her heart a small pinch.

Joe's face was white, as if stark with panic. He ran past her and grabbed a bystander, a tall woman with graying hair and a terrified expression on her face. "Ruby, are they all out?"

She looked pale and rattled. "I don't know. I think so. But what about the caterers?"

Ellie barely had time to register the group of vacationers — no, not vacationers, or maybe yes, vacationers, but definitely a select group of people clumped at the far edge of the round driveway, their almond eyes wide, some of them hugging each other. Standing farther away was a group of equally horrified ladies dressed for an afternoon social. She frowned as she turned back, surveyed the house, and took a quick inventory of the weather, type of structure, the color and thickness of the smoke puffing out the back of the house. "How did the fire start?"

"I'm not sure," the woman answered. "It's in the back near the kitchen. The sprinkler system should have kicked on, so I don't understand why it's still burning."

Accelerant. If the fire had fuel, even the sprinkler system might not be able to pour enough wet on the red to extinguish it. Ellie inspected her crew — Joe, Dan, Craig, Bruce. Doug Miller's truck streaked up the road, Mitch and Ernie crammed beside him in the cab. The pumper carried enough water for an initial attack, and she spotted the hydrant for the facility in the center of the driveway — obviously, they'd paid homage to code when they built this place. A fact that just might save their building.

She filed through her list of size-up questions — assessing the type of fire, the water, her crew, ability to terminate the fire. She mentally calculated the wind and the dry index for the day. The house sat well away from the woods that ringed it, but if the fire turned into an inferno, she'd easily have a woodland incident on her hands. They needed to contain the fire, then douse it — and fast.

The time she'd taken assigning her squads

into positions of responsibility paid off now. Craig's extra training with the pump operation showed as he hooked up the hoses, first to the truck, then spiraled them out to the water source in the center parking lot.

"Please, this is our home," the woman said in a tight voice.

"Stay back, ma'am," Ellie said. "Joe," she barked into her radio, taking off around the house, "you and Miller get in there and tell me what you see. Work your way to the heat, but be careful. I don't want any kamikaze fire-fighting. Stay safe. Open the windows as you go and get this place vented. Bruce, set up the hoses. Ladder crew, Dan and Mitch, get on that roof and open some vertical ventilation. Ernie, cut the gas and power to the house. I'm going around back."

The back of the house hinted at an ugly future. No windows blown out, no visible fire, but the second-story window directly above the kitchen exhaled yellow-black puffs of smoke. The panes rattled as the blaze fought for air. "We've got potential for a backdraft here, men. We need venting on that roof — now!"

Ellie knew that whatever had ignited the fire had eaten all the available oxygen in the room, starving it until it flamed out, leaving only a thick smoke of unburned particles.

194

But the heat in the room, rising to flash point, only needed a fresh breath of oxygen to explode and engulf the place in flames. Releasing smoke through the roof would lower the temperature, maybe allow them to save the house. "Joe, Doug, what do you see?"

Joe's voice crackled over the radio. "The fire seems to be in the back bathroom, but the smoke is thick and hot on the first floor. It's going to roll over soon."

Ellie pictured the toxic fumes that hugged the ceilings in the other rooms igniting and sending a ball of flame rolling through the house. "Stay low, Joe," she instructed. "Wait for the hose team to cool it down, then head upstairs. Any bodies yet?"

Joe replied in the negative, and Ellie debated pulling him out. The first rule of firefighting was to protect her resources — her men. She didn't want to risk Joe's life for a maybe. But with the fire still below flash point, perhaps they could buy some time.

"Craig, how are you doing on that water?"

When Craig's affirmative came back, she ordered in her hose team, Bruce and Guthrie, who seemed to materialize from nowhere. "Get in and cool down those ceilings. Work your way to the heat. I need a

195

second team on Joe and Miller, protecting that staircase. Is the second crew here yet?"

Craig gave a negative reply and Ellie cringed. The last thing she wanted was trapped firefighters. She'd give Joe and Doug another three minutes before she would pull them out.

She stepped back, watching Dan and Mitch attack the roof. Like lumberjacks, they took chain saws to the shingles, and the sickly smoke billowed out. She wanted to yell at them to be careful, to watch for the sudden burst of flames as the oxygen supply fed the fire, to beware of collapse. But the screams from the crowd and the urge to obey her own rules about not showing emotions at an incident kept her mouth clamped.

Still, the thought of Dan going through the roof nearly ripped her breath from her vise-tight chest.

She swallowed back her panic, forced her voice steady. "We need water fog as you go toward the back room," she ordered the hose team. "Bring that heat down." Instead of a solid stream on a fire, a fog of water would saturate the entire room, as Bruce and Guthrie worked their way to the hottest part of the blaze, protecting the other rooms. She hoped they remembered their masks, their SCBA gear. The memory of Dan tackling the Simmons house without his equipment flashed through her mind. The only safe way to fight fire was with smarts and caution, and she hoped she'd pounded that into their heads. The toxic smoke and searing steam could kill an unprotected firefighter.

She ran back to the front of the house. Craig was monitoring the pressure of the water as it fed into the hoses, ready on the relief valve should the pressure escalate above standards. Simon had arrived and was laying out a second hose, waiting for John. She prayed the guy showed up soon. They worked in teams of two, the front man working the nozzle, the other helping hold the snake of water that, once filled, felt like lifting a steel pipe. Steam hissed out of the roof, the open doors, the windows. Ellie felt a twinge of remorse for the destruction of the house. The carpets and furniture would be melted into a pile, everything covered with greasy, black soot.

She cast a glance over the inhabitants, and her heart fell. These adults were special . . . the pleading words of the woman returning. She frowned. "Is this a residence?" she asked into her radio.

Joe's voice came back. "Yes. For the

mentally challenged." With his grim tone, saving their house took on new meaning.

"Where's my second squad?" she yelled into her radio. They were going to save this house if she had to go in there herself and stamp out the fire with her bare hands.

Doug had exited without checking in and was helping Bruce with the windows on the porch. She counted the rest of her men. Two on the hose in the house, two on the roof, Craig at the pump. She couldn't see Joe. Anger flared in her chest. "Michaels, where are you?"

"I'm upstairs . . ." His voice trailed off.

"Joe?" Her voice betrayed an edge of panic.

"I'm here. I'm just . . . I'm coming out."

"Now! That's an order."

Silence hissed over the line.

She watched the men battle the house, organized chaos. Where was Joe? On the roof, Dan was chewing up a new section with his saw, venting more smoke. She couldn't see Mitch either.

Never had fear for her crew felt so invasive, like claws around her heart. She'd been a fire captain for three years in Duluth, and even then, while she cared about her men, she hadn't felt actual pain at watching them fight a fire. "Joe!"

198

Nothing.

"Joe?"

Dan stopped chopping, looked at her from the roof. "FAST team now," she ordered.

Was Joe wearing his PAL? Was he down? She started toward the door, desperation fueling her steps.

"Ellie, stop!"

Dan's voice in her ear made her freeze. What was she thinking? Dan was already halfway down the ladder. Bruce Schultz and Doug Miller, the other FAST team members, had also responded. "Get back, Ellie. We'll find him."

Ellie stared at the smoke tunneling out of the doorway. It stung her eyes even from twenty feet away.

"You do your job; we'll do ours." Dan ran up to her, took her arm, pulled her back. He looked downright fierce in his turnout gear, mask, air pack, and the definite glower on his face. "You're not going in there."

Before she could sputter a response, Joe appeared in the door, on all fours, holding something to his chest. Dan let her go and ran up to him. Joe got up and sprinted out the door, not even coughing.

Relief spilled through Ellie. "You're in big trouble, Michaels," she growled as she sent the FAST crew back to their positions.

■ ■ ■ ■

Dan had tried not to panic. He really did. He tried to let her do her job, to let her stalk around the fire without his interference. For a couple of seconds he even forgot she was down there, and then he'd hear her voice over his radio and the worry would return with a shudder.

He died a thousand deaths when she rushed toward the door. Where was the woman's common sense? She had him dreaming of his SCBA gear in his sleep — what was she thinking heading into the blaze without it? Besides, such situations were why she'd trained the FAST team — to rescue fallen firefighters. The system worked . . . if the fire chief did her job and kept her panic under wraps.

The fire had been doused, with damage only to the bathroom, kitchen, and two upper bedrooms. Unfortunately, the rest of the residence, at least on the kitchen end of the building, was a soggy, oily mess. Dan finished fixing the tarp onto the hole he'd just made in the roof, then climbed down the ladder.

Joe was wrapped in conversation with Ruby and his brother, Gabe. Dan recognized the item Gabe clutched to his chest — a picture of Joe and his brother as children, standing with their mother, taken shortly after their father had abandoned them. No wonder Joe had risked his life for the snapshot — the brothers knew the importance of saving memories. If Dan remembered correctly, their mother had died shortly after Gabe moved to the Garden, a permanent residence for mentally challenged adults.

It was also a strawberry farm, and Dan didn't even want to imagine what the firemen might be doing to the fields in back. He shot a quick prayer skyward that their garden had been spared.

Ellie was supervising the overhaul of the place, the walk-through that would guarantee every ember had been extinguished, every hot spot cooled. She barked orders like a five-star general, reminding the crew of the most elementary task. Tear open the mattresses from the damaged bedrooms, open the eaves, and fog out the house with huge fans. Her commands saturated the wet, smoky air.

Did she think the Deep Haven Fire Department was totally incapable? that she'd spent the last month training a bunch of chimpanzees? that they couldn't figure out which end of the axe to use? Somehow they'd survived, with nary a casualty among the crew, for the last three years without her. They'd muddle on somehow.

Now that Dan had his emotions safely under lock and key, he could admit, only to himself, that frustration hadn't been the primary emotion ravaging his nerves. Fear, pure and simple, had grabbed him by the throat when Ellie ran toward that house. Every golden moment they'd spent together flashed past his eyes. In the thirty seconds it took for him to get down that ladder, he realized that fear had nothing to do with protecting Ellie, a member of the fairer sex.

It had to do with protecting himself. The blinding pain he'd experienced watching her fling off safety and run into danger told him he'd invested more into their friendship than he'd intended.

He should have recognized that fact last Sunday when she all but bolted out of the church to avoid him. He still hadn't recovered from the ache that nonverbal rejection had left in his heart.

Dan tromped over to Craig Boberg, who was slowly draining one of the hoses. "Fine way to end your shift, huh?"

Mild-mannered, blond Craig, with his basketball height and years of experience, smiled slightly. "Are you on tonight?"

Dan nodded. And if he had it his way, he was going to corner that spitfire chief and force her to tell him why she'd turned the cold blast on. It didn't escape him that this was the second time he'd thrown caution to the wind when it came to Ellie Karlson. In fact, just being near the woman had him off balance. The same qualities about her — courage, determination — that drew him to her also scared him numb. From the moment he'd met her, he couldn't seem to rein in these spurts of emotion. It bothered him more than he wanted to admit. His ability to order his actions, his words, had always given him a sense of control. Of righteousness.

But being with Ellie made him feel the blood in his veins, the air in his chest. Her chilly roundabout felt like a slap.

He watched her as she exited the house and stomped through the muddy pools in the yard toward Joe and Ruby, the house manager for the residence. Ellie looked like a woman on a mission, her fire-chief face pasted on. Dan tightened his grip on his axe and headed into the house, suddenly wishing he could extinguish the fire she'd ignited in his heart.

11

Ellie stood, hands on her hips, staring into the remains of the lodge. She hoped Doug and Mitch were going through the electrical wiring like she asked. She'd caught their rolled eyes at her request but decided to ignore it in favor of doing a thorough overhaul. The last thing she wanted was to return here in a few hours to douse smoldering flames in the eaves.

Two police cruisers had arrived while she and Chief Sam were taking Ruby's account of the fire.

The poor woman, who, Ellie suspected, usually managed the place without breaking a sweat, stood clenching and unclenching her fists as she spoke. "We were in the back having our annual harvest party." Her hazel eyes looked like they could be etched with wisdom but today were overshadowed by horror. "I went in to get a refill of potato salad from the fridge when I saw the smoke."

"Where did it seem to be coming from?" Chief Sam asked. His presence at the scene and the respect he gave Ellie bolstered her lagging sense of victory. Yes, they'd saved the house, but thirty or so mentally challenged adults would have to add this tragedy to their repertoire of struggles.

"I think it must have started in the bathroom. I smelled smoke, and when I opened the door, the entire room went up. Poof, just like that." She shook her head, and despair leaked out of her expression. "I closed the door and ran."

"You did the right thing." Ellie logged her words, then frowned. "The bathroom? Did you see anyone inside, someone who could have set the blaze?" Her mind tracked back to the Simmons fire and the fact that it too started in the bathroom, smoldering until it found enough oxygen to flash over.

"No, I saw no one. We were all outside. I thought the caterers had gone home. I told them I would clean up. It cuts costs that way."

"Caterers?" Sam asked, glancing at Ellie. "Smoky Joe's BBQ?"

"Yep, that's them. They host our party every year. It's sort of a tradition with us, and the residents love it so." She glanced at her group of residents. "I feel just sick for them."

Ellie couldn't agree more. And the fact that Joe had a brother here only added to her nausea. She wanted to fire the fireman or at least hang him by his toenails for snatching up that photograph from his brother's room. But the poignant scene of his handing it to Gabe turned her fury down to low boil. She'd give him a warning. Maybe.

"Did one of the caterers use the bathroom?" Chief Sam asked.

Ruby shrugged. "I was outside in the back. I did hear their truck leave, though."

"I'll do a walk-through later after the smoke has cleared," Ellie said. "We'll get to the bottom of this. Don't worry."

Four hours later, as Ellie hauled out the hoses for drying at the fire station, the blaze at the Garden hung in her mind like the smell of creosote. Something didn't sit right. The fire starting in the bathroom, the evidence of a fueled flashover. She still hadn't received word about the Simmons debris she'd sent to the fire marshal in Minneapolis, but fifteen years of experience poked her.

She lugged the last of the hoses into the

three-story hanging room. She'd already inspected the other hose hanging from the ceiling like a snake in a tree. Hand over hand she wound the next hose along, inspecting for tears, cracks, and other pressure-related weaknesses. The Deep Haven equipment wasn't new by any means, but if it was cared for it should last. She hooked one end on a pulley and hoisted it in the air to let it dry. A horizontal dry would be better, but this option would at least keep it out of the sun.

When she walked through the garage to the kitchen, she noticed through the open doors that Franklin had decided to leave his mark on their polished floor. Poor dog had been neglected in the aftermath of the incident. With a sigh she grabbed a mop, dragged the bucket over to the puddle, and began to sop it up.

"Now that looks more like woman's work than what I saw today."

Ellie turned and dread hit her like a wrecking ball. Mitch Davis, his timber-sized arms folded across his chest, leaned against the door to the kitchen. His dark brown hair had been washed and slicked back, his chin freshly shaved. He had the aura of a very wet, clean mastiff. "Hello, Mitch. What are you doing here?"

The look he gave her made her feel about two inches tall. "I'm on the schedule."

She tried not to scowl. She'd attempted to maneuver Mitch's schedule so she never had to be in the station during his shift. Obviously, she'd overlooked his name on today's roster. "Okay. Well, the turnout gear is piled in the laundry room. If you could get going on cleaning it, I'd appreciate it."

"In your dreams," he said.

She took a deep breath. Why, oh why, did he have to bare his teeth at her every request? She finished cleaning, then plopped the mop back into the bucket, wheeled it over to the wall. "Right. Well, that's part of your job, and I know you did it when Halstrom was chief, so please —"

"Oh, honey, I think that you can probably take care of that. I mean, what's a woman for?" He lifted one side of his mouth as he said it — half smile, half sneer.

"Don't think I won't fire you, pal," she said in a glacial voice, wondering if she could back up her words. It was common knowledge that Mitch had more experience and training than any man on her crew. "Laundry. Now." She strode past him, fighting to keep herself glued.

She felt Mitch's gaze on her back, hot and not at all gentlemanly. Scheduled or not, she wasn't spending the night with Mitch the Menace on the premises. Lifting her chin, she marched to the schedule sheet. Her heart fell slightly when she saw Dan's name penciled in. No wonder she hadn't noticed Mitch's name. Yes, she'd definitely be hightailing it back to the hotel. Not that Dan made her skin crawl, like Mitch did, but the last thing she wanted to do was face Mr. I'm-Here-to-Save-You, especially after her near dash into danger — or being accused of it. She'd felt like a disobedient kindergartner when Dan barked at her in front of her crew. It made her want to strangle him.

Except it felt strangely . . . sweet. And that fact had her emotions in a tangle.

She moved into the kitchen and opened the fridge. She had specifically purchased a number of frozen dinners to help the guys adjust to their new routine. "I stocked the fridge with sodas and sandwiches. You should be set until tomorrow."

"What? You're not staying over?" The way he said it and the proximity of his voice made her freeze.

"Uh, no." She turned. Yep, Mitch had closed the distance between them, and the dog in him had turned predatory. She tried not to feel like cornered prey as she leaned back against the sink. "I stayed here last night, and . . . well, I don't think it's . . ." Her voice trailed off when he took another step closer. The smell of beer leaked off him, and her fear morphed into fury. "You've been drinking!"

He advanced, wearing a lazy smile. "I'm stone-cold sober, baby. But maybe you need a drink? Something to make you a little less tense?" He reached out and touched her shoulder.

She always thought that the expression "cold with fear" was just that — an expression.

But no. Ice raced through her veins, and she actually went numb. Mitch's hand tightened, and the other reached behind her and braced on the counter, neatly pinning her to the sink.

"Please don't, Mitch," she said just above a whisper. Where was the girl who'd fended off a camp full of smoke jumpers and hotshots, and managed to maintain one of the few unsullied reputations in six different EMS departments across the state of Minnesota?

That gritty girl had obviously jumped up and ran for the hills, leaving behind this wimpy scarecrow of a woman. Swallowing hard, Ellie somehow slammed her hand against Mitch's chest. "Leave me alone, Davis."

"No, you don't want that, do you, Chief? See, I've seen you making friendly with our good ole pastor. By the way he looks at you, it seems to me it's more than firefighting tips you're handing out. I was thinkin' that maybe you'd like to share . . . you know, win over a few more converts to your way of thinking? Sort of a firefighter perk?"

She'd had her share of ugly propositions. But the way he said it — condescending, ridiculing — jump-started her muscles and pumped courage into the cowering biddy inside. Ellie slapped him hard. The sound rang through the station as his head jerked. When he met her gaze, fury filled his eyes. An expletive left his mouth, but she'd already ducked under his arm and was halfway across the station. "You're fired, mister!" she yelled, right before slamming the door and throwing the lock.

Her heart hammered against her chest, and she held her breath, listening. She heard another foul word, then, "You'll regret this!" The entire station shook as he slammed the door. She closed her eyes, her breath ragged and hot.

Obviously she'd bitten off way more than she could chew. What had she been thinking when she practically begged Romey to hand her this position? That she could actually pull it off and become the first female fire chief in the state of Minnesota?

She tottered over to her chair and sank into it. Great, just great. What had she just done? Brutus or not, Mitch knew how to fight fires and she needed him. She hung her head in her hands. After reconsidering, Ellie decided to place the oaf on disciplinary probation, giving the dog a cooling off in hopes that she wouldn't have to permanently cut loose one of her most capable captains.

A rap at the door nearly sent her out of her skin.

"Mitch, I told you to leave!"

Silence. Mustering her nerve, she rose, stalked to the door, unlocked it, and yanked it open.

Dan stood in the doorway, looking clean, sweet, and way-too-heroic in a gray T-shirt and enough muscles to communicate that he could toe up to Mitch without flinching. Except he was a *pastor*. "Ellie, are you okay? I just saw Mitch leave, and well, he looked like he could spit nails."

He looked so gentle standing there with his hands in his jeans pockets, his brow furrowed, concern in his eyes. Words locked in her chest, and she tightened her jaw before it shook.

He ducked and looked her square in the eyes. "Did he hurt you?" His concern changed into the slightest flicker of fury. He stepped back and took his hands out of his pockets. They clenched into fists. "Did he?"

She gripped the doorframe, hoping he wouldn't see her shake. "No." But it came out in a whisper.

He obviously didn't believe her because his face twisted and a growl emerged. "What did he do?"

She closed her eyes. "I just want to go home." Then, suddenly, she slid to the floor, touched her head to her knees, and began to sob.

Dan died just a little watching Ellie crumple and her shoulders shake. He crouched beside her, his heart aching. "Ellie, what's the matter?"

She shook her head.

He touched her shoulder, longing to draw her into his arms. "Please, tell me."

"I can't do this, Dan. What am I doing here?"

Her quiet voice shook the emotional bedrock he'd held on to for dear life this week. She had no idea how hard it had been for him not to hold her hand, touch that silky brown hair, tuck her under his arm as he walked her along the shoreline to her hotel. And if she kept crying, he wasn't sure he wouldn't dive over the line she'd drawn and drag them both into deep trouble. He braced himself, hanging on to his honor with both fists.

"No one listens to me, half my squad either hates me or thinks I'm some sort of female mutant, and I can't help feeling that someone is setting these fires deliberately, but I don't have a scrap of evidence to track him down. I'm failing this town."

Dan sat down opposite her, took her hands, and searched her beautiful blue eyes. They were red-rimmed, and tears trailed down her cheeks. Seeing Miss Grit shatter made him feel raw and a little afraid.

"Why do I do this to myself?" She raised her hands as if talking to heaven. "I know I'm going in over my head, and yet I sink myself before I even start."

"What are you talking about?"

She turned to him. Her eyes were glossy and dark. "I'm just tired. Tired of trying, tired of fighting. Tired." She took a deep breath, and when she exhaled her shoulders slumped. "Maybe I should quit."

He tucked a stray lock behind her ear, and

she responded with a melancholy smile. "Maybe you're just trying too hard. No one expects you to save this town or us. You're a good leader, and sooner or later the rest of the guys will see that."

She looked away from him, her jaw quivering. "I doubt that. All they can see is a lady trying to do a 'man's' job."

"I see a firefighter who's trained for years, who is trying to help this community stay one step ahead of disaster."

"What if I lead you right into disaster instead?" Her voice had dropped so low it sounded like a groan. Her expression hovered on the edge of more tears.

"That's not going to happen."

"Yeah, well, you can't tell the future. I have a tendency to react first and think later." She ran her finger along the carpet. "Like today, when I nearly ran into the house after Joe." She raised her eyes to his and gave him a disgusted look. "I'm in over my head here. I should have never come. I should have listened to you when you said, 'over my dead body.' "

Why did she *always* have to return to that idiotic, brainless sentence? She had no idea how he longed to rewind time and erase it from the logs. Why couldn't she remember how he'd said she was the woman of his dreams instead? Unfortunately, *that* line had been carefully blotted out of the memory of their relationship. It was certainly more accurate. Especially now when the vulnerability that lay on the surface of her expression had him wanting to wrap her in his arms and never let her go.

"Seth was right all along."

Her words hit him like a two-by-four across the chest. He actually gasped, a puff of painful understanding. These tears had something to do with her past. *With her brother.* As Ellie closed her eyes, leaned back, and wrapped her arms around her waist, Dan glimpsed again a raw vulnerability, and it made him ache.

"How was Seth right?" he asked carefully.

She blew out a breath and shook her head. "Firefighting isn't a job for a woman. I'll just get people hurt."

Ouch. He reached out and touched her arm. "Your brother told you that?"

Opening her eyes, she nodded. The pain in them appeared deep, and tears pooled along her lower lids. "I was nineteen. Done with my freshman year in college. I'd hiked out to Colorado after exams to join the Rocky Mountain Hotshots. It's a firefighting team. My brother had just finished smoke-jumper school."

She looked at him, but her gaze seemed farther away, past him and unfocused. "Seth was my hero. He did everything right. He wasn't only a great firefighter, handsome and fun, but he had this thing going with God that seemed to emanate from his pores. I figured if I could tap into his world, I'd find it too."

The fact that she wanted to know God better took his breath away. Ellie seemed so . . . so . . . put together. Determined. Spunky. And now she wanted to be passionate about God?

He was in deep, deep trouble.

"So what happened?" he asked, as if she hadn't just pushed him another step off his "just friends" position.

She pressed her fingertips under her eyes, then wiped away the moisture.

Dan guessed at the truth, hoping to unlock the words that seemed to be clogged in her throat. "He tried to send you home."

She nodded. "Nearly tackled me, more than once, but I . . . had a mind of my own. I wanted to be a firefighter. Like our dad."

"Or . . . like Seth?"

He'd hit a bull's-eye from the way she flinched. She didn't meet his eyes. "Yeah, I guess."

He felt the torment in her simple words,

and it made him wince. "Oh, Jammie Girl. Just because life seems to have hit the skids here in Deep Haven doesn't mean Seth was right. Women *can* be excellent firefighters." He couldn't believe those words actually exited his mouth, but for the first time, he believed them. She was good — too good. Too good to quit, for him or anyone else. The shadows of the evening streamed in through the tall firehouse windows, drenching the floor and her weary expression in somber tones.

"I don't want to mess up," she said on nothing more than a breath. "I can't."

He frowned, not sure of her meaning. "He should have seen you today, Ellie. You knew what you were doing, and you helped us save the Garden. He would have been proud."

Her chin trembled.

"Hey." Dan leaned close, lowered his voice. The hint of smoke still in her hair despite the scent of fresh soap wheedled past all his safeguards. He took a breath. "I was proud."

"You were?"

With that she completely destroyed the porcupine firechief image. She was just Ellie, finally, the woman who wanted to find a niche here, the woman he'd seen the first night, reaching out with compassion as he landed at her feet.

He could barely speak through his thickening throat. "Well, except for the part where I nearly had to tackle you."

She grinned, wobbly as it was, and gave him a shallow punch.

"But, yes, you know what you're doing. You're not going to mess up. I know you're going to keep this town out of trouble."

Her smiled faded. "I don't know, Dan. I think I might be bringing it right to your doorstep."

He touched her cheek, turned her to face him. "What are you talking about?"

She shook her head, looked away, turning red.

Realization came to him like the flow of lava, thick and hot. "Is this about our . . . uh . . . friendship?" The flare of memory of Mitch leaving the firehouse looking like he wanted to kick his dog made Dan sick. "Did Mitch . . . Ellie, did he say something crude to you?"

The twitch in her face at his words made him want to put his fist through the wall. His bottled-up emotions tore at him, and he didn't feel at all pastoral. "What did he say?" he growled.

She hung her head. "He was right. I

should have seen it sooner. I knew better."

Fear gripped him by the throat. "Knew better?" *Oh, please, don't say* —

"I shouldn't be cultivating a friendship with one of my staff." When she looked away from him, he felt as if he'd been one-two punched square in the chest. "I . . . I mean . . . I can't be your friend but —"

"Wait, Ellie. Listen, I don't know what Mitch said to you, but he isn't right. You do need friends. Everyone does. Just because you're my boss doesn't mean you have to hang a 'black plague' flag around your neck. I enjoy hanging around with you." Okay, he teetered on a lie there . . . being with Ellie felt about a thousand times more wonderful than just "enjoying" her company, but now — or perhaps never — wasn't the time to tell her that he'd missed her the last few days. That the gap she left in his life felt like a sucking chest wound, and he'd do just about anything to close it.

He took her hand, traced a vein. "Listen to me. Yes, you do break the mold, but you're doing your best, and you need to trust God to help you do it. Don't worry about Mitch or Ernie or town gossip."

"Town gossip?"

Oh no, had he said that? He made a face. "Well, the ladies at church saw us bicycling

220

last Saturday. I had a few questions on Sunday."

"Sorry."

He cupped her chin. "Why? I'm not. I'm glad to know you, to be your friend."

She smiled, but her chin quivered. "Why, Dan? Why would you face town ridicule to be seen with me?"

A dozen answers flashed through his mind, and none of them had to do with pastoral care. *Because when I'm with you everything seems a thousand times more beautiful. Because underneath that armadillo shell is a woman of laughter and grit and tenderness.*

And because when I'm around you, I feel . . . alive.

But those reasons felt too fresh, too close to his chest. He let his pastor mode kick in. "Because you're my friend. And I don't care what others think."

Somehow that seemed to satisfy her in a sad, melancholy way. Her expression spoke of relief, resignation. Exactly the type of response a "just friends" friend would hope for. So why did it hurt so much to look at it?

"Thanks. I feel better." She stood. "You're a good . . . friend."

He felt as if he'd been kicked in the teeth

221

yet was supposed to be happy about it. "You're welcome," he stammered.

She moved into her office and closed the door, leaving him in the hall wondering why he hadn't taken her in his arms and kissed her.

Then he broke out in a cold sweat that he'd even seriously entertained that thought in the first place.

12

Ellie hunched at her desk reading the incident reports from the fire at the Garden. According to Ruby and two other eyewitness accounts, no one had been inside the house before they saw the smoke. Even Dan and Joe, who had been at the barbeque, couldn't recall seeing the fire before Ruby did. Only one witness piqued her interest. Bonnie. Ellie now remembered seeing the accident victim, her arm in a cast, huddled in the group of horrified onlookers. The report identified Bonnie as a member of the board of the Garden.

Ellie was glad to see that the woman had made sufficient recovery to resume her life. She hoped Bonnie had also learned a valuable lesson about drinking and driving. Ellie had to wonder why a woman who had supposedly embraced the values of the church had fallen into a place of despair so deep she used alcohol to try and claw her way out.

Then again, everyone had their own method of grief therapy.

She was halfway through the report about the Simmons fire from the fire marshal in Minneapolis — finally — when a knock spliced her thoughts. She looked up, then smiled. "Hey, Liza."

The potter looked her usual flamboyant self today in a pair of hip-hugger jeans, a beaded belt, and a hot pink, peasant-style shirt. She'd swept her black hair up in a matching pink scrunchie, and her eyes danced with friendly mischief. Ellie felt downright dowdy in her black work pants, boots, and blue firefighter's shirt.

"Hope I'm not disturbing you," Liza said as she sat down in a folding chair across from Ellie's desk. "I haven't seen you for a while and thought I'd drop in. Are you in hiding?"

Ellie laughed, masking how close Liza's words landed to the mark. Since the incident with Mitch nearly a week ago, she'd narrowed her social life down to late-night walks with Franklin. And he wasn't much of a conversationalist. "Are you out shopping?" She indicated the bag Liza had tucked beside the wooden chair.

"No." Liza picked up the bag, set it in her

lap. "It's a gift, actually." She grinned as she reached into the bag. "A spaghetti bowl."

Ellie's mouth sagged open a second before she took the bowl with Liza's trademark seagulls and shoreline. Its weight surprised her and Ellie nearly dropped it. "This will feed an army, Liza. Thanks. Wow . . . I'm speechless."

Liza put the bag down. "I thought firehouses were known for their spaghetti."

"And their chili. Unfortunately . . . I don't cook. I don't have one Martha Stewart bone in my body." Ellie made a face that had Liza laughing.

"Well, leave it for Dan. He's a great cook."

Ellie didn't comment. She'd been having mixed feelings about the pastor — feelings that made her melancholy one minute, angry the next. Their conversation last week had left her just outside the circle of frustration. Dan had his opportunity to . . . to . . . deny that their friendship was part of his ministry SOP and didn't. She should have never bought into the sweet charm of Mr. Do-Right. He hadn't even followed her into her office.

When she *did* sneak out an hour later, his silence had stabbed at her. He'd been reading his Bible on the sofa and barely lifted his head to say good-bye.

What did she expect? That he'd declare his feelings for her? Tell her his emotions pushed the line of pure friendship? For a second when she told him about Mitch, she'd seen protectiveness rise in his eyes. And it felt . . . good. Too good.

It would behoove her to remember that the man's job, after all, was to make people feel welcome, to embrace them into the community.

She shouldn't have expected more.

Dan was her friend. *Just* a friend. That would have to be enough.

"I confess. I'm here on a selfish mission," Liza said. "I missed you in church last Sunday, and with Mona going through this dark time, I needed some girl talk. Can you sneak away?"

Her words touched Ellie. "I'm game. I've been here since 6 A.M., trying to unsnarl the mystery of the Simmons and the Garden fires. My brain feels deep-fried, and my muscles have rigor mortis."

Liza laughed. "Let's get outta Dodge then. I'm on dog duty. Do you think Franklin would hanker a run?"

Ellie closed her file. "I didn't know you had a dog."

"It's Joe's. A stray named Rip he picked up a couple of years ago. A Lab." Liza walked to the door, held it open.

"Well, maybe he can get Franklin moving. My dog seems to be in a coma. I nearly have to drag him out of the room for his twice-a-day walk. You'd think I was overworking him." She nudged Franklin from his curled position under her desk. "Get up, you oaf."

The basset hound groaned. Ellie reached down, grasped his collar, and forced him to his feet. "You're acting like an old man. C'mon; let's go chase some seagulls."

The dog looked at her with disdain. Ellie chuckled and snapped on his lead. He followed her with great reluctance, if the sighing was any indication.

She caught up with Liza outside, where a chocolate brown Lab sniffed at a nearby bench.

"Rip, I presume?" Ellie asked, falling into stride as Liza angled out toward the beach. "And how did he get that name?"

"He destroyed a pair of Joe's pants the first day they met. Joe is pretty particular about those jeans. Guess he'd climbed a few mountains in them and wasn't thrilled about Rip's alterations."

"Really? Joe seems like such a homebody type. I can't imagine him climbing any mountains."

Liza laughed. The wind played with her

hair, lashing about her face as they veered off the sidewalk and onto the rock. Liza unleashed Rip and let the dog run. Franklin plodded along unhappily. "Joe is a best-selling author. Before he came to Deep Haven, he traveled the world and wrote fiction stories about those travels."

"Joe Michaels, Mr. I'm-going-to-be-a-father-and-I-can't-wait-to-get-home-to-my-darling-wife Joe Michaels?"

Liza's half-sided smile looked more serious than amused. "That's him. God did big stuff in Joe's life when He sent him here. In all our lives, really, but Joe especially found some kind of peace. It turned him from a wanderer to a man passionate about his family. That's probably why their loss has hit them both like a steamroller."

"Their loss?" Ellie's stomach tightened.

Liza stopped, picked up a stick, and threw it for Rip. Her eyes were moist when she looked at Ellie. "Oh, that's right. You don't know."

Ellie shook her head. A sick feeling seeped into her bones.

Liza took the stick from Rip, who'd retrieved it, and threw it again. "We prayed for them Sunday morning in church."

Ellie tried not to let worry sharpen her words. "Is Joe okay?"

Liza sighed. "Yes." Her voice thickened. "Mona lost their baby. It's been difficult. Especially since the baby didn't seem to have any of the symptoms they feared . . ."

"Symptoms? Do you mean because of Joe's brother?"

Liza frowned at her. "You know about Gabe?"

"I met him at the Garden fire. Other than being pretty shook up he seemed like a nice guy. Were they worried their child might have Down syndrome?"

Liza nodded. "But it turns out the miscarriage had nothing to do with the baby."

Oh no. Ellie felt slightly weak asking, "What do you mean?"

"Mona has endometriosis. It's so severe she'll have a hard time conceiving again, if at all."

Liza's love for her friend showed in the grief flooding her dark eyes. Ellie couldn't dodge the sharp twist of loneliness. "I'm so sorry. That's tough."

Rip danced with anticipation, barking encouragement, so Liza threw the stick. Franklin had flopped down at Ellie's feet.

"Tell me how things are going at the shop. I saw your new collection."

"With the moose? I love it. I was inspired last summer while on a canoe trip with

229

Wilderness Challenge, a camp just up the Gunflint Trail. We were out in the middle of Pigeon River when suddenly this huge bull moose walked out into the river and stood there, staring at us. I think my heart stopped for a full ten minutes as I simply watched him. Have you ever seen a moose up close?"

"Uh, no." Ellie made a wry face. "In fact, I've never even seen one at a zoo. I've seen a few antlers, however." She thought of Mitch's truck and the rack she saw on the hood.

"They're magnificent animals," Liza said. "I started a new line when I returned. I'm going to unveil a twelve-piece clayware set in my winter catalog. I'm hoping to beef up sales and interest in my main line."

The afternoon sun hovered over the far western rim of the lake, dabbling the waves with golden kisses. The fragrance of wood-smoke and autumn tinged the air and tugged at Ellie's roughened nerves. She felt herself relaxing into Liza's friendship.

"So, you're holed up in your shop?" Ellie found a piece of driftwood and waved it in front of Franklin's nose, hoping to drum up a response. "I'm honored that you emerged to drag me out of my cave."

"Oh, I finished my last order and shipped it off to be fired." Liza gave her a scalawag look. "Besides, all work and no play makes Liza — and Ellie — dull girls."

"Well, you'd have to try pretty hard to get me out of my dull rut. I'm afraid I'm a lifer."

Liza laughed. "Oh, please. I'd say you're just about the most exciting woman in town. You hang around fires bossing men around, you get to rescue people, and you've got a hook into the heart of the most eligible bachelor in town. I guess you're the envy of every woman within one hundred miles."

Ellie gaped at her. "Hardly. First of all, I don't get to boss the men around. They won't even listen to me. Secondly, I don't rescue anyone; I supervise. And thirdly — what bachelor?"

Liza shook her head. "You're kidding, right?"

If Liza named Mitch as her favorite admirer, Ellie was going to drop into a ball and wail. "No."

"Dan. You can't see the way he looks at you? I see him scanning the audience every Sunday. Don't tell me you don't see him light up when he notices you."

Ellie stared at her scuffed work boots. "He does that with everyone. He's very friendly."

"Wait. Are we talking about the same Dan

Matthews? Mr. Reserved?"

Ellie blinked. "I guess I wouldn't call him that."

Liza laughed. "My point exactly. Dan has a . . . reputation for his cool demeanor. He doesn't get riled or overly excited, and he's not the kind of guy who wears his emotions on his sleeve. I think he has to consult ten different theology books and pray for a week before he opens his mouth."

Ellie had seen plenty of emotion in his eyes when she told him about Mitch. And the night at the Simmons fire when he blurted out dreams and threats. And what about — "But he *is* emotional. I saw him put his arm around that girl who works for you, and they're going to a wedding toge—" She bit off her words, cringing.

Liza's eyes were wide and full of mischief. "Katie? They have mutual friends. He probably hadn't seen her in a while, and yes, they're carpooling to the wedding with us . . . but it's not a date." She smiled, and it looked downright sassy. "You're jealous."

Ellie frowned and tugged on her dog's leash to pull him to his feet. "No, I'm not. I'm just facing reality."

Liza laughed, and the outburst startled a group of seagulls that had been following them. "Ellie, you're a hoot!"

"Liza, really, Dan and I are just friends." She didn't miss how her voice turned sour on the last two words. She turned away, suddenly aware of how her throat constricted, as if saying those words left her bruised and swollen. What a fool she'd been for reading into Dan's innocent affection. "He treats everyone that way."

"What do you mean you're 'just friends'?" Liza demanded, one eyebrow up. "I saw you biking, and Joe told me you played hockey together. Dan doesn't share his hockey fanaticism with anyone. Babe, somehow you got into his world."

Ellie harrumphed. The last thing she needed right now was to dig up the memory of his antics on the ice . . . or off. The way he'd held her had felt so . . . so . . . perfect. She gritted her teeth against a betraying expression. "It doesn't matter. I can't date one of my firemen."

Liza bent down and rubbed Rip behind his ears. His dog tags jangled. "Why? It's not like you're in the army or anything."

"It wouldn't be right. How will any of the guys respect me if they think I'm favoring one of the men?"

"So you do like him."

"I didn't say that."

Liza caught her by the arm. "You do; I

can tell. I mean, what's not to like? He has gorgeous eyes and deep chocolate hair —"

"Wide shoulders and a kind smile," Ellie added softly.

Liza smiled smugly. "So, is there a romance smoldering at the firehouse?"

Ellie shook her head. "No. Dan is . . . wow. I mean, yes, if I were in the least persuaded to invest in a relationship, I might consider Dan. But I need a man who isn't afraid of letting me do my job. Dan says he supports me, yet I can't help but notice the slightest bit of doubt that edges his expression, like he's one breath short of wanting to drop to his knees and beg me to quit. The second I mean more to him than a fellow firefighter is the second he'll be sabotaging my work. Begging me to switch professions. Become a cookie baker or a Sunday school teacher."

"Neither of which are bad things, El." Liza laughed. "And the way Dan cooks, you have no fears, believe me." Her expression sobered. "Dan's not a male chauvinist. He sees your abilities. He wouldn't ask you to be less or more than you are."

"Now. But if I let our friendship progress, he'd stop seeing that and instead see his loss. Dan's a hero, right through to his marrow, and that means protecting the woman he loves. It can't be me."

"Hogwash."

Ellie blinked at Liza's response.

"Dan's not asking you to quit your job, nor would he. I think you need to give him another chance."

"He didn't have a first chance, Liza. He's not interested."

Liza smirked. "Oh, really? Would you be willing to put that theory to the test?"

Ellie felt like she'd been sweet-talked into a land deal in the Florida Everglades. She narrowed her eyes. "I'm not interested in getting my heart carved out here."

Liza rolled her eyes. "Will you just trust me?"

Ellie wrinkled her face. "I'm not sure. Are you trustworthy?"

Liza gave a mock sigh. "I set up Joe and Mona, and now they're living happily ever after. And Noah and Anne hung out at the Footstep of Heaven while they figured out they should tie the knot. Surely you'll trust me when I tell you I think you and Dan are a perfect match."

"There's no match, Liza," Ellie countered, but the smallest ember of hope had burst to life in her heart.

"We'll see. So, here's a question, and of course it's just hypothetical." Liza steered them toward a picnic table. She sat down opposite Ellie. "If you fell in love with the right guy, would you give it up? stop fighting fire? change professions?"

Ellie appreciated Liza's bluntness but looked away anyway. Across the street, the local dime store had set out a rack of out-of-season summer clothes. They flapped in the cool breeze. The smell of smoked fish from Mack's Smoked Fish Stand laced the air. Her stomach jumped to attention. "No. I can't. I . . . have to do this."

Liza folded her hands on the table. "Why? What is so important? I mean, yes, I can't imagine doing anything other than throwing clay, but if I met the right man, I might consider surrendering it. Especially if God gave us a family."

Ellie sighed. How to explain to Liza how the legacy of firefighting drove her, how she had made unspoken promises one blistered day in Colorado? "I guess it's in my blood, that's all. I have a desire to do something with my life, something that makes a difference. And for me, this work matters. At least I hope so."

Not far away, an American flag snapped in the wind.

"Do you fear that it doesn't matter?"

Ellie hid a wince. She considered Liza,

wondering at the tinsel strength of their new friendship. "Maybe. I have to admit there are moments, times when I lie awake at night wondering what would happen if I rang the bell tomorrow. Gave up. Picked another profession, like teaching or maybe investigation. But . . . I've been fighting fires all my life." She ran the strap of the leash through her fingers. "If I gave it up now, I'd lose everything."

Liza reached across the table, took her hand. "Hardly. You wouldn't lose one second of those fifteen years. Not one. You've saved lives and made a difference. And every second you spent doing that matters. Nothing we do with God is wasted."

Ellie's face twitched. "I'm not sure. Why is it that people spend their entire lives trying to help other people?"

"Depends on the person. A Christian works from totally different motives than a non-Christian. One of the bad reasons is to try and earn special favor from God. Like a barter system. We can't earn God's grace or His forgiveness. You should ask Mona about that. She's shared her testimony a few times, but the gist of it is that she went looking for God's forgiveness, and it was already there."

Liza's words resonated deep in Ellie's heart. She knew all about wanting to earn

God's forgiveness, longing to embrace it, and knowing she didn't deserve it. But somehow her question felt deeper. "For the person who is already . . . um . . . forgiven. Why then? I mean, if we can't earn God's love, if it's already there, why does a person like Dan spend his entire life in ministry?

"Or her entire life fighting fires and rescuing people?"

Ellie gave a huff of agreement. Liza squeezed her hand. "I'm not entirely sure, but I think it has to do with the great thorn in the flesh."

"The what?"

"Paul's great thorn. You know the apostle Paul had a thorn of weakness, something that made his ministry difficult. Three times he asked God to take it away. And God answered, 'My gracious favor is all you need. My power works best in your weakness.' See, God promises that when we are weak, He'll fill in the gaps. Our 'work' for Him is the perfect way to see Him at work in our lives. He gives us a task to do, but without Him, we can't complete it. God amazes us with His grace, and in that act, we draw closer to Him. It's what Dan's been preaching about — John 15. We have to abide with Christ to accomplish anything of worth in this life. Without Him, our work means nothing."

Ellie couldn't look at Liza and the keen intensity in her eyes. Oh, she remembered the verse . . . in fact the part about the useless branches being cut off, gathered into the fire, and burned had seared her mind late into the night. She couldn't escape the feeling that, despite her outward activities, she was a "stripped for burning" branch.

Liza continued, "I think our work for God actually helps us love Him more, abide with Him more. The more we seek to serve Him, the more we need Him. It's a circle of joy. And that makes our work for Him worth the sacrifices we make."

Ellie managed a weak nod. She couldn't embrace all of Liza's words, but she recognized tidbits she might ponder while alone and staring at the sunset. "I'm probably just tired. I've been keeping some late hours."

Liza nodded, but her dark eyes seemed to look right through Ellie, and in them Ellie recognized argument. "I know what you need," Liza said, her posture changing, her expression turning sly.

"I almost hate to ask." Ellie took her first full breath since sitting down.

Liza grinned and her eyes sparkled. "A party. C'mon; it's time to put your theories about our pastor to the test. In fact, let's call it a dare."

13

"Can you catch the door, Dan?" Marnie Blouder hollered from the fellowship hall in the basement of the church, jerking Dan out of his daydream. Again, trapped by Ellie.

He hadn't seen her in nearly a week, yet every day she tangled his thoughts into knots of regret. Yes, he cared for her. More than he should. He should have run after her last Tuesday night after her encounter with Mitch the Brute. Should have thrown open her door or at least banged on it. But the stoic pastor in him grabbed him by the throat and death-locked him in indecision, hesitant to risk offense.

Where was the man who had broken free of his stoic exterior and chased after Ellie at the hockey rink? or yelled at her over the radio at the Garden fire, desperation in his voice?

He tried not to think about how he'd sat

outside her door and heard her muffled sobs or the haunting sound of her playing some classical music, telling him just how much she hurt.

He'd sat awake more than once over the past week, listening to the waves, thinking about the moment when he should have —

"Dan! The door!" Marnie appeared in the foyer, looking exasperated and one thread away from unraveling. Her gray hair had uncurled from its hair combs, and her round, lined face held the last fragments of patience.

"Sorry." Dan headed toward the entrance doors and opened them for the catering crew. The breeze filtered in along with the smell of barbeque. He saw Guthrie Jones unloading the white van. The man looked tired today. Dan had heard he struggled with some ongoing disease, but he'd never learned the details. Whatever it was, it had Guthrie looking pale and drawn. Dan only knew him through Cindy Simmons, but he guessed his sister's injury weighed on him. Last reports had Cindy still on the critical list at the burn unit.

Earlier in the week, Dan had visited the two Simmons boys, who had been upgraded to stable and moved to the pediatric ward. They, along with their sister, Angelica, comprised the entire patient count in the pediatric department, but until they located a foster family, the hospital had agreed to keep them admitted. However, the day loomed when Angelica and her brothers would need a family to care for them until their mother recovered. Dan spent most of his free time worrying about whom to ask. In the small town, few people had the resources to feed and keep three small children.

"Let me help you there, Guthrie," Dan said. Guthrie breezed past him, holding a tray of steaming barbeque meat, and didn't spare Dan a glance. Dan stared after him, wondering what he'd done to miff the boy.

Two more caterers, dressed in Smoky Joe jackets and carrying potato salad and rolls, followed Guthrie down to the fellowship hall. The smell of dinner curled up from the basement, tugging at Dan. While he stood in the vestibule acting like a bellhop, he noticed the van from the Garden roll in with Ruby at the wheel. Right behind them came Joe and Mona and a trail of other cars.

Lord, please let this night be a success. Grace Church had agreed to host the fundraiser to help with the cost of repairs on the Garden lodge, paying for the buffet out of the benevolence fund. With Joe Michaels

243

raffling off a set of his Jonah series books, Liza donating a place setting of her new design, and a host of other businesses offering goods or services, Dan hoped the Garden would easily reach its goal of five thousand dollars. It turned him inside out to see the hope-filled faces of the Garden residents as they filed in. Gabe, Joe's little brother, gave Dan a teary hug.

Now why couldn't Dan be more like Gabe? The man wore his feelings on the outside of his body and without fear. Just being around Gabe felt like hanging around sunshine — even when Gabe wore his trademark Michaels stubbornness. The man treated people like gifts . . . and wasn't afraid to show it.

Not Dan. The second someone got too close — specifically, someone with tawny brown braids, stormy blue eyes, and a smile that could rattle a man clear down to his bones — he tucked away his feelings and donned his pastor garb. Slow, steady, reliable Dan. The town safety net. Except — hadn't he shown his feelings at least twice around Ellie? Hadn't he barked at her when she'd bolted toward the burning house and chased after her when she'd marched out of the hockey rink? Or even further back, nearly a month ago, hadn't he declared the feelings bubbling through his heart before they'd had a chance to harden? *Are you a dream?*

He wondered now if his heart and mouth hadn't reacted to something his brain was only now realizing. If so, he'd better figure out a way to push his feelings to the surface. It wouldn't take the rest of the single males on the volunteer force long to figure out that Ellie Karlson was just about the best thing to ever happen to this town.

Dan trod downstairs with the rest of the crew. The long Sunday school tables ringed the room, in half-moons facing the front like stadium seating. A podium, decorated in balloons and a spray of pumpkins, gourds, and dried chrysanthemums, betrayed Mona's touch. Dan spotted her talking with Edith Draper. Mona still looked drawn, her cheeks gaunt, grief written in her eyes. She caught Dan's eye and smiled. It seemed more polite than happy, and Dan returned it in kind.

He wished he could walk through this darkness with Mona and Joe. He'd visited Mona twice since the miscarriage, but although she was on her feet and tending the shop, her smile felt forced at best. Joe had mentioned she spent long hours in her room, curled on their bed, sobs leaking out from under the door.

Dan still hadn't found the right words to comfort them.

He made his way over to Edith, who was stacking paper plates onto the buffet table. "We've decided we can do without fancy tonight, Pastor," she said in way of greeting. "Less to clean up."

Edith Draper, town organizer, woman extraordinaire to the rescue. She'd invited Mona to this town two years ago, and the year after that, her niece Anne, who'd found true love with camp director Noah Standing Bear on the Gunflint Trail. "How are Noah and Anne?" he asked, ripping open the paper napkin bag and stacking the napkins in baskets.

Edith glowed at the mention of her niece. "I can't believe they're getting married next month. I feel like I've been waiting forever. And I haven't been down to Minneapolis in nearly a year. I can't wait to see my sister. She's still working at the homeless shelter she and her dear husband ran all those years." She shook her head. "I told her she needs to quit and move up here. I just hate to see her all alone."

Dan laughed. "Edith, if anyone can talk her into it, you can."

She shot him a quizzical look as he turned

and went into the kitchen to retrieve the silverware.

The increasing murmur of voices told him guests had begun to fill the basement. He heard deep groans, saw Bruce Schultz holding court by the windows, probably telling the story of the Garden fire. Memory flared, and Dan saw Ellie, the hot breath from the blaze pushing back her hair, her face blackened, her eyes fierce when she looked up and spied him on the roof one second after he'd told her to halt. The vulnerability and shock in that expression still rocked him.

With a whoosh, it all made sense, and he knew why she wanted to give up. Why she couldn't believe he'd want to be her friend. Why she fought so hard for respect. He slowly put down the package of forks.

She didn't think anyone cared.

The woman had come to this town alone. And so far, no one had gotten close enough to her to make a difference. To make her hesitate before she ran into a fire.

He wanted to rewind time, to see himself pound on her closed door, no, force it open, take her into his arms, and show her how much he . . . cared.

Oh, he cared all right. So much so that daydreams of her intruded into his sermon preparation, into his hockey games as he ricocheted shots off the goal pipes, and into his thoughts as he lay awake staring at the ceiling. Even into his food preparation — would she like bacon on her omelette?

"Dan! Can you bring me that silverware?" Edith's presence, standing with her hands on her polyester-clad hips, exploded into his thoughts. He managed a grim smile and shuffled out to the hall.

Next time he saw Ellie he wasn't going to let her slam the door in his face. . . . Oh no, he was going to —

"Hi, Dan."

He turned and went weak. Ellie smiled at him, looking sweet and even a touch shy, and why not? She wore a very, very unmasculine black dress with a burnt yellow sweater and the slightest edging of fear in her beautiful eyes. Her hair lay unbraided around her neck, framing her face. He nearly lifted his hand to touch it. But this . . . lady . . . wasn't really Ellie, was she? This woman smelled like sweet apple blossoms and had not a hint of smoke in her wake.

Unless he considered the air between them. He felt himself turning red, as if she could read his thoughts and the way he wanted to grab her hand and escape to some quiet place, away from prying eyes and expectations. He'd spread out for them a blanket underneath the stars in a spot overlooking the lake and stay there. Forever. No fire chief. No pastor.

Just Dan and Ellie. Starting over. This time without stereotypes, without expectations. With emotional honesty. "You look . . . beautiful."

She sparkled. "Well, it just shows that I can use a bar of soap."

And how. He managed to grab his voice just as it was about to flee. "Yeah. Hmm . . ." Okay, so that wasn't really his voice. More like sounds of delight. He cleared his throat. "I don't suppose you'd be willing to . . . go for a walk with me . . . after this?"

He nearly danced through the fellowship hall when she nodded.

Ellie wavered between wanting to crawl under the table, hightail it home, or enjoy the way Dan kept sending warm smiles in her direction. She felt like an idiot. Why had she allowed Liza to talk her into wearing this outfit? It wasn't as if she didn't own at least three work suits. If she wanted to get dressed up, a smart navy blazer over wool gabardine pants would have done the trick.

But no, Liza had to dress her in whimsy, take down her hair, and apply makeup — as if she didn't know how to do it. Well, okay, it wasn't her SOP in the morning to put on mascara, but that was mostly because, in the heat of a fire, the smoke and soot would send makeup down her face in sweaty trickles.

It felt odd to see Dan light up when she walked into the room. She desperately hoped that it had to do with seeing her and not with the layer of foundation and brown eye shadow. Or perhaps *odd* wasn't exactly how she felt. More like warm and fuzzy, with a thrill of adrenaline running up her spine and through her veins.

He'd invited her out for a walk.

She smiled, goofy and large. There she went again, acting like a smitten teenager. She should put a sign on her chest . . . single and desperate. Only, she wasn't desperate. Had never been. She was perfectly content with her life, thank you very much. She didn't need a husband to horn in on her time, her goals. She didn't need a man to tell her what to do or try and get in the way of her job.

Then what was she doing here, picking at her potato salad, watching Dan mingle with his parishioners? He had a natural warmth, a smile for everyone, a handshake, a one-armed hug for the ladies. He exuded a gentleness that made people drop their guard.

At least she had.

Long enough that his friendship had seeped in and filled an empty place she didn't realize she had. Enough that his absence hurt — no, ached. And enough to climb into a dress and discover whether Dan Do-Right was simply flexing his ministry muscles, or if he truly had a special place in his heart for his new fire chief.

Liza and her double-dog dares.

Ellie couldn't decide which one she hoped for — her brain and her heart were already duking out that war as she tore apart her dinner roll.

Ellie waved at Liza, who was setting out her pottery on the display table, and then at Ruby, the woman she'd met at the Garden. It tugged at Ellie's calloused heart to see the outpouring of support for the Garden from the Deep Haven residents. The town obviously embraced the burdens of its community members with no hesitation to sacrifice.

It made Deep Haven feel like a place she wanted to call home. She could use some old-fashioned, small-town comradery, over-the-picket-fence-type of friends, the safety that came with neighbors and shopkeepers knowing your first name. Perhaps in Deep Haven she could finally put Seth to rest. Fulfill her promises and find peace.

The fact that the town pastor kept her pulse a little on edge didn't dampen that scenario in the least. As if reading her thoughts, Dan turned and gave her another warm smile, those smoky gray eyes alive with mischief.

Oh, he packed charm in that look, and she desperately hoped she wasn't walking right into heartache.

"Ellie! I'm glad you could make it." Bruce Schultz sauntered up to her, holding two saggy paper plates. They looked like they might collapse any second, and Ellie squelched the urge to reach out and catch the dinners before they landed on the floor. "And you're looking spiffy tonight."

If her captain felt surprise at her appearance, he masked it well. He put down the plates and sat across from her. "Ellie, have you met my wife, Ruth?"

"Uh, no." Ellie held out her hand to a woman who seated herself next to Bruce. A purple pantsuit, blue-dyed hair, shining brown eyes, a dab of blush on her cheeks, and a wide grin gave her a jolly appearance.

"Glad to meet you, Ellie. Bruce speaks highly of you."

Ellie measured Ruth's words for disdain, criticism, or disapproval. So far, nothing but enthusiasm. "Thank you. Bruce is a great asset to the team."

"Oh, honey, he's been fighting fires for so long, I believe he could do it in his sleep."

Ellie made a face of mock horror. "I hope not. Sleeping firemen are pretty ineffective."

Ruth blinked at her.

"Uh, that was a joke. I'm sorry." Now she *really* wanted to hide under the table. Thankfully, Ruth and Bruce chuckled, probably out of pity. Well, she never rested on her PR laurels.

"Are you going to bid for anything?" Ruth asked, pushing around her baked beans with a plastic spoon.

Ellie shrugged. "I really like that quilt with the Bible verses on it." She noticed Katie had pinned up the treasure Ellie had seen in Liza's shop. By the way Katie gestured as she held court before a small crowd, she was rehashing her "the truth will set you free" speech. It touched a place deep inside to see Katie's enthusiasm at donating her hard work to the Garden's needs.

Maybe the truth of God's unfailing love did set Katie free. Free enough to donate her time, her work, her ambitions to the Lord. Ellie watched the joy radiating from her face and wondered if she hadn't hit upon a secret beyond worth.

"So, do we have training this weekend?" Bruce's voice broke her away from her thoughts.

"Just a few hours in the morning. I know how precious Saturdays are."

Or, rephrased, she had surrendered to the fact that half the team took off the moment lunch hour hit anyway. This week they'd work on woodland-fire suppression. With the fire-threat index rising in the north woods, so did their need to prepare for forest fires near the town.

"Are you the lady fire chief I keep hearing about?" An elderly woman with a round, pleasantly lined face and a smile that felt like an embrace sat down next to Ellie. "Edith Draper. Welcome to Deep Haven."

Ellie shook her hand. "Glad to be here," she said, meaning every word. Especially when Dan looked across the room and riveted her with another wide smile. "Very glad."

14

Leaves chased each other down the street, and the moon lit a path of heavenly brilliance along the boardwalk as Dan walked Ellie home. He'd deliberately parked at the far end of the beach so they could stroll the long way to the hotel. The fragrance of woodsmoke and the nip of an impatient winter tinged the air.

When they passed in and out of pools of golden lamplight, Dan stole glances at the woman beside him. She had her arms crossed, perhaps fighting a chill, and the smallest smile playing on her lips. Looking down as she walked, her expression seemed as if she was tossing around amusing thoughts inside that intricate mind of hers.

"Did I mention that you look incredible tonight?" Dan said, digging up words through his churning emotions.

She wore a lopsided smile. "A few dozen times. But don't quit."

He laughed. "Okay." Somehow their friendship had taken a wild turn, and if he didn't know better, he'd think Ellie was . . . reaching out to him. In a way that had his heart doing cartwheels. "Thanks for coming to the benefit."

"Do you think they raised enough money?" She rubbed her hands on her arms. He debated, then in a burst of courage, put his arm around her.

She didn't resist. He'd been right — she fit perfectly in the hollow of his one-armed embrace. He could barely keep his voice steady. "Yes. The Lord really opened hearts. I saw people there who only come down the trail once a year for supplies."

"You're kidding."

Dan shook his head. "Ruby and her gang are special members of our community. I suspect they'll be back in their home within the month."

"Joe is a surprising fellow. I didn't know he wrote the Jonah series. I read one once . . . something about Russia."

"That would be *Siberian Runaway*. He actually went there and herded reindeer."

"Amazing. He seems to have found a home here. Too bad about their baby."

Dan's hand moved up to her neck, tangling his fingers into her silky hair. "Yes.

256

Mona's taking it pretty hard, I think. I can't help but feel I'm supposed to do something . . . I don't know, to help her get through this. But I'm at a loss to know what." He hadn't realized how healing — or gut-wrenching — it would feel to admit his inadequacy aloud. He braced himself for indictment, but when she looked at him, he saw empathy.

"I'm sure it will come to you."

He managed a one-sided smile of agreement, amazed at how much he wanted this woman in his life. Being with her felt more than just comfortable. It soothed the aches of his failures, balmed his empty places, and filled them with the tender caress of hope.

"Liza told me that she might not be able to have any children."

Now *that* he didn't know. "You and Liza are getting pretty close."

She looked up at him, surprise in her gaze. "Yeah, I guess so. She's . . . infectious."

Dan laughed. "That's a good word. It'll be a strong and brave man who wins her heart."

Ellie's slow smile had him wondering exactly what she thought. "You're not interested?"

He frowned slightly. "No. I guess I'm interested in . . . someone else."

Her mouth formed a perfect, silent *O* before she quickly looked away. Even in the darkness, he saw the faint reddening of her face.

"Do you think I walk down the street with my arm around everyone I meet?"

The twitch in her expression told him he'd hit the mark. The wind left him briefly. "Ellie, wait. I hope I haven't given you the wrong impression over the past month."

She moved away from him. He touched her arm and stopped her. "You're important to me." He hooked his finger under her chin and gently tugged her gaze to his. The fear in her eyes turned his throat raw. "I should have told you that last week," he said softly.

"You did."

"Not like I wanted to. Not like this."

He looked into her eyes, and before he could put a halt on his unleashed emotions, he leaned over and kissed her. She tasted fresh and sweet, and as he wove his fingers into her hair, she trembled, just enough to let him know that his touch affected her. He started to move away, but she leaned forward and kissed him back. *Kissed him back.* He stepped closer, wanting to put his arms around her, but stopped when she put her hands on his chest. For a second he feared she'd push him away. Instead, she curled her hands into his shirt and held tight. He put one arm around her waist, the other around her shoulders, and she relaxed against him.

It made his heart soar clean out of his chest.

With more strength than he thought he had, he pulled away and leaned his forehead against hers. His breath felt hot in his throat, and he tried to hide how incredible it felt to hold this woman, this fireball, in his arms. Blinding. Terrifying. His chest nearly exploded with sheer joy as she let out a soft sigh.

"Well, I guess that's not quite what I was expecting, but I like it," she said softly.

He wanted to pick her up and twirl her. Ellie Karlson in his arms. Yes, oh yes. Until this moment, he hadn't realized how dark his world had been without her. "I'm sorry. I should have asked before I —"

"You have my permission." Delight tinged her eyes.

He couldn't help it. He kissed her again, and this time freed the emotions bottled in his chest. Time stopped as they stood just outside the bath of lamplight, with the moon and stars as their audience and the waves as sweet accompaniment to the emotion of the moment. When he pulled away, and this time put space between them, his pulse felt like it might send him skipping down the street.

She took a deep breath, but a smile graced her lips.

He cupped her face in his hands. "You're beautiful. Have I told you that yet?"

She blushed. "No, I don't think so."

He laughed, full and loud and freeing. "Ellie, you're . . ." He stopped. *What? Amazing? A dream come true?* ". . . unexpected."

She raised her eyebrows. "Now that's something I've never heard. Gutsy, stubborn, and a troublemaker, yes. But never *unexpected.*"

He let out a breath of relief. She was unexpected. He longed to give her more. Tonight she looked . . . feminine. Tomorrow, however, she'd be wearing her imitation of a man's outfit and racing into danger again.

It didn't sound like a match made in heaven. He tried not to let voices from the past filter into this delicate moment, but he couldn't silence them as he slowly lowered his hands.

Tonight was a dream. He wouldn't think about tomorrow.

He took her hand. "So, what are we going to do about . . . us?"

260

"Us?" she teased, but he heard the pleasure in her voice. They began to walk, his thumb rubbing her hand as he held it. Her grip was strong and solid, just as he would expect.

"Well, just so I make myself crystal clear . . . I don't run around town kissing every pretty girl I meet."

"Not a new evangelism technique?"

He laughed. "Hardly. Believe me, I'm not known as a ladies' man."

"Well, that's good. I mean, a pastor has to make a few concessions." Her expression was teasing when she stopped and faced him. "But in all seriousness, we need to make three rules." She held up her fingers in a Girl Scout sign.

"Rules? We can't live by grace?"

She grinned, shook her head. "Rule number one. At the firehouse, no hint of our, um . . . friendship. Aside from the fact that the guys would never let you live it down, all their respect for me would be shattered —"

"Ellie, I don't think —"

"Number two." She held up her hand to silence him. "Don't protect me."

He recognized the fierceness that lit her eyes and winced. "C'mon, just a little blocking? To keep you out of trouble."

261

She glared at him. "Don't mock me. I know you . . . or I think I do, and I have this gut feeling that getting into a relationship with me is going to seriously test your abilities to let me do my job. But —" she raised her finger and gave him a definite schoolmarm look — "if you can manage to keep those protective instincts under control, I'm willing to follow my heart a little bit here."

"Follow your heart? Oh, I like the sound of that." He grinned and moved to draw her closer. She put her hand on his chest to push him back, but she smiled, as if charmed. The thought of not swinging her into his arms or not keeping her out of the line of fire deflated his joy, just a little. How was he possibly going to follow rules one and two? By the grace of God, he supposed. He blamed the moonlight framing her face and the shine in her eyes for the way he nodded, stupidly agreeing. "And rule number three?"

Her smile faded, and sadness hued her eyes. "No promises."

He felt as if he'd been punched right in the sternum. "What?"

She shook her head. "I can't promise you tomorrow. I don't know if I'll get the job in this town, and if I don't, I'll need to move on."

He tried not to let her words dig into the already wounded, soft tissue of his heart, but he wanted to let out a groan. Why did all the women he cared about prefer adventure over him? He took a deep breath and refused to nod. "Ellie, listen. I told you already, I don't kiss just any pretty girl who gets close to me. That kiss meant something . . ." His throat tightened and, fearing what his idiotic mouth was about to commit him to, he reined in his words. "I mean . . . I know I don't have a right to kiss you without a promise in pocket. But the intent is there. You're more than unexpected. You're a . . . a surprise. A good one. One that I think God intended." Her eyes glistened in the soft light, beautiful and filled with unshed emotions. It bolstered his courage. "I was sorta hoping that . . . well, you felt that way too."

Soft tears layered her eyelids, dripped onto her cheeks. "It did mean something to me." But her tone didn't match her sweet words. "Dan, I can't stay in Deep Haven without a job. Firefighting is my life." Her voice fell. "It's all I have."

He wanted to grab her up and plead with her. *No, you have me.* But he obviously wasn't enough for a woman like Ellie. His throat burned as he locked those feelings in his chest and forced a nod, knowing that the woman he wanted was slipping through his fingers.

And he was allowing it. That realization ripped open all the old scabs, the old hurts. The old desperation.

Not again.

"Ellie, I understand. Well, not totally, but I'm trying to understand how much fire-fighting means to you. However —" he ran his fingers down her cheek and cupped her face in his hands — "will you let me try and talk you into sticking around Deep Haven? Please?"

She swallowed. Her indecision rattled through him, but he pinned his eyes on hers and searched them. He saw her longing and enough fear to make him wonder if yes, he could change her mind. Maybe. "I won't make you promise. But let me try, okay?"

She closed her eyes and nodded.

He kissed her. And this time tasted the salt of her tears.

She swept her arms up around his neck and held him tight, long after the kiss ended. "I do like it here."

"Here in my arms?" he murmured into her ear.

She sighed, deep and long, and he hoped that meant agreement.

"Ellie, can you hand me a bunch of those sixteen-penny nails?" Dan dropped his hammer into the slot on his tool belt and reached down from his perch on the ladder propped against the side of his house. Or at least the shell of the house. The structure had potential, however, with its four walls now standing and Dan finishing tacking the plywood to the roof joists.

Ellie crouched at the base of the ladder and picked up a rickety box holding nails as long as her finger. "These?"

"Yep." Dan descended a step to grab the nails from her. "Thanks. I really appreciate your help today."

Oh yeah, she was a huge asset. So far she'd managed to ram his thumb into the roofline while handing up a sheet of plywood, nearly toppled him off the ladder when she accidentally jostled it, and let her dog gulp down the homemade brownies in Dan's lunch bag. He should be thrilled she was here.

With his lopsided grin and the way those gray eyes twinkled whenever he looked in her direction, well, she just might buy his words. His devastating looks, coupled with the brilliant blue sky and the view of reddened maples, golden oak, and poplar trees gilding the hills surrounding his property, had convinced her that she'd spend every Sunday afternoon helping him build his dream cabin.

Unless, of course, those Sundays ended with an abrupt cancellation of her employment. Which might happen if she didn't get to the bottom of the recent fires and if Romey's daily telephone calls to her office were any indication.

The ladder squeaked as Dan descended. "Ready for another sheet of plywood?" He looked like a modern-day warrior this afternoon, obliterating the tidy-pastor image he'd accomplished this morning in his tweed jacket and dress pants. Now his blue thermal shirt, his worn blue jeans, and work boots turned him into a rogue construction worker, and a slight five o'clock shadow gave him a rough-edged look. The breeze played with his hair, turning it into a nest begging for a woman's touch.

Ellie stuck her hands in her pockets and nodded.

"Great." Dan grabbed his water bottle off the ledge of the open window frame and downed a gulp. He wiped his mouth on his sleeve. "I think one more Sunday afternoon and I'll have this place roofed in. I might hire one of the guys in town to do the shingling."

Ellie ambled over to the stack of plywood, bent, and gripped her edge. "Why are you doing this by yourself? You should ask some of the guys at church to help you."

Dan lifted his edge. "Got it?"

Ellie nodded, noting how he took the job of walking backward. Dan emanated chivalry with each step, yet he let her pitch in. The combination had the power to tangle her heart.

Will you let me try and talk you into sticking around Deep Haven? Please?

Yes, she was in deep trouble. Especially when she realized she'd spent a good chunk of time wondering where her keyboard might fit in the 28 x 52-foot bungalow and how nice it might be to play Chopin while overlooking the lush panorama of Lake Superior.

"So, why don't you let them help?" she asked again as Dan climbed the ladder, still holding his end.

"I dunno. I just want to do it myself, I guess. Free time is a precious commodity. I don't like to interfere."

Yeah, that sounded like the man she was beginning to know. Considerate to a fault.

So considerate he hadn't tried to break her rules. Not once in the two days since their beautiful stroll down the boardwalk under the waxen moon did he do more than smile knowingly in her direction at work.

Of course, by the thunderous tone of her racing pulse, she didn't doubt that the entire station could guess that she had serious, dangerous feelings for the local man of the cloth.

"What did you think of the sermon today?" He levered the plywood onto the roof, his muscles stretching the sleeves of his shirt. It conjured up the feeling of those same arms around her, holding her tight, evoking every urge to surrender, to let him protect —

"Ellie?" Dan peered down at her, and she realized she was staring.

"Um . . . it was interesting. Usually missionaries are so . . . uh . . ."

"Boring?"

She shrugged, feeling heat edge up her face. "I guess. This guy and his family intrigued me, however." She envisioned the man — dressed in blue dress pants, a light blue shirt with a silver tie — his blonde wife, and their four sons, who'd sat in the front row like angels, beaming as their father preached. The picture of a well-behaved and well-groomed family. For a moment, she wondered if their behind-the-scenes life matched the Sunday service performance.

"Why, exactly, would a man drag his family overseas for nearly a decade and subject them to illness, trauma, and poverty?" she asked, voicing her question. "How do they do it?"

Dan put a wad of nails in his mouth, and Ellie watched as he pounded them in at the base, then climbed onto the roof and finished at the top. He moved like a carpenter, as if he'd been born with a hammer in one hand and glue on his boots. It didn't do her heart any good at all to see him climbing around fifteen feet above the ground.

And just how would she feel when he was wearing a turnout coat and armed with a chain saw, smoke billowing out of the windows below him? The wind hissed through the leaves, and she crossed her arms against a sudden shiver.

Dan finished pounding in the last of his nails and climbed down the ladder. "One day at a time, I suppose."

"Huh?" Ellie frowned at him.

Dan frowned back, tease in his eyes. "The missionaries? They get by one day at a time, holding on to God's love. Trusting in His grace to keep them going."

"Uh, right."

He smiled, stepped close, and suddenly she found herself in his arms. He smelled so profoundly masculine it nearly swept her heart right out of her chest. Oh yes, she liked these arms around her. Probably too much. He swept back her hair and kissed her in the soft well behind her ear, just above her neck, sending a ripple of pleasure down her spine. Then he met her eyes. "I think that's how it's supposed to be, whether you're a missionary or not. Hanging on to God one day at a time, so we can see Him in our lives."

She heard whispers from her chat with Liza and swallowed hard. *The more we seek to serve Him, the more we need Him. It's a circle of joy.* She'd spent more than a few moments pondering that paradox, unsure as to how God could be seen in the stress and sacrifice that accented her daily life. And joy? Yeah, right. She hadn't felt joy since . . . well, never, really.

Ellie hoped her confusion didn't show on her face.

Dan gently tucked her hair behind her ear, his eyes roaming her face. She attempted a smile, but he kissed her, this time on the lips. Gently. As if he cherished her, as if nestled in the embrace of rich forest colors, the smell of autumn, the song of the trees, they'd found a simple, quiet peace. Just Ellie loved by just Dan.

Loved?

She stepped back, away from his embrace, her heart pounding. "I've never heard that story he preached on before. King Uzziah?" Ellie's voice came out just a tad too high, on the fine edge of vulnerable. Oh, brother. The last thing she needed was to start hoping this man loved her.

Except hadn't she begun to entertain those very hopes the moment he took her in his arms on the boardwalk, with Lake Superior lapping the shore?

Why, oh why, couldn't she listen to the voice of common sense screaming in the back of her brain?

Dan looked at her, the faintest hint of hurt in his expression, then turned back to his work. "Yeah, he chose an interesting passage, that's for sure. Chronicles 26. I remember when our seminary professor preached on it once in chapel. I always felt a bit sorry for Uzziah, and I prayed that I'd never take my eyes off the source of my strength and hope."

He'd picked up one end of plywood and stood there, waiting patiently. Ellie swallowed her heart back into place and grabbed her end. *Take his eyes off his source of his strength. Oh, Seth, if only you could meet this guy.* She muscled the plywood over to the ladder and watched Dan carry it up. *You'd love him.*

Just like me.

No.

Definitely not. No.

But if he smiled at her one more time, the sun framing his wide shoulders, she just might be a goner.

15

Ellie felt as transparent as a piece of Saran Wrap. This relationship wasn't going to work. And it wasn't Dan's fault. The poor guy did his dead-level best to toe the line when they were together. Could he help it that every time he looked at her with smoke in his eyes or a grin on his whiskered face, she turned into a soggy pile of goo? She couldn't think with Dan in her presence.

Ellie clunked her head down on her desk, listening to him laugh in the kitchen, and groaned. Her lack of focus had been dreadfully evident during the drill on Saturday when she'd nearly set the field to inferno as she watched him and his team battle the blaze. Something about the way he faced the fire without fear, the determination on his hard face while he battled with a Pulaski, a two-sided axe used for clearing brush, sent shock waves through her. She'd fought hard to pull herself together to order the second line to attack with retardant.

If she thought that having to watch him during the drill left her weak-kneed, his easygoing laughter around the firehouse deleted any hope of getting work done. After their building "date" on Sunday, one she could barely get out of her mind, she'd sat in her office all day Monday, listening to him joke with Bruce or razz Craig during a dangerous game of darts. The most she'd accomplished was to write a report of the Garden fire for the fire marshal's office and send the forensic office another box of evidence.

She'd highlighted her suspicion that the fire may have been — again — an arsonist's handiwork. The debris and burn pattern in the Garden's bathroom smacked of familiarity, and if the forensics office confirmed traces of alcohol, she'd have to face reality. Deep Haven had an arsonist in their midst. A fact that had her hanging her head in her hands.

Dan was so much like Seth it dug her breath right out of her chest. Thankfully, despite their conversations, Dan didn't probe her silences or try and unearth the source of her comments or questions. Nor did he add to Liza's words, although she hadn't been able to expunge them from her mind.

Liza had proved accurate on one account — Dan was a great cook. He'd made her dinner every night this week and walked her home under the starlit sky. And last night he'd whisked her away in his VW, up the shoreline to Paradise Beach, a patch of shoreline covered with pearly, Superior-smoothed stones. As the sun simmered over the horizon, he'd spread out a picnic of Italian sandwiches on focaccia bread, a strawberries-and-spinach-leaves salad, and homemade chocolate-chip cookies that had left her dumbfounded for the better part of ten minutes. Dressed in a thick Minnesota Wild jacket and with the wind raking his dark hair, he looked nothing like the groomed pastor who manned the pulpit every Sunday.

Then again, looks could be deceiving. Here she was hiding in her office, trying to pull off the steel-toed, fire-chief routine, thinking only about diving into Dan's arms the second she snuck away from work, which had become more of a habit than she realized. She had no doubt that he wielded serious power that could make her sink roots in this town, and if she didn't have her lifetime goals hanging over her head to yank her back to reality, she would have surrendered happily to his charm.

The fact that he'd also kept his promise about not protecting her felt — respectful. Despite the fear in his eyes, he'd held his emotions in check as she'd dangled herself down a fifty-foot cliff to rescue a trapped climber. And when she answered the call to scoop a couple of overboard fishermen from the drink out in the bay, she'd returned to find him onshore, his face grim, his hands in his pockets. He'd said nothing, and although his smile felt forced, she knew he just barely had a grip on his promise.

She couldn't decide if she admired him for it or if, deep down, she longed for him to shatter that promise and haul her to safety. But Seth had already done that, and one life given for hers seemed one too many.

Lifting her head off her desk, she stared at the newest edition of *Firehouse Magazine,* attempting to read an article about hazardous-materials management.

Dan's voice filtered into her office along with the smell of sizzling omelettes. The man was enticing her with food. It worked. Her stomach groaned, loudly enough to wake Franklin, and when she realized she'd read the same sentence three times, she accepted defeat.

Ellie opened her office door. "You're trying to kill me."

Dan looked up from the stove, where eggs popped and sizzled. The smell of bacon and onion frying was enough to send her to her knees begging.

"Hardly," he said, a crooked smile on his face. His eyes, however, twinkled, and she couldn't escape how devastatingly handsome he looked in his uniform — black pants and blue shirt with the sleeves rolled up to the elbows to reveal his hockey-player forearms — and his wide I-can-carry-your-burdens shoulders. It nearly took her breath away. She managed to cross over to the table and lean on a chair.

"I didn't know you were on today," she said casually. *Liar, liar.* But she didn't want him to think she'd memorized — no, dreamed — about working with him for the last five days. Just having him around made her day seem bright and sunny, even amidst the thunderclouds of unsolved investigations, firemen who continued to harass her, and one very angry Mitch Davis, who had placed a complaint about her with the mayor. Oh, joy.

Dan folded the omelette, slid it onto a plate, and set it in front of her. "You need your nutrition. You're wasting away."

"Oh yeah," she said, nodding, "I'm a regular skin and bones after the way I've been eating this week. You know, you might want to think about feeding me once in a while."

He laughed. "I'm at your service, Jammie Girl."

She always turned to indiscernible mush when he called her that. "Thanks for the omelette. Is Bruce around?"

"He's upstairs reading, I think. I saw him with a fire-fighting strategy book."

Ellie forked her omelette. "Yeah, I gave it to him. He said he'd be interested in applying for a deputy fire chief position. I thought I'd help him prepare for the test."

He sat down opposite her with his own omelette. "Good. You carry too much. You need some assistance." He covered her hand with his. "Not that you aren't up to the task." His eyes glinted with tease.

She stuck out her tongue at him.

"Let's pray for lunch," he said, and before she could agree, he bowed his head. "Lord, thank You for this time with Ellie, for Your provision for another deputy chief. Please help her to share her burdens with others. Please bless this food, in Jesus' name, amen."

She frowned at him when he raised his

head. "Do you really think I carry too much?"

His incredulous, eyebrows-up expression made her squirm.

"No, really."

He laughed and shook his head. "Ellie, you're not happy unless you're doing three things at once. While one half of your brain is inventing new training for us, the other half is investigating the Deep Haven fires. You stay up past midnight and are out riding your bike at 5 a.m. You never eat unless I feed you, and you've filed more reports than Chief Halstrom did in his entire fifteen years as chief. Yes, you carry too much."

She grimaced. "I just want to do it right."

He nodded, but his expression had lost amusement. "When will it be good enough? When will you have done enough to make yourself happy?"

She stared at her food and didn't know the answer.

He reached across the table, brushing her closed fist with his thumb. "You're doing everything right, Jammie Girl. But leave the rest of us something to do, okay?"

She didn't look at him.

"Besides, I have to admit, you make a man wonder — will he be enough for you if you're not enough for yourself?"

She looked up. His eyes brimmed with compassion and a hint of fear. She wanted to reach out, rub his cheek, and tell him how he *had* been enough — more than her wildest dreams, in fact — all week. But his words resonated deep inside and drummed open a secret chamber in her heart.

Why *wasn't* she enough for herself? The question clawed at her. Did she fill every spare moment and then some with additions to her to-do list to fill an empty place inside?

No, of course not. She was happy. Content. Thrilled with her life, thank you. After all, she'd finally made it to the top — Deep Haven fire chief.

So why, then, did panic grip her chest every time she looked down from her perch?

Her appetite vanished. Pushing her plate away, she was about to form a negative response to Dan's invasive question when the alarm sounded.

Structure fire on Main Street.

Ellie wore her firefighter's face — gritty and fierce. She'd snapped on the persona the moment the service tones chimed. Thirty seconds later she was in her turnout gear and sitting in the officer's seat, calling in the page for another squad.

Her instincts proved correct as usual. Dan drove the rescue vehicle and only had to follow the billow of black smoke to find the source. For a chest-gripping second, he'd thought the smoke came from the Footstep of Heaven Bookstore. It wouldn't be the first time the DHVFD had responded to Mona's address to fight a fire. He vividly remembered the scene, nearly three years earlier when they'd answered the call and found a fire chewing up the back of her house. But quick thinking and plenty of water had kept it from turning the Footstep — and the neighborhood — into a conflagration.

They'd need more than that to stomp out the inferno eating the General Trading Store. A two-story log building that once housed voyagers in town to trade furs and other wares from Canada, the General Store now sold everything from postcards to moccasins to art. It easily hosted the most business in town, and no tourist left Deep Haven without a licorice twist and a General Store satchel bulging with purchases.

There would be no shopping today. Smoke billowed out of the upper-level window, and flames leaped from a ground-story wing on the lake side. Next to it, Mack's Smoked

Fish Stand had succumbed and now shot flames thirty feet high.

Dan screeched up behind the pumper engine and hopped out. A crowd had gathered in the Red Rooster parking lot across the street, and he motioned for them to get back as he ran to the engine. Ellie was already out, assessing the situation. He heard her voice over his radio calling in the units from Moose Bay and St. Francis Township and asking Marnie to dispatch the rest of her squads.

"We might have to shoot for containment on this one," she said.

Dan snatched his air pack and his chain saw and ran for the thirty-foot ladder, assuming Ellie would want him on the roof. For once, he wished Mitch were here. But Ellie had placed the oaf on disciplinary probation, deciding to give the dog a cooling off in hopes she wouldn't have to permanently cut loose one of her few capable captains. Outside a fire, Mitch made even the pastor in Dan want to turn him into mulched meat. But working on the crew, Mitch had a cool head, fire savvy, and courage.

"Joe, Doug, give me an assessment and search the place," Ellie barked. "Listen, I don't want any kamikaze firefighting or

Lone Rangers. You see a tight spot, you back out, understand?"

Dan watched Joe and Doug head into the fire, armed with their axes and SCBA gear. While they did a room-to-room search, he'd climb to the roof and start venting so the gathering smoke might escape and lower the possibility of flashover.

Ellie stalked the perimeter of the building, her radio to her mouth. "Simon, cut the power to Main Street. Then find the gas main and shut it down. If this thing goes up, it'll take out the entire business district."

A canopy of black, toxic fumes was quickly blotting the firmament with trauma, choking out the daylight and littering the air with ash. Dan saw the owner of the Loon Café standing white-faced on the corner. Dan's jaw tightened as he climbed the ladder. This blaze could level Deep Haven's tourism trade and bankrupt the little town.

"We have wind off the lake pushing the smoke toward the city. The flames will want to run that way. Be alert, men. Craig, get another line into the lake. Bruce, you and Guthrie lead —"

"We need a master stream, pronto!" Mitch's voice boomed over Ellie's. Dan turned, halfway up his ladder, to spot Mitch on the ground, dressed in his turnout gear and helmet, equipped with a radio.

"Mitch, if you want to help, join Dan on the roof," Ellie growled in a dangerous voice. She looked like she wanted to rip his eyes out, but she stood her ground in the middle of the street. "Guthrie, get a spray on the store."

With a sick gut, Dan watched Guthrie aim a hose toward the store. "No — !" Ellie's voice came a second too late, and Guthrie opened the stream. The force of water knocked him flat, and he landed in the dirt. The hose sprayed like a snake through the air.

"Get the hose!" Ellie yelled. Dan saw her start for it, then stop. "Bruce, grab that hose!"

Bruce tackled the hose, shut off the nozzle. While the steam hissed, everyone stood frozen. The fire crackled and spit at them.

"Okay, men," Ellie said stiffly. "We're okay. Bruce, Guthrie, drag the line into the building, but don't open stream until you're in position."

Bruce ran forward with the hose, Guthrie on his tail.

Dan climbed to the roof, planted his feet, and ripped the cord on his saw. Smoke billowed out of the ventilation as he cut a line. "Be careful, Dan," he heard softly in his ear. He didn't look at Ellie and wondered if he'd actually heard it, but the words slowed his heartbeat, made him check his footing. He wasn't unaware that the trusses could already be weakened, and he could plunge right through to the ground.

"Mitch, what are you doing?"

Dan looked up. He spied Mitch on top of the engine, fixing the monitor for a master stream shot at the building. Designed to blanket the building with water, the fixed sprayer atop the pumper was only used for surround and drown, a last-ditch effort to put out the fire when containment was the only goal.

"Mitch, get down!" Dan saw Ellie running toward the engine, scramble up it. "Are you crazy? If you put water on the smoke, it'll drive the fire down, right at our men." She reached him and grabbed at his jacket.

Dan nearly leaped from the roof when Mitch pushed her back. She landed hard on the cab of the engine. Mitch's words over the open radio made Dan wince. "I've been fighting fires in this town for nearly a decade. You're the idiot who keeps sending our men in there to —"

"I found a body. A woman." Joe's voice stopped them all short. "Upstairs."

Ellie bounced to her feet. "Simon, get an

egress ladder up to that window. Bruce, Guthrie, I want water on that staircase. Keep the fire away from the second floor while Joe and Doug bring her down."

She pointed at Mitch, her face fierce, and even Mitch stopped. Dan recalled the day in the hospital when she'd verbally mopped the floor with him, and he silently hooyahed his girlfriend. *Get 'em, Ellie!*

"You wanna help?" she barked at Mitch. "Help Dan on the roof." She stalked past him and climbed down from the rig. "I need a second line! Where's my squad?"

John Benson ran up, pulling on his turnout coat. Dan chewed out another hole while John laid down another hose line. A cheer went up from the crowd in the parking lot when Joe and Doug appeared at a window. Joe climbed out to the ladder, then reached for the victim and carried her down over his shoulder, fireman style. John helped hand her over to Steve Lund, paramedic. The two firemen then turned to run back inside.

"Look out!" Ellie hollered.

In a collective breath, everyone froze as the front entrance of the store, an archway of river rock, collapsed.

"Bruce!" Ellie's voice betrayed panic.

Dan crossed the roof on pure adrenaline. "Bruce!"

286

No reply.

Dan stopped long enough to connect gazes with Ellie. He saw in them his worst nightmares. "No, Ellie, don't."

"We're shorthanded, Dan. Keep cutting," she said into the radio. Crisp. Tight. Low and dangerous. He watched in paralyzed fear as she dashed to the engine and grabbed her SCBA gear. "Joe, help me."

Instinct took over. *Sorry, honey, but there is no way you're going in there.* Fire licked out of the first-story windows, and smoke billowed from the second story like a giant coal furnace. "No, Ellie!"

Ellie didn't even look up. She dropped her helmet and pulled on her mask, her Nomex hood, then grabbed her helmet back up and reached for her axe.

Dan didn't take a full breath as he slid down the ladder. He hit the ground running. John Benson and Joe had seized the other hose line and were wrestling it toward the side entrance of the building. Ellie hustled one step behind them, ready to spring forward the second they turned on the water.

"The first rule in firefighting — don't go in without a buddy!" Dan screamed while he rounded the building.

Ellie whirled, and for a second her eyes

widened, shock written on the small square of her face behind her mask. Then Dan tackled her. Full out, down to the ground. Pinned her tight.

He shocked even himself. Pulling a deep breath, he scrambled off her. "You're not going in there."

She sprang to her feet, hustler that she was, and if it weren't for the fact that Joe and John were already moving into the building, he had no doubt she'd have decked him right there.

"C'mon," he said roughly and charged into the house.

Ellie stood there, gasping. Her bones ached, and her pride smarted. First Mitch and now Dan? Tightening her grip around her axe, she followed him into the fiery tomb, pressed through gray smoke, and immediately dropped to her knees. In a blink, the daylight vanished. Her flashlight dug out a lit path barely large enough to make out her hand in front of her face. A swirl of writhing smoke pressed against her mask, separating her from Joe, John, and Dan. Their voices cut out, eaten by the fire, and the immediate isolation turned her skin clammy.

How she wished for a thermal imager — a handheld device that could pinpoint temperatures and help her crosshair a body or two. But Deep Haven's firefighting funds had already dipped in the red after her purchase of PASS devices for every man. Something she would never regret, especially hearing the full alarm of Bruce's PASS screaming, telling her he'd been down longer than ninety seconds.

Taking a deep breath and deliberately slowing her breathing, she recited her thermal layering — three hundred degrees one foot above the floor, five hundred degrees five feet up, and twelve hundred at the ceiling. She hugged the floor, one hand on her axe, the other reaching out for the hose line. Inching forward, she veered toward what she hoped was the wall, aiming to keep one hand against it. Dan crawled ahead of her somewhere in the cloying heat, lost in the blackness. She kept her breathing calm, refused to try and discern the objects she ran against — a table, a chair, a rack of clothes?

"Find anything, Dan?" she yelled.

"Negative." Dan's voice sounded constricted, as if terror had him by the throat. But she knew him better — the only terror that choked him was the fact that she'd darted in on his tail.

She'd have to fix that.

She bumped into something, wondered if it could be the stairs. Climbing up she immediately felt the heat press against her, then the hard bump of a wall. A chair. She dropped to her knees and pressed on.

Blackness swirled around her, despite the steam John and Joe churned up with their spray. Her flashlight a pitiful beacon, she fought the sense that the room might be shrinking, trapping her, and crawled faster.

The wall ended, whatever hallway they'd traversed now merging into a larger room. She aimed for the hose line Bruce and Guthrie had dragged in, praying she'd trip over it.

When something fell hard against her, she instinctively threw up her arm in a protective move, expecting the ceiling to rain down. Instead, an arm ranged past her peripheral vision. She clamped onto it, reeled him in. She nearly cried when Guthrie shoved his mask up against hers. She squeezed his shoulder, turned, and hauled him toward the door.

Heading away from the fire seemed easier, less like having to tug her courage along with her body. She followed the hose line toward the dent of light, the ease of heat. Ellie muscled Guthrie out into the smoke-filled sunshine just as the man began gasping, his air pack near its last puffs.

She tore off his mask. "You okay?" She clutched his coat and yanked him away from the fire, while he back-pedaled to keep up. "Steve! C'mere and check on Guthrie!"

A second later, the nurse from the hospital, complete with a helmet and a turnout coat, rushed over to Guthrie as he crumpled onto the street. Ellie didn't miss the mix of pure fear and hero worship on the young firefighter's face as he stared up at her. She crouched beside him and patted his arm. "You did well, Guthrie. A real hero."

He smiled and coughed as his lungs spewed out the toxins that had seeped through his mask.

Ellie sprinted back toward the building, and Dan nearly bowled her over, dragging Bruce out, holding one of Bruce's arms over his shoulder. Barely conscious, Bruce had lost his helmet. Burns laced his neck, ugly red and black curls of skin. Ellie dropped her axe and grabbed Bruce's other arm. Together she and Dan carried him to the rescue squad. Steve had already affixed an oxygen mask to the victim Joe had rescued and had her on a litter, ready for transport.

Monte, an on-call paramedic from St. Francis Township, ran over and helped them lower Bruce to the ground. The man had lost consciousness, and his body sagged like a dead man's. Ellie removed her mask and helped Monte ease off Bruce's equipment. Bruce had suffered second-degree burns on his ears, forehead, and scalp.

"I found him facedown, a part of the ceiling joist pinning him to the stairs." Dan flashed a look of agony at Ellie, and she too easily remembered the day Dan had found her, similarly pinned.

"He may have a spinal injury." Steve ran over with a C-collar and snapped it on while Monte opened Bruce's jacket.

Steve looked up at Ellie. "We'll take it from here. Go."

Ellie had frozen as she stared at Bruce. The man was a carpenter by trade. What would he do if he'd been seriously injured? If he couldn't walk again? The image of his blue-haired wife, Ruth, her round, smiling face telling her that she'd heard good things about Ellie filled her mind. Oh yeah, great things. Like how she put her men in danger.

She turned away and hurried to the front of the building, her radio to her mouth. "Joe, John, you'd better be on your way out."

"Right behind you, Ellie," came Joe's voice, and she glanced over her shoulder to see them running away from the blaze.

Flames licked out of every window, smoke filled the harbor, blackened the sky. Mitch had ignored her — or perhaps seen the writing on the wall — and sprayed an arc of water from the monitor on the engine. Another hose team composed of Ernie and Simon now doused the smoke shack. She hadn't even known they'd arrived.

She stood watching her crew and knew she'd failed them. Mitch had been right. They should have remained on the perimeter and launched a big water attack. Instead she'd launched a Custer charge on the building and nearly gotten Bruce and Guthrie killed. In the distance, she heard the whine of the Moose Bay Fire Department. At least they could assist with the containment. She eyed the sparks that littered the Loon Café. "Joe, John, go lay some containment spray on the café before we have another catastrophe."

She backed up to see the damage. The General Store was a bonfire, the fish house a charred frame, and nearly a hundred onlookers stared in disbelief at the buildings.

She wanted to drop to her knees and sob.

Dan came up to her, his mask over his face, his helmet in his hands. Concern darkened his already blackened, sweaty face.

"You okay?"

She blinked at him, frowned. Then his meaning rushed back to her. He'd tackled her. Tried to keep her from going into the fire. Now that he mentioned it, she ached from head to toe and right down to her heart. "Yes. I'm fine."

She turned away from him, watching the inferno, trying to gather the shards of her command and fighting the bitter nip of tears. "But after we're done here, you need to turn in your gear and your pager. You're fired."

16

Dan sat on a chair in the ER waiting room, his elbows on his knees, running his hand around the inside of his helmet. Joe had elected to pace away the stress of waiting for Bruce's prognosis, and Mona sat beside Ruth, holding her hands in a tight supportive clench. Only the second hand of the clock and the occasional ringing telephone dared interrupt their silent vigil. As usual, profound words eluded him, and the best Dan could muster for himself or Ruth was, "Please, God, let Bruce live."

Mona seemed to have the ability he lacked in comforting the elderly woman. She had wrapped her in a hug, squeezed tight, shed tears, and reminded her that God loved them. Mona should be the town pastor.

He tried not to think of Ellie's parting shot — *you're fired.* He deserved it, the rottweiler he'd turned out to be. He'd broken his promise to her; he'd done a flying tackle, right between her and her job. No wonder she looked like she wanted to chew him up and spit him out.

He'd kept his wary distance as they fought to contain the fire. The Moose Bay Fire Department had helped them wet down the café and World's Best Donuts, located just behind the General Trading Store. Neither building had been lost, although the store burned to its frame. He'd left shortly after the St. Francis Township Department arrived to help with the overhaul, the scraping up and turning over of the smoldering beams, opening the furniture and standing walls to reveal embers that might reignite. Ellie had picked up a long-handled axe and joined the crew, regardless of the fact that her own firefighters sat exhausted on their engine, drinking bottled water, defeat lining their faces.

Footsteps yanked him out of his despair, and he looked up to see Doc Simpson emerge from the ER rooms. His drawn expression betrayed the pain of treating two burn victims. The woman had been identified as a tourist. Her distraught husband had already called their physician in Minneapolis. Dr. Simpson wiped his hands on his wrinkled scrubs while he walked toward them. Dan stood, and Joe stopped pacing.

They drew close to Ruth and Mona, a tight circle of concern.

Dan nearly fainted with relief when the Doc gave a grim but hopeful smile. "He's going to make it. His burns aren't as bad as we thought. Second degree mostly, one section that will need some grafting." He folded his arms across his lanky body and pursed his lips. "But his back has me worried. He cracked one of his lumbar vertebrae."

"Is he . . . ?" Ruth started, her hand shaking as she held it to her mouth.

"We're hoping his paralysis is temporary. Sometimes, with time, the swelling reduces and movement returns. He has sensory functions; we know that. That is a good sign."

Ruth nodded, but Dan felt as if he wanted to find a broom closet, lock himself inside, and scream. Bruce, paralyzed? His stomach twisted and he was about to be sick.

"Excuse me," he said and nearly ran to the bathroom. Breathing hard and sweating, he banged into the room, locked himself in a stall, and braced his arms against the flimsy walls. Breaths came long and loud as he fought his writhing stomach. Bruce — kind, hopeful Bruce — didn't deserve this. But God didn't deal in fairness — if He did, ladies like Mona wouldn't lose their babies, men like Bruce wouldn't become paralyzed, and sweet children like the Simmons babies wouldn't suffer for their father's crimes. God dealt in comfort. In hope.

That thought and a multitude of deep breaths slowed the waves of nausea. Dan closed his eyes, dislodging the tears gathered there. They fell down his cheeks and off his chin. *Oh, Lord, what do I say to them? What?*

Silence pressed against him, spliced only by the dripping of a sink as Dan searched for words. None came. Finally feeling like his lunch might stay in his stomach, he left the stall, ran water from the sink, and splashed it on his face. Looking in the mirror, he decided he'd aged about three hundred years in the last two hours. Bags of worry sagged under his eyes, his unshaven chin had collected grime and ash from the fire, his hair stuck out in all the wrong places, looking as if it had been trampled by a moose.

He looked so unpastoral, the sight threatened hysterical laughter. What a joke. He didn't have the faintest idea how to comfort and lead his flock. They didn't teach Burn Victim 101 in seminary. He knew his theology . . . but how did a person quote Romans 8:28, even if he believed it to the marrow of his existence, when a man like Bruce faced a future in a wheelchair? Dan's attempts to comfort felt hollow and lined with failure and fear of rejection.

He looked uncannily and painfully like the man Charlene had left bruised and bleeding fifteen years ago. Obviously, he was as hardheaded as she'd accused him of being — and even less bright. "You're an island, Dan. You don't need anyone," she'd said, as sunshine brightened her green eyes and kissed the freckles on her nose, looking like a dream just outside his grasp. She'd stood there, hands on her hips, tears running down her face, and severed their relationship with the sensitivity of a hooded executioner. "And until you learn to reach out with authenticity, you'll never be the pastor you hope to be."

Ouch. Her words still made him wince. So he wasn't stellar at sharing his feelings or living on the cusp of his emotions. He liked to think that his temperate nature made him wise, respectable.

Hadn't Paul admonished them to be temperate and self-controlled? Then again, this was the same man who said he'd rather go to the fires of hell than see his fellow Israelites miss out on salvation. That didn't sound like a temperate man. Or perhaps passionate and temperate weren't opposites but two sides of a man's godly character.

Dan *did* reach out. He visited the poor, the sick. Wasn't he hiding out in the bathroom now, sweating out Bruce's pain?

Charlene's words dug at him while he scrubbed his face dry with a paper towel, making his appearance dreadfully worse, then marched out of the bathroom and down the hall. In the waiting room, Joe had Mona in a tight clasp as they leaned against each other. Although Mona looked like she'd aged a decade, she managed a weak smile. "Are you okay, Dan?"

His face twitched and he warred between the truth and his stock, pastoral answer. "No, actually. I'm . . ." He sank into a chair, buried his face in his hands. "I'm at a loss. I don't have any comforting Scripture, anything profound for Ruth or Bruce."

Mona knelt in front of him. She put her hands on his knees. "You don't have to say a word. Just do what you did when we lost the baby."

He frowned at her. He'd done nothing. Absolutely nothing. Words, theology, training failed him.

She smiled. "Dan, you cried. You knelt by our bed and wept. And that act alone told us how much you cared. How much God cared. You reminded us that we weren't going through this alone."

Dan stared at her, the frown tightening on his brow.

She shook her head. "Sometimes words aren't enough. Just *show* them that you love them."

The words from his sermon preparation flooded into his mind: *"This is My command: Love each other."*

Love? Of course he loved Bruce and Mona and his entire congregation.

"Love each other as I have loved you."

The thought swept through him like a hot breath. Love like God loved him. Sacrificially. With passion and mind-blowing dedication. Love enough to risk becoming a baby to a teen mother. Love enough to weep for Lazarus, enough to raise the son of the widow of Nain. Love enough to sweat blood in the garden of Gethsemane wrestling with His painful purpose. Fully wise. Fully self-controlled. Fully emotional. Fully God, reaching out with perfect love.

Charlene's words nailed him: *An island.* Dan never once stepped over his own line in the sand to risk his heart. His service to his flock was polite, not passionate. If he wanted to impact them, he had to invest in them. Perhaps he didn't have to produce

301

the right words but rather show the right emotions. He had to embrace them with the perfect, passionate, agape love of the Almighty.

Mona took his helmet and stared at it, resting it in her hands. "Sometimes I think you hero types give yourselves too much credit." She had a smirk on her face, but it faded in a second. "You know, you're just the messenger. You only need to deliver God's love. God will do the rest."

God will do the rest. Dan nodded, but the words stirred him. He'd been trying to be the picture of God in his flock's life for so long, he'd forgotten he was only the messenger. Dan wasn't responsible for solving their problems, just pointing them to the one who could.

Perhaps, instead of trying to solve their problems, instead of having the answers, he would simply be . . . himself. Transparent.

He touched Mona's hand. "How are you? I haven't . . . I should have . . ."

She turned her hand and held his. "Getting by, day by day, in God's grace. I know He has a family out there for us. I'm just waiting to see how He is going to accomplish that."

Dan stared into her green eyes, and her faith soothed the ragged edges of his heart.

302

"God bless you, Mona."

She smiled. "Oh, Dan. He already has." She looked at Joe, who stood a breath away. A tear caught on his lower lash. When he smiled at his bride, Dan's throat thickened. Oh, how he longed for a love like theirs, a love that could ride out the storms, a love that wouldn't fold against a stiff wind.

A love that would survive the refining fires. Obviously he hadn't found that kind of love with Ellie.

Love?

As Mona stood to hug her husband, Dan closed his eyes, bridling a soft groan. Yes, he loved Ellie Karlson. She'd stormed into his life with all the gentleness of a hurricane, yet he had never felt so breathtakingly alive. So hungry for a person's smile. So revived by her laughter. She challenged every assumption he held about women, but that seemed to only make his blood flow thicker, filling every gap in his chest. Ellie Karlson had leveled his defenses, and for the first time in his life, showing that love felt invigorating. Right.

And she'd just axed him out of her world.

He clenched his jaw against a rush of pain. Now was not the time to think about the gash she'd left in his heart. Opening his eyes, he swiped his fingers across them, then rose. He retrieved his helmet from Mona and, tucking it under his arm, made his way to the ER. He might not be able to tell Ellie how he felt, but Ruth and Bruce needed their pastor, their friend. He'd reach out with his emotions, mourn with them, and believe that God would do the rest.

Ellie stood in a huddle, conferring with the incident commanders from the St. Francis Township and Moose Bay Fire Departments. Over their shoulders, she watched steam and wisps of smoke spiral into the deepening twilight. Moisture saturated the air like the cough of a primeval beast, and the smell of smoke, melted plastic, and charred furniture clogged every breath. She felt as if she'd run about thirty miles, laden with her air pack and bunker pants.

Right now she needed to interview witnesses or at least gather names and confirm that the overhaul process could be terminated. Tomorrow she'd do a walk-through and see if she could pinpoint the source of the fire. On her first glance, she suspected it might have been ignited by the smokehouse that abutted the General Store. Mack's had burned clear down to the foundation, and only quick thinking on Mitch's part had kept it from igniting the café and sending the blaze along Main Street.

She wanted to huddle in a ball, hide under her helmet, and cry. She felt sick. Not only had she gotten into a near fistfight with one of her firefighters — who happened to be right — but a man on her watch had been seriously injured.

She'd hand in her resignation as soon as she filed her report.

"How's your man?" The fire chief from the Moose Bay Department, a squat, elderly, bear of a man who looked like he had a few thousand decades of firefighting under his belt, gave her a look of concern.

She shook her head. "I don't know yet. I'm headed up there after we're done here."

"What a shame. Keep us posted, will you?"

Ellie nodded, making a mental note to ask Romey to keep her in the loop after she left.

The Moose Bay chief shook his head as he surveyed the damage. "The General Store building has been a fireball waiting to ignite for years. I'm just surprised it took this long."

Ellie frowned. "Why?"

"Proximity to the smokehouse, wiring that dates back to the fifties. No fire escapes. A fire chief's nightmare. We were fortunate today. We could have lost more men."

Ellie didn't comment. One tragedy seemed sufficient. She stared at the steaming pile of charred timbers. The second story had finally caved in on itself, and the crew had to pull apart the timbers to douse the smoldering cinders. The onlookers had dispersed; only a handful remained to pull their coats around themselves and brave the slick wind to watch the process. Ellie noticed Bonnie in the crowd, her arm in a sling, her face red and puffy. Ellie couldn't ignore the fact that the woman seemed to pop up at every fire she'd been at in the last month.

"You've set a new record here, Karlson," said the chief from St. Francis Township, a burly Native American with the name Crow stitched to his jacket. He didn't wear a turnout coat like Ellie and had kept his distance from the flames, preferring to command from afar. But *he* hadn't lost any firefighters today.

"How's that?" Ellie asked, wishing she were curled up, nursing a hot cocoa with Franklin in her old apartment in Duluth. She wondered if she could get the place back.

"You've had three structure fires in one month. That's more than Deep Haven had the entire year last year."

"What?"

306

"Yep." Chief Crow nodded grimly. "Did you get the fire marshal in here for the Simmons fire?"

Ellie shook her head. "They wouldn't come. I boxed up the debris I found at the source and wrote a report. It came back just this week."

"And?"

"It indicated some sort of alcohol-based accelerant."

"Anything in the debris?"

"Yes. I found three tiny round aluminum balls, almost flattened disks. The funny thing is that I found two more of the same disks in the debris at the Garden."

The Moose Bay chief frowned. "Sounds like you could have an arsonist in your midst." His gaze tracked to the smoking remains of the General Store. "I'll be anxious to hear what you find."

"I'll let you know."

"Anybody here out to do you in, Karlson?" Crow's voice dropped, yet the question felt like a slug to her midsection.

"I . . . don't know." Mitch's voice echoed through her mind: *You'll regret this.* "Maybe."

Crow clamped her on the shoulder, pal style. "You watch your back."

She nodded, grateful for his words, but

the warning resonated. Someone wasn't trying to sabotage her job here, right? She felt
fragile and slightly ill as she turned back to
the fire scene.

If someone thought he was going to run
her out of town, he didn't know she'd been
born with steel encasing her backbone. If
he wanted a fight, she'd give it to him. Seth
hadn't called her Ellie the Mule-Headed for
nothing. His voice boiled in her head. Seth,
dressed in his smoke-jumper gear, the chop-
per churning up dust on the airfield: *Please,
go home, hotshot. You're going to get yourself
or somebody else killed.*

She hadn't obeyed then. She wouldn't
now.

Except his words had turned out to be
painfully prophetic.

17

The ghostly skeleton of the General Trading Store hull haunted the landscape of the Deep Haven shoreline while Dan drove toward Ellie's hotel. The wind stirred up char and ash and sent it against his windshield, as if in omen. Whitecaps brimmed on the lake, warning of a storm front, and the dark cumulus fought to blot out the silver moon. The perfect night to bare the wounds on his soul to Ellie.

The woman had a right to know why he cringed every time she answered a call, why he wanted to grab her and run whenever she started for her gear.

He loved her.

And just maybe, she'd listen and forgive him. Or, in his wildest dreams, she'd agree with him and chuck this entire dangerous profession and don the garb of a traditional woman —

Which was . . . ? He hadn't realized he

was so myopic in his thinking. Never had he seen a fire chief more dedicated to training the crew, more adept at sizing up a fire. Under Halstrom's thumb, they'd fought fires with all the organization of a badly played rugby match. But with Ellie, they had focus, jobs . . . a leader.

But he didn't want a leader. He wanted a wife. He wanted Ellie.

He'd never felt so empty, so desperately alone as when he'd sat beside Bruce's bed and seen Ruth hold his hand, praying for him. No wonder the Bible said that finding a good wife was akin to receiving favor from the Lord. Ellie surely felt like God's blessing in his life. When she entered his world, pure joy filled his lungs and he never felt so alive.

He pushed the accelerator down, poised on the lip of losing his nerve. A streetlight bathed the hotel porch in golden light, but on the second floor, only two window lights pushed against the grayness of the hour. Pulling up, he checked his watch and grimaced. Well, she hadn't gone to bed before midnight any other day this week. He prayed she wasn't curled up in her pajamas. He tried to tiptoe in his size elevens as he climbed the hotel's porch.

Easing inside, he flinched at a creak on

the second-floor landing, then crept down the hall. He stood outside her door like a thief, listening, his heart pounding against his sternum. No noise, but the light spilling from under the door fueled his courage.

He knocked.

A deep bark from inside nearly sent him out of his turnouts. Obviously the dog had come to life in the last few hours. Dan had serious suspicions that Franklin had entered senility or maybe ate tranquilizers with his breakfast.

The door eased open. Dan straightened his shoulders and tried not to look like he'd crawled out of the local dump.

Ellie's face appeared in the crack. Her hair hung wet around her ears. Droplets of moisture fell onto the collar of her bathrobe. "Dan?" A frown accompanied her question.

"Hi." He shifted from foot to foot wondering whose brilliant idea it had been to come tromping over to her place — obviously the desperate, emotional Dan who had decided to manhandle his life. A smart person would flee and salvage what little pride remained.

"What are you doing here?"

"We need to talk."

She sighed, not a good sign, and her face twitched, sadness in her expression. "I'm sorry I had to fire you."

"I'm not here about that." He wished he'd changed clothes. Why hadn't he thought to stop by the station, get out of his grimy gear, and take a shower before showing up desperate, his heart in his hands, at her door? "I want to talk about us."

She closed her eyes, as if in pain. "There is no us. It . . . won't work." She started to close the door, but he pushed his palm against it, wedging it open. The move surprised both of them — her eyes widened and his heart jumped into his throat.

"Please, Ellie. Just hear me out. Then you can decide what to do with . . . us. I'm sorry that I tried to interfere today, but I have my reasons."

She stared at him, as if searching for a good reason to believe him.

"I don't want to come in. I mean . . . I shouldn't." His voice betrayed him, the coward it was, and he mushed it back into service. "What I mean is, will you come with me someplace to talk?"

She looked down at his boots. "I'm tired. It's been an eternal, wretched day, and I'm exhausted."

"Okay. I'm sorry I bothered you." Dan turned and felt the door closing. But a spark of desperation inside him, the kind that made him drop to his knees and weep for

Mona and pray in earnestness for Bruce, made him stop and turn around. He shoved a toe over the doorjamb, and the door bumped against his boot. When he looked at Ellie, he saw tears pooling at the corners of her eyes. He took a breath. "Oh, Jammie Girl, forgive me. I know I didn't keep my promise to you, but please will you listen to me?" He fought the impulse to touch her cheek, to rub away the tear running down it with his thumb. But he'd leave greasy prints across her clean face. "Please?"

"You know, you shouldn't call me that in public. People might get the wrong impression." She said it softly with the slightest smile, and he felt hope ignite. "No promises, okay?"

Somehow, he nodded.

"Okay. Let me get changed."

Thank You, Lord. "I'll be downstairs in the car —"

"No. You go grab a shower and stow your gear. I'll meet you at the station."

Panic must have shown on his face because she smiled. "I promise." And held up three fingers, Girl Scout–style.

He nearly ran to his VW, then took the quickest shower in the history of mankind at the firehouse. When he emerged from the locker room, dressed in his faded jeans and a sweatshirt, Ellie was sitting at the kitchen counter, nursing a cup of cocoa, wearing her track pants, a wool sweater, and a down vest. Her eyes looked red and heart-wrenchingly puffy.

"Hey," he said softly, "let's get out of here."

She didn't object, which told him that she didn't want the guys sleeping upstairs to listen in on their conversation. "Where to?"

He grinned and for the first time in hours felt as if he just might live through the day.

Why had she ever fired him? The thought of not seeing Dan at the firehouse or on a call had dug a hole clear through her heart, and any thoughts of surviving that wound died a swift death as he drove them to the hockey rink and led her to the ice. Ellie felt dangerously close to weeping. She clung to the feeble hope that the brisk air and the breath of ice under a canopy of black expanse would help keep her emotional footing and hold her ground. He wouldn't sweet-talk her into getting his job back.

Even if he did wield a formidable arsenal. His faded, made-for-Saturday jeans, a navy sweatshirt that did nothing to hide his muscled chest and sculpted arms, and his tousled, wet hair that begged her touch were knee weakening. Added to the sizzle of some sort of secret in his smoky gray eyes, and she knew she'd have to cling to her armor. A smart girl, one using the good sense her mother gave her, would run back to her hotel, lock the door, and pray he didn't chase her.

Because if she stuck around much longer, she'd end up in his arms. Right where she wanted to be.

She took a deep, calming breath and followed Dan out onto the ice. In her boots, she had to stiffen her legs to keep from sliding but managed to keep pace with him. He headed for the middle of the ice, where the center red line crossed it. The memory of their first moments here and the way she'd let him hold her while she grieved Seth nearly unraveled her right on the spot. She crossed her arms in fortification. "What's up?"

She should have known this evening had danger written all over it when he'd hauled a blanket out of his VW, along with a cooler. He now spread out the blanket on the ice, as if laying down a picnic, then sat down, cross-legged. "Sit down, Ellie."

She felt her defenses crumbling like ricotta cheese. "I'm cold," she said stiffly, knowing she'd fold if she sat next to him. Somehow being in his shadow made her feel warm and safe, a feeling she hadn't known she'd needed until he stepped into her life.

And being next to him just might make her admit it aloud.

"Then come here." He patted the blanket next to him. Oh, the man had mischief in his eyes, and his slight smile had her brain reeling. Before her common sense could catch up, she had joined him. He smelled clean and fresh, and she suddenly wanted to forget everything and simply embrace this moment, this tiny patch of blanket in the middle of a landscape of ice.

"Hungry?" he asked and opened the cooler.

She hated how he always knew her weak points. Her stomach cheered in anticipation when she took a blueberry muffin. "How did you — ?"

"I stopped by the Footstep of Heaven on my way to the firehouse. Mona let me raid their fridge."

"Thanks," she said. She didn't have to tell him that she hadn't eaten after the fire — she simply dropped off her gear, checked the roster, and returned home to shed her stress in the shower. His smirk told her he already knew.

Or maybe it was the way she devoured the muffin.

He dug out his own treat and picked it apart.

Silence filled the expanse like a winter breath. Ellie shivered. "Did you bring me here to feed me?"

"Sorta. Yes." He set down his half-eaten muffin and slapped the crumbs off his hands. "Actually, I wanted to tell you a story."

"I'm listening."

He blew out a breath, and raw emotions flickered across his face. She lowered her muffin, her appetite gone.

"I'm really sorry I got in the way of your job today." He swallowed, and it seemed to echo through the building. "I panicked. I saw you running into the building, and I just knew that it was going to come down on your head."

Ellie slowly wiped off her fingers. "It's my job. You knew that before we started . . . well, whatever it is we were doing. Dating?"

He gave her a wry smile. "Sneaking around Deep Haven is more how it felt. I want to take you out, show up with you on my arm after church, tell the choir to stop fixing me up with the organist."

She laughed at the face he made.

"For that reason, I don't want my job back."

She blinked, not quite sure she heard him correctly.

"If my being a firefighter stands between us, then I don't want to do it. I love fighting fires. But I . . . love you more."

His words filled her ears, along with her pulse, and she stared like an idiot at him as if he'd just spoken Swahili. Then emotions completely betrayed her and filled her eyes with tears. "What?" she whispered.

He took her hand, and the warmth radiated clear to her frozen bones. "I love you, Ellie. I probably loved you the first moment I saw you, but I didn't know it, not for sure, until today." He ran his finger along the side of her face, hope in his beautiful eyes.

She swallowed, thinking she should speak. Say something. But she couldn't dredge up her voice from the tight clasp of fear that wound around her heart. He loved her? Oh no, now she was crying. She let go of his hand and cupped her face in her hands.

"Ellie? What's wrong? What did I say?"

She shook her head.

His arm went around her, and with a slight tug, she leaned against him. Of course he was solid and strong and everything she'd longed for. She cried harder.

"Oh, man, I have to admit, I didn't expect this response." He brushed her hair, and she couldn't help but let out a wretched whimper.

"What's so awful, Jammie Girl? Why are you crying?" He wiped away her tears with his thumb.

She felt like a blubbering fool as she snatched a napkin and wiped her nose. "The thing is, I'm not sure it'll work for you to love me."

He raised one eyebrow. "Why?"

She swallowed and her past hovered in front of her eyes like a phantom. She looked away, her voice thin in her throat. "Because deep down inside, I'm afraid that it's only going to get you killed."

He frowned now, and the way his thumb caressed her cheek, she had a hard time not throwing herself into his arms. "Does this have to do with Seth?"

She closed her eyes. "Love makes people do stupid things."

"Like tackling the fire chief before she's about to rescue one of my best friends?" He said it in a teasing tone, but seriousness laced his words.

She opened her eyes and saw his chagrined smile. "Yes. Sooner or later you're going to get tired of being afraid, and you're

319

going to try and stop me."

"Oh, I see." He tucked her hair behind her ear. "Seth tried to stop you —"

"Seth tried to rescue me when I got in over my head."

"And died saving your life."

She nodded, drawing her knees up to her chest. The chill in the arena penetrated to her bones, and she shivered.

Dan leaned close. "That's not going to happen to me, Jammie Girl."

"It might," she whispered.

He shook his head. "May I remind you that you fired me today?" He grinned, and framed in an array of whiskers, it looked just shy of scalawag. No, not shy of, completely. Utterly. And she was a goner. *Dan loved her.* She couldn't even begin to put a word to how that made her feel. *Afraid? Happy? Jubilant?*

Moving to face her, he sat knee to knee with her and took her hands in his. "Okay," he said, as if mustering some kind of inner chutzpah, "here's the story I promised. When I was a senior in college, I was engaged to a young lady named Charlene. She was beautiful and smart and a little sassy — sorta like you."

She narrowed one of her eyes. "I'm not sassy."

320

He laughed. It echoed through the building. "I'm not even going to go there."

Oh, she loved a man who made her laugh. *Loved.* She swallowed hard. "Now listen, bub —"

"Like I said," he continued, "we were engaged. I had our life all planned out and thought she would make a perfect pastor's wife. Charlene was strong and passionate —"

"Like me."

"Yes —"

"I was just kidding."

He cupped her face in his hands, leaned forward, and kissed her. She leaned into his touch, aware that her actions ran opposite of good sense. But she must have left that back at the hotel, along with her boring dog. Thankfully, he pulled away. "Shh. Let me finish."

She opened her mouth. Closed it. Nodded.

"So right before we were about to graduate, she drops a bombshell. I knew that Charlene loved to fly — she'd gotten her private pilot's license long before I met her, but suddenly she doesn't want to fly only Cessnas." His voice dropped, and she saw the old wounds in his eyes. "She wants to fly fighter jets. As in . . . the Air Force."

Ellie stared at him, and her throat began to burn.

"She tells me that we can still get married. I can join up and be a chaplain. While she flies jets." He closed his eyes. "I said no."

"You said no?" Ellie heard the sharpness of her tone and tried to regret it. But suddenly Dan the Caveman had resurfaced, the same narrow-minded —

"I was wrong."

Okay. She took a deep breath, trying to sort through her feelings to understand his.

He held her hands, and she felt him tremble. "We should have prayed about it, sought God's will together. I should have considered her needs, her desires, and tried to nurture them." He looked defeated as he hung his head. "A Christian husband looks to his wife's needs before his own, and I owed Charlene the benefit of a pause before I reacted."

"It went badly," Ellie said in a low tone.

"Yeah, it was ugly. She accused me . . . well, of some of the same things you did when you first arrived."

"Ouch. Wait, did you say something brilliant to her like . . . 'over my dead body'?"

"Round two was sort of a knee-jerk reaction." He appeared sufficiently chagrined,

322

and Ellie soundly enjoyed it.

"I guess girls like me bring out the best in you."

"Yeah, and being with you has reminded me of all my thickheaded tendencies. I don't like the fact that you're a firefighter, but if fighting fires is your life, I'm going to have to learn to deal with it. I can't help that I want to protect you, but I will try not to let it show. Even if it does rip out my heart every time I hear the sirens."

And the more he loved her, the more those sirens would dig into their relationship.

Ellie ran her hand down his strong arm, knowing what it cost him to open up his past and let her take a good look at his failures and his fears.

"So . . ." He lifted her chin and pinned her gaze with his. From a distance, those eyes made her heart skip, but up close, they had megawatt power to turn her into a smoldering pile of mush. "I have to ask . . . do you think you could learn to love the town pastor?"

She suddenly hated herself. Staring at him, she knew beyond hope that she'd fallen for this man. Hard. Fast. No turning back.

She loved the way he wanted to protect her, yet fought it. The fact that he took her seriously, yet knew how to tease her. Being around Dan felt like she held joy in the palm of her hand. But as much as she wanted to grab onto him and this life he offered, she couldn't. She'd made promises she had to keep. To herself, to Seth.

Oh, Lord, why can't I keep those promises here?

Maybe she could. Maybe Deep Haven would turn out to be exactly the place she longed for it to be. Maybe she could find peace on all fronts in this little town.

She reached out to Dan, cupped her hand behind his neck, finally able to twirl her fingers in his hair, longing to tell him yes. Yes, she already loved him. Yes, he was a gift in her life. Yes, yes.

Instead, she kissed him. His arms immediately went around her, pulling her to himself, and she felt his emotions in his gentleness, in his strong embrace, in the taste of his kiss. Sweet and strong. If ever she wanted to love a man, it was this one.

But tomorrow held no promises.

18

Ellie hadn't told him she loved him. She'd kissed him until he'd had to wrench himself free of his desires before he got them into trouble. And here he thought the hockey arena would be a safe environment to keep his feelings on ice.

Right. Just being with Ellie made his emotions ignite. And kissing her only added fuel to those feelings.

Dan took her to her hotel around 2 a.m., then returned to his dark parsonage and spent the rest of the night wondering why she hadn't answered his question.

She didn't love him.

Why did he always court rejection?

That thought found its way into his nightmares, and he woke raw and achy to the sound of someone banging the front door. He stumbled to the door and yanked it open. "What?"

"I see we have our happy pastor's face on

this morning. Oh, and you're looking spiffy. Sleep in your clothes last night?" Joe leaned against the doorjamb, arms folded in a way that made Dan want to deck him. Joe smiled, all teeth, looking like a hyena.

Dan glared at him. "Maybe." He glanced down at his attire and cringed. "So, yes. What are you doing here?"

"I'm your carpenter slave, remember? I promised you a day of free labor."

"Since when do slaves get to pick their day of service?" Dan scrubbed his hand down his face, noted that the sun glimmered from over the trees, and wondered if he'd slept into the lunch hour. With his stomach rubbing against his spine, it certainly felt possible. He should be grateful it wasn't Edith Draper standing on his porch, giving him a copy of Sunday's bulletin, or worse, reminding him he'd missed a meeting of the Advent committee. He stepped back to allow Joe entry.

"Since today is a holiday. Bolshevik Day."

"Excuse me?" Dan closed the door behind his way-too-springy friend and scuffed his way to the kitchen. "As in Communist Russia?"

"Okay, I know it's a bit of a stretch, but I needed an excuse. Power to the working class."

"Oh, please. Want some coffee?"

"Are you kidding? When I can drink Mona's?" He gave Dan a face that looked like he'd offered him roadkill. "So, tell me, why do you look like you slept under a canoe?"

Dan turned on the teapot, then opened his fridge. He'd have to make do with two eggs and a hunk of Gouda. "I was out late."

Joe pulled up a chair, turned it around, and sat on it backward, draping his arms over the back. "Mona said you raided our fridge."

"I stopped by to see Ellie."

Joe's mouth opened, and the smile that followed looked downright sinister. Dan had no doubt that if he didn't elaborate, he'd find Liza on his doorstep next, threatening to break Dan's arms if he shattered the town fire chief's heart.

And what about damage done to the town pastor's heart?

Dan cracked the eggs into a bowl, whipped them, then shredded the cheese as Joe's gaze burned into the back of his bed head. "Okay, fine. I did a stupid thing."

Joe held his hands up in surrender. "Did I say anything?"

"Just listen. Last night after I left the hospital I went by Ellie's hotel room and talked her into going down to the ice arena

327

with me."

"The ice arena? Oh, you're romantic, pal." Joe shook his head.

"Hey, at least I didn't take her to a dump on my first date."

"No, you skated circles around her and made her cry." Joe licked his finger and made an imaginary mark in the air.

"Thanks for bringing that up. Did you come over to make me feel like refuse, or are you going to be my friend here?"

"Is there a difference?" Joe grinned, again, all teeth.

Dan threw a smelly dishrag at him.

Joe ducked, laughing. "So what happened, Casanova?"

Dan pulled out a pan, set it on the stove, lit the burner. "That's where I'm sorta confused. I told her . . . well, that I loved her."

Joe didn't say a word. Didn't breathe. Didn't laugh. Nothing.

Dan glanced at him out of the corner of his eye and saw that his friend's eyes were wide. "Joe?"

"You used the *L* word? Wow. You must be serious about Sparky the Fire Chief."

Dan glowered at him as he melted a pat of butter in the pan. "Have you known me to ever date someone in Deep Haven?"

"That's what you were doing? Dating? I thought it was more like a short-order-cook thing you had going."

"Dating, Joe. Discreetly."

"Are you going to give me one of those eggs?"

"No." Dan poured the eggs into the pan. They sizzled and crackled as he grabbed a spatula. "So, there I am, pouring my heart out to her, and she starts . . . crying."

"Crying? Happy tears like, 'Dan, you're the guy I've been waiting for all my life'?"

"No. Wretched sobs. Like, I've wrecked her life. And then she blurts out this horrible thing about how her brother loved her and died trying to rescue her, and then suddenly, she's —"

"Wait. Pause. Slow down. Her brother *died?*"

"Yes, it was in a forest fire." He opened the cupboard and pulled down a plate.

"Whoa, and she's a firefighter? Doesn't that ring some sort of pastoral counselor bell with you?"

Dan stared at him, brow tight.

"You're going to burn those eggs, pal." Joe got up, stepped over to the stove, turned down the heat. "I'm only saying that there's something behind that scenario. Something more than just being afraid you're going to

329

die in a fire. I'd do a little digging."

"Yeah, well, here's the really strange part. I tell her I love her, she breaks into gut-wrenching tears, tells me about her brother, and then she *kisses* me."

"And the strange part is . . . ?" Joe sprinkled the cheese on the omelette and took the spatula from Dan. "Go sit down."

Dan obeyed, shuffling over to the chair. "Well, it felt . . . weird. Like what I said sorta bounced off her."

"She didn't tell you she loved you, did she?" Joe had taken a towel and flung it over his shoulder, a regular Galloping Gourmet. He shook his head as if in disapproval. "Didn't anyone ever tell you not to show your cards until you know you can win?"

Dan frowned.

Joe scooped the omelette out of the pan and plopped it onto a plate. "The reason you feel weird is because your timing is off. You gotta wait until she's ready. Kind of like fishing. You have to let them want the bait and then hook them."

"Did some old geezer on an Alaskan fishing boat tell you that?" Dan reached across the counter and grabbed a fork.

Joe leaned against the counter, wiping his hands on the towel, grinning. "Don't run down old Volodia now. He's got a woman in every port and plenty of experience."

"Not the type I need. Hey, I just thought if she knew how I felt, maybe . . ."

"She'd run into your arms?" Joe came over and joined him at the table. "I'll bet you even thought that she'd hang up her bunker pants and join you in planning the Christmas pageant."

Dan grimaced. "Does it show?"

Joe patted him on the shoulder. "Only to your friends. And anyone who saw you tackle the poor woman yesterday. Were you a defensive end?"

"Very funny. Okay, I can admit I don't love her profession, but I'm not going to stand in her way. Besides, she fired me."

Joe whacked the table, laughing hard. "The good thing is that now you two can be seen together in public without the choir starting a prayer chain. Enjoy it. Your termination will last for about three days. Believe me, she'll need you on her side with Mitch stalking her like a hound dog on a rabbit."

A chill ran up Dan's spine. "What?"

Joe nodded morosely. "Yep. Craig dropped by the Footstep this morning. Told me that last night after the fire Mitch was down at the Billy G's waxing eloquent about her follies and how the last two fires have been arson."

"Arson? You're kidding. I suspected the Simmons home, but the Garden?"

"Yep, and just between you and me, I wouldn't put it past Mitch to do something to drive her out of town."

Dan shook his head, suddenly not hungry. "No, not Mitch. He's light on working brain cells, but he wouldn't deliberately hurt anyone, would he?"

"Ruby said he came by on the day of the fire while the caterers were setting up to warn them about the dry season and not to build their usual bonfire."

"But what about Leo Simmons's house?"

"You know they were drinking buddies. And you'd recently gotten Leo on the wagon."

"But arson — Leo *died* in that fire. And the kids and Cindy are still in the hospital. Why would Mitch do something like that?"

Joe pulled the plate over. "You're not going to eat this?"

Dan yanked it back. "I am."

"So maybe the Simmons fire was an accident. Mitch went over to talk to him and threw his cigarette into the trash."

Dan cut up the omelette, wondering if food would slow the slide into nausea. "Do you really think someone is setting these fires on purpose?"

"I don't know. Maybe. Ellie's a good fire chief, but she doesn't have everyone behind her, and frankly, with Bruce lying in the hospital, things could get ugly around here. Mona and I are praying for her." Joe stood up. "You about ready to head out, master?"

Dan nodded and finished the omelette.

"Hey, Dan, I have an idea for you." Joe leaned against the kitchen counter with his hands in his pockets. "You want Ellie to fall for you?"

"Yeah, of course."

"Then get behind her dreams. Really, 150 percent. Help her find the arsonist. Maybe then Deep Haven will see what you see . . . a woman with smarts who can handle this job."

So she could break his heart every time the alarm bells chimed? Dan gave a wry nod, not sure if he wanted to see Ellie's dreams come true or pray that they would change. "Good idea."

He set the plate in the sink and snatched his grimy baseball hat off the top of the fridge. Thankfully, he left his tools in the VW for just these types of occasions. Grabbing his work boots, he was wrestling them on as the telephone rang. He hopped over to it on one foot. "Hello?"

He lowered his foot when the voice on the other end identified herself as the administrator from Duluth's St. Margaret's Hospital. Dan closed his eyes while he listened to the news, pain radiating through every nerve. He hung up slowly.

"What is it?" Joe stood in the door, concern on his face.

Dan took off his hat and tossed it on the table. "Cindy Simmons passed away last night."

This time the dream started with the fire. Ellie nearly felt the heat of it as she stood on the ridge, a yellow bandanna around her mouth, her Pulaski dangling in her hand. She watched the wall of flames, nearly half a mile away, devour the side of the mountain, barreling toward the gulley. Her lungs burned when she gulped air, her heart still racing with the fear that had driven her from the fire line she and the other Rocky Mountain Hotshots had been clearing. Now she stood mesmerized by the fury of the blaze. Mad for oxygen, the flames charged down the mountainside, jumping from one treetop to the next, shooting up fully grown trees like torches. Even from this distance she heard it rumble like a freight train, chewing up the tracks toward her.

"Run, Ellie!" In her dream, it was again Fire Mike, her captain, although she knew he'd long ago run back to hustle the other hotshots up the mountain. Inside, a voice pulsed, sounding like Seth's. "Get to the firebreak!" Only the cleared field and her fire shelter could save her now. Adrenaline poured into her limbs, but still she stood gripped by the wall of flames. Other hotshots ran by her; one caught her arm. She wrenched free.

Always in the dream the screaming started the moment she took a step away from the flames, toward escape. On the back side of subconsciousness, she recognized the screaming as only the howl of her heart, but in her dreams it sounded guttural, desperate, afraid. In her dreams, as in history, she hesitated.

It was in this hesitation she felt the invisible cord between her and her brother knot and pull taut.

"C'mon, Ellie," yelled Fire Mike, and then he appeared next to her to grab her arm, drag her along.

Their fate crackled on Mike's two-way as the smoke jumpers relayed a panicked request to the escaping hotshots. One of their own had run down the mountain. One of their own, desperate to save the hotshots blinded by the ravine. One of their own, searching for his sister. Had they seen him?

Seth.

Right then sanity lost its grip. She wrestled free from Fire Mike. He let her go, fear winning over valor. Turning, she raced toward the fire. *Seth!*

Even in her sleep, she felt her breathing quicken, her heart tight, heavy. Her face burned; tears sizzled on her cheeks. The fire had reached the gully now. Spears of pure flame arrowed into the sky, sparks spiraling through a wall of smoke and ash. Her lungs burned from the heat. "Seth!"

And then someone emerged from the smoke. His brown jumpsuit sooty, his eyes blinded with tears . . . he ran up the hill toward her.

Seth.

Even now she had a hard time blinking back her disbelief. Tears etched trails down his cheeks, and his blond hair had curled, as if burnt. Her big brother. Hero. Larger than her dreams. He grabbed her arm and motivated her up the hill with a speed that seemed superhuman. She screamed more than once at the wall of fire licking their heels. He didn't slow even when she stumbled but nearly yanked her arm from its socket.

The fire roared behind them, a firestorm that bent the trees in half and heated the air into a furnace. "Over here! We have no time!" Seth flung her onto a bald spot of earth, and the next moment he shook out her fire shelter and flung it over her. "Turn your face into the ground. Find cool air." Then he went to deploy his own shelter.

Cocooned inside the silver "shake and bake," she stretched out and held down the cover with her hands and feet and dug her nose into the precious cool, breathable air found six inches into the ground. She didn't have time to think as the fire roared over her. Fiery tongues lashed the shelter, the ferocious wind licking at its prey. Ellie shook, her nose in the dirt, her hands pressed against the edges of the shelter. *Please, God!*

"Keep your breathing shallow; don't suck in too much air." She heard Seth's voice in her head and wondered how far away he'd deployed. His voice sounded pained, a scream against the thunder. She closed her eyes, concentrated on breathing, not daring to think what might have become of her had her brother not found her.

Sweat trickled down her face. "I'm sorry, Seth. I'm so sorry." Even in sleep, Ellie felt

337

as if she might be burning up, turning black. Her fingers ached, and her muscles cramped. She heard herself sobbing. Then, suddenly, all went quiet, as if the tornado had spent its energy. Even in the grip of sleep, her textbook classes took over, and she reminded herself to stay in her shelter until the toxic smoke had cleared, the air cooled to a breathable temperature.

This time, however, it wasn't Fire Mike who found her. The dream morphed, and as she stared, blinking against the lingering smoke, Dan pulled back her shelter, knelt beside her, and delivered the news.

Seth was dead.

Ellie blinked. Daylight flooded into her hotel room. She lay on her stomach, breathing into a small moist well she'd dug into the center of her pillow. Drenched in sweat, she trembled from head to toe.

They told her later that they'd found her curled in a ball under her shake and bake, sleeping like a child. What they never knew is that she'd climbed out of the shelter and found the other silver tent . . . the one that held the burned corpse of her brother. He'd gone in the fire after her, to save the hot-shot crew he knew she was on, and hadn't had time to deploy his shelter after saving her life.

She unlocked her fingers from their death grip on the pillow and eased herself off the bed. Her heart beat like she might still be running, and in her thoughts, she was. Running from the memories. Running from the grief. Running with only her promise to fill in the gap Seth's sacrifice had left in the fabric of the world.

And standing on the rim of the blackened horizon, watching her flee, stood Dan.

The image faded as Ellie pushed her fists into her eyes. The memory felt achingly real each time, and yet this time panic rushed in its wake. She'd spent half the night fighting reality, wondering if she could simply unload her burdens and settle down with a man who embodied everything she ever wanted. Gentle. Kind. Protective.

Yes, protective. The fact that he'd tried to save her life not once but twice had found fertile soil in her heart and seeded all sorts of warm, feminine feelings. Feelings she'd buried for fifteen years.

She wanted to cling to his promise that he'd support her and fight the innate masculine impulse to throw himself between her and danger. Believe that yes, they could carve out a niche here. Dan and Ellie. The man had a way of making her feel like only she could unlock the sunshine and bring warmth to the day.

Maybe, just maybe, they had a future. If she landed the position as full-time fire chief, if she managed to untangle the mysteries behind the Deep Haven blazes, and if Dan could stand in the shadows and let her do her job . . . yes, they might survive this.

But her promises came first. As she'd stood on that blackened hillside, watching them bag her brother's body, she'd made a vow. And not even her Benedict Arnold heart, the one that wanted to run after whimsy and true love, could keep her from fulfilling it. She would be the son, the next generation firefighter her parents lost. Seth wouldn't die in vain.

Some things were simply more important than true love.

So, she'd have to pray she got the Deep Haven job. Full-time. Permanent.

She touched her lips once, remembering Dan's kiss, his arms around her, and stumbled to the bathroom to get a shower.

19

Ellie had finally arranged her galley-style office to her contentment. Three pictures — two of historical firehouses and one of her dog — hung on the wall. She'd commandeered an armchair from the living room, found a standing lamp in the storage shed out back and replaced the shade, and thrown down a homemade rag carpet she'd found in Liza's shop. Small changes, but they softened the morgue effect inherent in the warehouse office and made her not hate spending hours attached to her computer, reading reports.

She held a cup of cocoa between her hands, relishing the sunlight that streamed through the wide window and fell across her new desk — an old kitchen table she'd seen for sale in Deep Haven's Hidden Treasures store. Even if her employment in this town didn't take, she'd drag the oak table back to Duluth or wherever she landed. It would be a memento —

Oh, who was she kidding? She had enough mementos etched in her brain — Dan cooking omelettes for her, Dan going one-on-one with her in hockey, Dan tackling her in front of the entire town, Dan wrapping her in an embrace that made her forget time and grief.

Those memories embedded themselves in her heart in a way she knew she'd never break free. *Lord, please let me keep this job.*

She'd been flinging one-line prayers heavenward in alarming frequency these days. And somehow, cracking open her soul in hope had her glimpsing God in unfamiliar places. For example, in a friend like Liza who popped into her office this morning to bring her a muffin, tell her that she was rooting for her, and to inform her that Dan was busy planning the funeral of a victim of the Simmons fire. Ellie tried not to be interested, but the fact that she hadn't seen him since the ice-arena escapade two days ago nagged her. It helped ease her pain that he'd left three messages on her voice mail while she'd been at the General Trading Store doing her walk-through.

She and Craig managed to narrow the source of the fire to a utility room in the General Store. The melted gas meter suggested a leak — the intensity of the heat would have warped the metal — and with the smokehouse ovens neatly butted up to the outside wall, Ellie didn't have a difficult time making the leap to the heat source. Heat + fuel + oxygen = chemical reaction. The fire tetrahedron.

She had high hopes that this fire had been accidental. Not arson.

Except she couldn't shake the image of Bonnie standing in the parking lot, the wind blowing her dark hair into tangles, her gaze glued to the blaze. Didn't Dan say that she'd recently separated and that she and her estranged husband owned the store together?

It bothered Ellie enough to place a phone call to Sam the police chief to discuss her suspicions.

What she'd discovered had Ellie sipping her cocoa now in deep contemplation. Bonnie and her husband, Matt Williams, owned not one but two Deep Haven businesses. The General Trading Store and Smoky Joe's BBQ.

Ellie's heart went out to Bonnie. Matt sported a new woman on his arm these days, an act that surely cut into Bonnie's emotions. Even if no love remained in a marriage, seeing her not-yet-ex-husband happy in another woman's arms could curdle a wife's judgment. Maybe push her into a crime of passion.

But arson wasn't usually a crime of passion. Arsonists set fire to disguise a crime, to recover insurance money, or occasionally just to watch the action. These criminals set fire only to watch it live, breathe, then die. They had a fascination with fire and firefighters that made their crime a game. They set fire to woo the flames and admire those who faced them.

She stacked the reports from the three fires in piles across the top of her desk and began a list of similarities.

Footsteps, then a knock at the door, drew her away from her thoughts.

Her pulse jumped when Dan entered, a smile on his groomed face. "Hi." He'd cleaned up well since the last time she'd seen him — not that she'd minded the faded jeans and tousled hair package, but this version, with the burgundy shirt, tweed jacket, tie, and suit pants turned him into Mr. GQ Pastor. Except for the twinkle in his eyes, she wouldn't suspect he was the same man who had kissed her breathless just two nights ago.

He looked too . . . clean.

She had that weird sensation of dating a

monk and tried to shrug it away. "Hi, there."

"You busy?" He sauntered in, his hands in his pants pockets, a look of vulnerability on his face.

"No. Yes, well, not too busy for you." Oh, brother, she wanted to bang her head on her desk. But he smiled at her words, and she decided that the blush pressing her skin told him she'd let her mouth run ahead of her brain.

"What are you working on?" He sat down in the armchair, put his hands on the arms, gripping them loosely.

"The fire reports. I'm trying to find a link between them."

He nodded like this was riveting information. "So, what do you have?"

She eyed him, not quite sure if she should divulge the information now that he wasn't a firefighter. But she could use another head. "I've got two that started in the bathroom, with an alcohol accelerant. In the debris of the Simmons fire and the Garden fire I found small, round aluminum disks. And my list of onlookers and interviewees places Bonnie Williams at both the Garden fire and the General Trading Store fire. I looked up her address on her interview form and discovered that Bonnie rents a house only a block away from the Simmonses'. Do you know — did she know Cindy?"

He'd gone slightly pale at her summary. "They were friends, but only because Guthrie worked for Smoky Joe's and Bonnie owns the catering company."

"Guthrie? I don't see the connection."

"Guthrie is Cindy Simmons's brother. Occasionally Cindy would fill in for him if he had to care for their mother or even help out at the fire station."

"Did he spend a lot of time at the station before he passed his exams?"

Dan's color had returned, thankfully — it couldn't be easy to hear about the involvement of a parishioner in a murder case. "I hadn't really thought about it. Yes, maybe. He seemed to get on well with Chief Halstrom. And a few times he helped out on the volunteer crews when we had a forest-fire issue. I think he was even given an award once for citizen involvement."

Ellie reached into her personnel files to dig up Guthrie's file. How had she missed that?

Dan crossed his arms, and his expression darkened. "Ellie, I have to ask you — do you have any reason to suspect Mitch?"

Ellie searched his face and slowly nodded. "He threatened me the night I . . . I . . ."

"What did he do to you?" Dan asked in a dangerously low tone. He hadn't moved from his relaxed position, but his hands had tightened on the arms of the chair.

Fear rippled through Ellie at the intensity in his gray eyes. "He, uh —" her mouth dried, and she looked away — "propositioned me."

"That's a polite way of saying he was his rude and vulgar self and forced himself on you."

"I got away. Nothing happened," she said quietly.

But Dan had his eyes closed, his jaw clenched. It rattled her to see him struggle for control. *I love you,* he'd said. Did he love her so much he'd toss out his pastoral reputation to defend her honor?

"I'm fine, Dan, really."

When he opened his eyes, she saw the pain in them. "I'm sorry, Ellie —"

"That some men are swine?" She smiled, hoping to unravel his anger.

"Yeah, I guess," he said but didn't return the smile. "Mitch may be more than a farm animal, honey. He's going around town saying that someone is out to get you. That the fires are personal."

She leaned back, crossed her arms, and scowled. "Hardly. The Simmons fire happened before I got here, and since then only the Garden fire is suspected of arson. I doubt someone is trying to drive me . . . out . . . of . . . town." She leaned forward. "You don't really think someone would do that, do you?"

Dan swallowed, looked out the window where the wind tumbled leaves down the street. "I hope not."

That vulnerable look had returned. It made her ache. Something about this man made her feel cherished, and the realization made her tremble.

She'd never felt cherished in her life. Appreciated, yes. Occasionally. Thanked, more than once.

But cherished? The feelings she'd been trying to douse for three days — no, nearly three *months* — burst to life in full flame inside her. She loved this man. Desperately. Completely. She turned away from him before he could see her feelings written on her face and gathered in her composure.

Love wasn't going to solve their problems. It wasn't going to keep her in Deep Haven.

She took another sip of her cocoa. "I heard that Cindy Simmons died," she said, as if she didn't want to leap the desk and get lost in his arms.

"Yes. I heard yesterday morning. I spent

the day working out the funeral arrangements." Suddenly he looked drawn, like he mantled some unseen load. "Her kids are orphans, and I'm not sure what to do."

"Don't you have a social-services department in Deep Haven?"

"We've been working together. Problem is, the daughter has Down syndrome and the boys need ongoing medical care. Pretty tough to place."

"There's no one in Deep Haven who would take them? Someone who has a heart and an understanding for those with Down syndrome? I have a hard time believing that there isn't a solution after I saw the outpouring of community support for the Garden." She took another sip of her cocoa.

Dan stared at her, his eyes wide.

She stilled, wondering what he saw with those beautiful eyes of his.

"That's it! Of course. You're a genius." He stood, his hands clenched as if in victory. Then he leaned over, ringed her face with his fingers, and kissed her. She closed her eyes, loving the touch of his lips on hers, relishing this moment —

"Hello?"

Ellie recoiled like she'd been punched. Dan turned. Eyebrows drawn, one hand white-knuckling the doorknob, Guthrie

Jones stood in the open doorway. His expression told Ellie he'd seen the kiss and wasn't thrilled. The man always reminded her of a darker version of Greg Kinnear, unexpected and eager, a smile on his face. But this version didn't resemble the firefighter who more than once had sat in her office and quizzed her about firefighting tactics. She'd thought it endearing, even encouraging.

Now a chill ran through her. "Can I help you, Guthrie?"

"No. I guess not." He shot a death-ray look at Dan, then glanced back at Ellie. "I just wanted to see if you were free."

"Sure." Ellie leaned back, hoping Dan would sit down and pretend that no, the air didn't sizzle with both guilt and not a little frustration.

"No, that's okay." Guthrie's gaze felt like a thousand needles on her skin. "I see you have more important things to do." He nearly slammed the door.

Ellie froze in her chair.

Dan stared at the closed door. "So much for keeping this thing quiet."

God picked the right day to give Deep Haven a taste of Indian summer — a stretch of warmth on the far edge of October that

350

had everyone basking in the memory of lazy summer days. Only a light breeze rustled the leaves bejeweling the parking lot as Dan stood in the vestibule of the church, the door open to let in the warm air. He stood slightly behind the Jones family — Cindy's widowed mother and a very distraught Guthrie, who had spent most of the service rocking in his pew — to lend support and accept condolences while the congregation filed out to accompany the casket to the cemetery.

Dan watched out of the corner of his eye as Joe and Mona herded Jordan, Jeffrey, and a squirming Angelica out of the service. Second-degree burns on the little boys' legs and lungs had healed, and Doc Simpson had whispered in Dan's ear their readiness for discharge.

Dan hoped by asking Joe and Mona to babysit today, it would pave the path for the question that had him on his knees through the night.

They'd make wonderful parents.

Please, Lord. He took a deep breath and forced out another smile when Edith Draper stepped up to him. "Nice job, Pastor," she said in her usual cheery, frank tone. "By the way, I was in Duluth this week, and I picked up some supplies for Anne and Noah's reception. I put them in your office since I couldn't find you yesterday to unlock the kitchen."

Dan didn't rise to the unspoken question in her breezy tone nor the twinkle in her eye. He could spot a fishing trip when he saw one. "Thank you, Edith. I'll be sure and deliver it. Although Bonnie should have keys — she's on the hospitality committee, and they were setting up the funeral reception today."

She gave a flustered smile. "Of course. I'll talk to Bonnie." He didn't miss the wink she gave him as she trotted out to her car. Deep Haven's matchmaker.

Or perhaps that title belonged to Liza, who followed Edith's spot in line and didn't even bother to skirt the topic. "So, did you see Ellie today?"

"Nice singing today, Liza," he said in reply, commenting on her beautiful rendition of "It Is Well with My Soul." The last thing he needed was to entangle himself further into Liza's matchmaking efforts. Only, how could he not spot Ellie in that two-piece navy suit? He supposed she hoped to snuff out any hint of weakness and femininity. A work suit. Too bad it only turned her eyes into a knee-weakening blue.

"Are you going to bring her to Noah and

Anne's wedding?" Liza pressed on, raising an eyebrow. He had the uncomfortable sense of being a piece of clay on her potter's wheel.

"Uh, I hadn't thought of it." He groaned inwardly at how easily he folded to Liza's prodding.

"Hmm." It was what she didn't say that made him shift uncomfortably.

"Do you think I should?" Oh, that sounded so . . . desperate. The last thing he wanted was Liza managing his romance. Then again, she and Ellie were getting fairly tight. Maybe he should listen to her advice. He worked up a smile.

"Oh yeah, Preach. A good wedding gets under a woman's skin." Liza nodded, a mischievous glint in her eye. "Take her to the wedding."

Dan nodded, suddenly enjoying Liza's teasing. The thought of Ellie on his arm made him tingle. He could get used to having his name linked with hers, knowing that at the end of the day she came home to him. He could make her dinner and listen to her as she talked about —

Firefighting? Her latest dangerous escapade?

His smile fell. Okay, so maybe theirs wasn't a match made in heaven. Yet. But for the right man, perhaps in time she'd give it up. However, that's what he'd thought about Charlene. But hadn't he told Ellie he had been wrong? that her profession didn't matter?

He shook Craig Boberg's hand, forming a smile, but inside he felt uneasiness rubbing against the soft edges of his heart.

It didn't matter. *Really.* He'd made that decision the second he took Ellie in his arms. She may not have told him she loved him, but her response spoke volumes. He didn't have to love her job, but a future with Ellie was worth falling to his knees in prayer every time she got a call.

Dan walked into the vestibule, where Joe stood with Mona, the baby, and the boys. Dan bent and shook Jordan's hand, then gave Jeffrey's shoulder a gentle squeeze. "You boys know your mama loved you, right? And that she's with Jesus?"

They nodded, and their solemn expressions knocked him back on his heels with a fresh wave of grief. These boys deserved a loving mother like Cindy. They deserved a father who cared enough to teach them to be men of God. Dan stood and looked at Joe and Mona and felt his throat thicken. "Do you suppose that after the interment, I might have a word with both of you?" He ran his hand over baby Angelica's head as it bobbed on weak neck muscles. She smiled — a toothless, innocent toddler grin.

Mona tucked the child's head into her shoulder and nodded.

The late afternoon graced them with fragments of sunshine between gray clouds while they laid Cindy Simmons to rest beside her husband. Dan had debated that decision, but Marilyn Jones, Cindy's mother, insisted that Cindy would stick by her husband even in death.

"She ran a good race," she said to Dan as the guests departed, some for home, others to the reception at Grace Church. "She trusted in God 'til the end."

Dan embraced the frail woman, touched by her faith. "Yes, she did. Even when Leo served his time, even after Angelica's birth, she trusted in God's strength to get her through each day."

Marilyn nodded, her hazel eyes so much like Cindy's, always glowing with hope. She'd aged a decade since her husband's death to cancer five years earlier. Her gaunt face betrayed long days and the ever present worry about Guthrie's dangerous profession. But she modeled a faith that tugged at Dan's soul. "My daughter won't be forgotten, not on earth —"

"Nor in heaven. I am sure God welcomed her with 'Well done, good and faithful servant.' "

Tears edged down Marilyn's wrinkled cheeks. "Thanks, Pastor. I needed that."

She moved away, and Dan wondered for a moment how he'd come up with those words. But he hadn't thought them — he'd *felt* them. Perhaps that made the difference.

The murmur of somber voices emanating from the church basement told Dan that most of his congregation had beat him back to the church. He went into his office, took off his suit coat, and draped it over a pile of boxes that sat in the corner. Reading the labels on the sides . . . *napkins, candles, tablecloths,* a small box that had *warning* on the front of it snagged his attention. Dan opened it and found a box of Sterno canisters, used for keeping food hot while it was served. The hospitality committee certainly covered all their bases.

Closing his door, he prayed that Mona and Joe were downstairs, enjoying being parents for the day.

The hospitality committee had scrambled their resources and put out a buffet to rival Smoky Joe's. Potato salads, baked beans, sloppy joes, and fruit salads. In the middle

of the table a basket of white lilies, snap-
dragons, and gladiolas gave the room an
aura of hope. Of heaven. Just what Cindy
would have wanted. Dan spotted Joe heading to a round table, three cups of punch in
his hands. Dan caught his eye and waved
him over.

Joe delivered the drinks, then skirted the
tables and followed Dan back into the
hallway, where the din subsided. "How are
you doing?" Dan asked.

"Good. I'm hurting for those boys,
though. They have a rough road ahead of
them."

Dan nodded. Now that he'd screwed up
his courage, he wasn't sure where to start.
"I've been praying for quite a while about
what to do about the kids, and I'm wondering if . . . well . . ." When he looked up, the
concern in Joe's face bolstered his words.
". . . if you and Mona would consider
adopting them."

Joe's jaw didn't actually drop, but he
looked at Dan with such a stunned expression it didn't have to. "Are you serious?"

"Yes. I can't think of a better couple to
raise these youngsters. Especially Angelica.
They need to stay together, and you and
Mona would be great parents."

Joe moved out of the way to let Guthrie

pass him into the men's bathroom. "I don't know. I mean, yes, we'd like to be parents someday. But Mona's still grieving. She's not ready to try again." His face twisted.

"I understand. The thing is, I already talked to social services, and they're willing to approve you as temporary foster parents until you get your paperwork finished. You could take the kids home today."

"Today?" Joe's expression hinted at fear. "Wait —"

"You don't have to make a permanent decision today. I just hate to take them back to the hospital."

"You didn't find anyone else to watch them?"

Dan shook his head. "Marilyn is too weak, and her siblings are gone. We'd have to move them to Duluth into their social-services department and hope they could find a way to keep them together."

"They'd never see each other again." Joe folded his arms and leaned a shoulder against the wall. "We do have an extra bedroom. I could move out my computer."

"I could commandeer a crib from the church nursery."

"I'll ask Mona." A smile tipped his lips. "In the short term, I think we could work it out."

"God bless you, Joe. Thank you."

"I think we're the ones getting the blessing here." Joe took a deep breath, nodded.
"And we'll pray about the long term." He
clenched his jaw, as if to force back the swell
of emotion. "Thanks for asking, Dan."

20

Ellie raised her face to the sky and gazed at the periwinkle clouds, fat with precipitation, letting the waning hint of summer soothe the ragged edges of her sorrow. Burying victims had never come easily — the fact that the woman had been the mother of three young children sliced deep. Franklin nosed around the beach as if searching for exactly the right nook to do his business.

Ellie crossed her arms and sat on a large boulder, watching the seagulls as they scrutinized Franklin's movements. When their beady eyes settled on him, they'd cry out, lift into the air, and resettle themselves on the waves, where they scolded him from a distance, riding the swells with regal disdain. Thunder rumbled through the mottled sky.

Cindy Simmons had left her mark on the world, as evidenced by the closed businesses on Main Street and the line of cars that had exited the church parking lot and followed the hearse to the cemetery three miles up the Gunflint Trail.

Ellie had lingered at the edge of the crowd, not wanting to intrude, hoping to pay her respects, mostly doing her duty as the town fire chief. A few had acknowledged her: John Benson, Ruth Schultz, Craig and his wife. She'd made eye contact with Dan more than once, and the grief in his eyes felt like a seeping wound.

"C'mon, Frankie, hurry up." She clapped her hands, the urge to return to the church nipping at her. Dan looked painfully wrung out, and she wanted to shed the fire chief attire, don her jeans, and just hold his hand while they walked along the beach. She couldn't erase the sorrow, but she longed to help carry it.

On days like this afternoon, as the slight wind carried the breath of autumn around the mourners, she wished she had a different job. One minus the loss of life but with the joy of service.

Joy? She huffed a disbelieving laugh. She hadn't felt real joy in her job since . . . well, never. Firefighting wasn't something she chose . . . it chose her. Her debts compelled her into service. Not to atone but to give

Seth's death significance. Dan's eulogy tumbled through her mind, along with the verses he read in Philippians 3: *"I am focusing all my energies on this one thing: Forgetting the past and looking forward to what lies ahead, I strain to reach the end of the race and receive the prize for which God, through Christ Jesus, is calling us up to heaven."*

Cindy Simmons had run well and long. She'd won her prize and left behind fans and an imprint in the community. Children and family who loved her. Ellie pushed the toe of her pump through the stones. If she were to die today, what would she leave?

Nothing but a fat basset hound and a trail of moments she hoped counted in her favor in God's tally book. He couldn't deny that she'd tried. Still, she couldn't help but wonder if all her hard work in this life had accomplished exactly nil. She'd have a sum total of two at her funeral. Her parents, burying the last of their children.

What had Cindy done that left an entire town grieving her loss? Ellie mentally cataloged the speakers from today's service. The choir director, a Sunday school teacher, Cindy's mother. All relating stories about Cindy's love for her family, her church, her community.

Perhaps it wasn't so much *what* she did

as *how.*

"Lord," Ellie said, lifting her eyes to the horizon, where the sun sizzled and a magenta canopy bled into darkness, "You know I came here wanting to make a difference. I wanted to serve You in Seth's place. But I feel like I've been running in place? I've done nothing but stir up a strong wind. I want to make a difference in this life. In this town. Please, show me how."

The waves washed the shore. Seagulls cried, the dog snuffed at her feet. Ellie closed her eyes, still for what seemed like the first time in weeks — no, months, even years.

Abide.

She opened her eyes, even looked behind her, wondering if perhaps someone had spoken it aloud. *Abide.* She frowned as familiar words flooded her mind: *"Those who remain in Me, and I in them, will produce much fruit. For apart from Me you can do nothing."* Dan's sermon. It had bothered her before. It didn't feel any safer now.

If she didn't abide in God's love, did it mean her hard work meant nothing?

Certainly God didn't discount the thousands of lives touched by people, such as herself, who reached out simply because they wanted to change the fabric of life? If

363

she didn't do it while in the embrace of the Almighty, did that mean she added nothing to her spiritual bank account?

Or rather, perhaps it meant that if she didn't abide, she missed out on the joy. She again recalled Liza's words about our works on earth being something that drew us closer to God. Could it be that abiding made the work — any work — meaningful? Even if it was washing dinner dishes after Wednesday night prayer meeting or serving on nursery duty.

The entire concept twisted her brain, and in her distraught condition it made her feel about three million years old. She kneaded away a pulsing headache with her fingers.

Maybe her problem wasn't so much lack of abiding but wondering if she was good enough for God's attention in the first place.

Franklin plodded over, spilling rocks, an apple core in his mouth. "Oh, gross. Give me that." Ellie pried it out of his mouth, made a face, and pitched it into a nearby trash can. "That's it. We're outta here." She snapped on his lead and trekked back to the fire station. The hotel desk clerk's patience had started to wear thin so she'd had to keep Franklin holed up in her office. A few more weeks and she'd know if she was going to be looking for rental housing or packing her Jeep.

It felt like an eternity.

Or way too soon to say good-bye. She wanted to belong here. To stand by Dan's side at the back of the church and invest in the lives of his congregation. The urge to be a pastor's wife didn't push her to her knees at night in desperate petition, but perhaps then she'd find that tendril of joy that seemed elusive in her lifelong profession.

Or maybe she'd find true love. Maybe being in Dan's arms would give her the peace that seemed slightly out of reach.

She should stop fighting. Tell the guy she loved him. She certainly acted that way, kissing him without declaring her heart. Her mother would be aghast at her behavior. Well, *she* was aghast. In truth, she ached to tell the man she loved him, but she hoped he could see through her to her heart. Dan seemed to know her every other thought. He knew when to hold her hand, when to stop her in midsentence and tell her to slow down.

No one but Dan could drive her to her last nerve one second and make her laugh the next. Could move her to tears and make her feel like only she could unlock the sunshine. That somehow she was a part of the oxygen in his every breath.

Not even Seth.

Oh, I wish you could know him, Seth, she thought as she let herself into the quiet-as-a-tomb firehouse. She'd approved Simon's and Ernie's requests to attend the funeral, but it seemed odd they hadn't returned yet. She'd track them down at the church and give them her fire chief nudge.

She changed into her flats and put on a pair of dress pants she kept in her office closet. Tucking in her blouse, she grabbed her jacket and her keys and headed back to the church, hoping for time with Dan.

Maybe tonight she'd tell him she loved him. Throw her future to the wind and embrace the moment.

To her dismay, cars still overflowed the parking lot, but she found a spot at the far end. Rain spat on her as she ran for the church. She heard the murmur of voices downstairs — obviously the reception was still in full attendance. She felt and looked like a drenched hamster. She'd simply wait for Dan in his office. She'd done that once before after work — he'd sent her there while he met with the worship team.

Easing open the door, she stepped inside, flicked on the light. The overhead fluorescence bathed the room, and she couldn't escape a slight rush of clandestine adrenaline. She hung her coat over the edge of his desk chair, then sat down in it.

Dan sat here. The image of him bending over a Bible or with hands folded in prayer started a flow of warmth through her. Dangerous Dan the Preacher Man. What a paradox. A delightful, charming package that no woman in her right, sane mind would say no to.

And he loved her. No, *cherished* her.

Yes, she'd tell him she loved him and pray that God worked out their future.

Dan's slightly open window allowed in a breeze. It chipped at Dan's coat, piled on a stack of boxes, and suddenly the coat slid to the floor. Ellie rounded the desk to pick it up, set it on the stack, and froze.

The small box on top was open, and the warning label on its side screamed out like a siren. She peeked at the contents. Tiny boxes of Sterno canisters, and one was missing. Ellie stared at the empty space, a sickly acid welling in her throat. Sterno canisters. Filled with alcohol. Made of aluminum that, when burned in twelve-hundred-degree temperatures, would melt into tiny aluminum disks, the kind she'd found at the Simmons and Garden fires. Her chest tightened, nearly cutting off her air.

Surely there was an explanation.

She checked the pile of boxes. Paper napkins, tablecloths. Innocuous supplies. She picked up a box that held a canister and turned it in her hand. Dan would have an explan—

"Fire!"

The panicked voice came from the basement, along with a smattering of screams growing louder.

Ellie raced to the office door, and the stampede up the stairs nearly flattened her. "Stay calm! Walk!" she ordered. More people died from panic than from being trapped. She heard the church door open, more screams.

She pushed against the crowd, gripping the metal rail as she hurried down the stairs. "Let me through!"

She smelled the smoke before she saw it — the sickly sweet odor of burning plastic. Gray tufted the ceiling of the basement, thickening down one hall. As she shoved her way toward the source, she recognized Ernie and Craig herding people toward the back exit. "Where is it?" she yelled.

"The bathroom!" Joe grabbed her arm, pulled her out of the crowd. He and Guthrie were busy uncoiling an emergency hose from its place on the wall. Glass lay shattered at their feet. Guthrie glanced at her with a pained look.

"Where's the fire extinguisher?"

Joe wrestled the hose toward the bathroom door. "Dan has it!"

Ellie's gaze tracked to the door, where smoke huffed out in ugly, dragon breaths. "He's in there?"

"He found it."

Ellie stopped for a second, letting suspicion seize her around the throat. No. Dan *could not* be an arsonist.

Then simple and pure fear put her feet into action. *Dan is in there.*

She ducked into the bathroom, to Joe's dismay. Dan was crouched by the door in the three-unit bathroom, battling the flames that fought to find fuel in the Styrofoam ceiling tiles. Ellie hit her knees, keeping low. Blue flame lashed out at her in greeting, heat instantly turning her face red. "We gotta get out of here." In this compact space, the toxic fumes could sear their lungs quickly. Dan swept the base of the fire with bursts from the fire extinguisher, foam coughing out of the nearly empty can.

"I need water!" he hollered, turning. Tears dribbled out of his eyes from the smoke.

"Joe's right behind us!" Ellie clutched his shirt, aware that it was soaking wet from perspiration, and tugged him toward the open door. A spray of water shot over their heads as they backpedaled out. They leaned against the wall, coughing, while Joe and Guthrie advanced into the room. Smoke, then steam billowed out, the dragon hissing and fighting its demise.

Craig Boberg braced his arm against the wall, breathing hard, a *V* of sweat on his dress shirt. Mitch stood behind him with a pale expression waxing his usual sneer.

"Is everyone out?" Ellie asked between coughs.

Craig nodded, watching Joe and Guthrie. Steam spiraled out now, along with a haze of moisture.

"Get me the axe," Ellie ordered Craig. "We need to open the ceiling and make sure we stopped it."

As Craig handed her the axe, she turned to Dan. He sat, sooty and exhausted, his arms dangling over his knees, looking like he'd wrestled a grizzly.

If he thought the fire wore him out, just wait until they were alone, and she was able to vent the fury, the hurt that boiled through her chest. She saw the color of the flame, even smelled the alcohol as it burned. If this fire wasn't started with the missing Sterno canister, she'd turn in her badge and start flipping burgers. She barely forced out the words through her clenched teeth. "You . . . don't go anywhere. I want to talk to you. Better yet —" she faced John — "get Chief Sam on the horn —"

"I'm right here." Sam stepped up behind John.

"Good. Take . . . Pastor Matthews into . . . custody. I'll talk to him down at the station."

She didn't miss Dan's or the rest of the crew's open-mouthed shock when she marched into the sodden, charred bathroom with the axe, knowing she'd have no problem sending it through the wall and probably into the next county.

As usual, Ellie drove Dan's emotions to the edge, then nudged them over. "What?" Dan sprang to his feet, knowing in the back of his mind that he wouldn't handle this well. "Custody?" He shot a look at Sam, who hadn't moved but let shock suspend him into hesitation.

"Ellie!" He charged after her into the bathroom. The smoky, sooty moisture stung his eyes, the smell burning his nose. Through the mist he could make out her outline taking aim with an axe. He grabbed it on the back-swing.

"Hey!"

He snaked his arm around her waist and picked her up. She slammed the heel of her shoe into his shin as he dragged her out of the room. "You stubborn . . ."

"What?" she hissed when he put her down in the hall. She rounded on him, and he kept a firm hand on the axe, just in case. The fire in her eyes told him something other than panic over another possible arson blaze had her spitting mad.

At him. He shot a look at the assembly of firemen, all rooted to the spot and obviously as eager as he to hear her explanation. He turned his back to them, lowered his voice. "Ellie, what is it?"

Joe stood in the door of the bathroom. "The fire's out. Guthrie will open the ceiling." He reached over and took the axe from Ellie. She glowered at him a second before she released it. Then, hiking her hands onto her hips, she gave Dan a jaw-jutted, melt-him-on-the-spot glare.

"I think you need to cool off," he said, bracing one arm above her on the wall and hoping to keep this conversation semiprivate. Fat chance, with the crowd moving in to close the huddle.

Her hair hung in damp waves around her face, and she shook. Seeing her fight with some sort of emotional carnage made him feel weak. "Why, Dan? Why? You promised you'd stay out of my way."

"What — ?" He frowned at her.

"Oh, don't tell me you don't know what I'm talking about. I caught you, Mr. Lies-all-lies. I saw the evidence upstairs, and I bet that after the smoke clears we'll find the one missing Sterno canister smoldering under the sink." Her eyes narrowed, but her voice lost its steam as if she were trying to stuff her horror back into her chest. "Won't we?"

Dan shook his head, scrubbed a hand through his hair. "Sterno canister?" His memory tracked back up to his office, to the open box. "Hey, no. There's an explanation —"

"I put it together. I read the interviews. You were at the Garden before the fire, and more than one person said you were in the house. Alone."

"I was there to help."

"And you yourself said that the Simmons fire was all your fault." The look in her eyes — betrayal, disbelief, *fury* — swept the breath right from his open mouth. "Don't tell me you don't remember." She looked past him at the crowd of men. "At the hospital. You said to me, 'It's my fault.' "

He scrambled to dredge up the moment

but came back empty. "I don't remember."

"I shouldn't have believed you." Moisture filled her eyes, and she blinked it back. "For a guy who was supposed to love me, you've got a pretty warped way of showing it."

He flinched, feeling as if she'd kicked him in the teeth. "I do love you," he said in a low tone.

"Yeah, right. So much that you're trying to scare me away, or better yet, trying to destroy my reputation. Were you thinking that I'd chuck this wild fancy of mine, don a prairie skirt, and start leading the women's Bible study?"

A chuckle from somewhere behind him didn't help the situation. But the thought of Little Miss Fireball wearing petticoats, running around barefoot and pregnant did strike him as — he smiled against his will.

Wrong thing to do. He could see her unraveling, had glimpsed the same, desperate expression the day he'd chased after her in the ice arena, as if he'd inadvertently ran right into her secrets and opened all her wounds. Fighting the urge to put his hands on her shoulders and order her to take ten deep breaths or maybe a thousand, he doused his smile and looked her square in the eye. In his best calm-pastor tone he said, "You're jumping to all the wrong conclusions here, El."

"I told you love makes people do stupid things." A tear slid down her cheek and she let it roll, a bad sign that said she didn't care who saw her heartbroken. "But three strikes and you're out, bub." She closed her eyes. "It's over. Save your explanations for the grand jury."

"Ellie, listen to —"

"Dan, stop." Chief Sam's grip on his arm jerked him back to painful reality. "Let's just go down to the station. Wait until . . . things cool down."

Wincing, Dan looked at Sam. His friend wore a look of empathy, but Dan saw business in his eyes. "She's wrong."

The chief nodded. "C'mon."

Dan looked at Ellie and knew desperation and heartbreak lined his face. He wanted to rip his arm out of Sam's grip, scoop Ellie up, and run. She wasn't thinking clearly, reacting in standard Jammie Girl–style with her emotions instead of her head. It was no surprise that her brother had died rescuing her from herself.

That thought stopped him still. She stared at him, eyes wide, tears edging them, and he knew she saw his realization. Ellie knew her faults. She knew she had caused her brother's death. And knowing her guilt made her sacrifice her life trying to fill the gap.

"Oh, Ellie, please. I know you're desperate to find the arsonist, to prove yourself here, but this isn't the way. Stop trying so hard. You'll find the arsonist, I promise."

"I already did," she said coldly.

"Please believe me. I didn't do this."

"I saw him in the bathroom earlier. Before the fire." Guthrie Jones said it quietly but loud enough to ignite a hot murmur through the group.

If any doubt lingered in Ellie's eyes, it vanished in a blink. Only a harsh glitter remained. "I'm not desperate. I'm just seeing the truth for the first time. You might have loved me, but it was on your terms. I can't be the girl you want me to be."

He touched her hair, and she recoiled. It felt like a dagger through his chest. "I love you just the way you are."

"Yeah . . ." She nodded. "Right."

Sam tugged on his arm. Dan pinned her with one last look, praying she'd see the truth in his eyes.

She folded her arms across her chest and looked away as Sam led him out of the church.

21

The rain had stopped. Only a heavy fog and the very present hover of winter tinged the air. The clouds emptied, and they hung deflated in the sky, tearing into the fabric of the starry heavens. Ellie stood in the back entrance of the church, arms around herself, embracing her now destroyed blouse, her filthy, probably ruined dress pants, holding back a chill that emanated from her bones.

She'd found her arsonist. The man she loved. She wanted to curl into a ball and howl.

"Chief, the smoke is nearly gone. Do you want me to load up the fans?" Guthrie asked from the doorway. He looked ragged around the edges, with soot smudging his face, and moisture and char tangled in his brown hair, but he had energy radiating from him like a hot ember. Guthrie had not only followed the fire into the joists between floors, killing it as it tried to attack the insulation, but he'd then set up fans and chased the smoke out of the building.

One by one she'd dismissed the fire crew to their homes. Only Guthrie and Mitch remained. Why the big man had stayed to help, she didn't know, but she'd decided to be grateful, albeit wary. At least she had Guthrie nearby if Mitch decided to unveil some ulterior motives. "Yes, thank you, Guthrie."

"No problem, ma'am," he said and walked away.

"Guthrie?" she called, hoping to catch him.

He reappeared in the door. "Chief?"

She worked up a smile. "You did great today. I think you're turning into quite the firefighter."

His genuine grin seemed to balm the wounds Dan had inflicted.

"Thank you, Chief." He hesitated, and a sheepish smile appeared. "Do you . . . uh . . . need a ride back to the firehouse?"

"No." His concern touched her. Now here was a fellow who had real potential to be a gentleman, a stellar example of a Deep Haven firefighter. "Thank you, though."

"No problem," he said, shrugging. But disappointment tinged his eyes, enough that she actually felt guilty. Had she somehow led Guthrie to believe she felt more for him than was appropriate? Then again, she hadn't really put on the brakes with her relationship with Dan. The entire town probably knew by now that they'd been in love . . . no, that *he'd* been in love.

How could she love a man who would stop at nothing to derail her dreams?

She rubbed her arms, listening to the whir of the fans decelerate, the scrape of folding chairs being moved, grunts as Guthrie carried the fans up the stairs. She should be helping him, but frankly, she dreaded the next hour. Somehow standing here under the stars, wondering where her life had turned south, felt a thousand times simpler than filing charges against Dan for arson. Somewhere inside her she wanted to cling to the filament of hope that she was wrong.

Not that he'd ever forgive her.

She gulped a breath of sweet, rain-scented, autumn air, thankful they'd been able to contain the fire. She hated to think of Grace Church as a crisp scar on the hill.

But without their pastor, where would the congregation be?

Dan's sins would leave a painful gash on the community. Not to mention her own heart. His words still throbbed. She wasn't desperate. She simply put 200-percent effort into her job. Why not? How else was she supposed to make a difference, stand in the gap between life and death? She'd made promises to Deep Haven, to her firemen. To Seth. To God.

Seth's life for hers. She wouldn't have chosen it, but that's the card she'd been dealt so she'd added it to her hand without even considering discarding it.

Even if she did feel exhausted and alone at the end of the day, at least she'd done her best, invested her life in trying. That should count for something when she finally hung up her helmet. She may not leave behind a family, children, even a legacy in the Sunday school department, but she will have saved lives. Protected Deep Haven from more deaths.

She should have listened to her instincts and realized love wouldn't fit into her life.

Scraping up her courage, she entered the basement and pulled the door shut behind her, locking it. The fans had scattered the smell of smoke across the cinder-block hall. Moonlight pushed in through the windows, falling on the overturned chairs, the half-eaten plates of food, the cold beans on the buffet table. Maybe tomorrow she'd help the hospitality committee clean up and apologize to Bonnie for suspecting her. That was, after she finished meeting with the county attorney and outlining her case against Dan.

Pushing hard against her writhing stomach, she started up the stairs. A bulky figure stood at the top, just outside the fan of moonlight. She paused. "Hello?"

"It's me, Mitch." He moved into the light. His eyes studied her outline, spurring a flare of panic.

"What is it?"

"Can I talk to you?" His voice sounded . . . sober. Not a hint of snarl. Then again, maybe fatigue had dulled her senses.

She braced herself and climbed the stairs slowly, hoping Guthrie still lingered in the parking lot. "What do you want?"

Mitch blew out a breath. "I wanted to apologize." He stuck his hands in his pockets, a nonverbal I-won't-touch-you communiqué that she read with relief.

"Apologize?"

"For . . . coming on to you at the firehouse."

"Oh, that." She swallowed, glanced at the door, at the safety beyond. She didn't know how many times a woman had been attacked in the church vestibule, but she didn't want to start any statistics.

"I . . . had been drinking. And I was angry.

I promise, I wouldn't have hurt you." His face twisted, and the remorse in it almost touched her heart.

"I suppose you want to be let off probation?"

He shook his head. "I deserved it. I just . . . well, I thought you couldn't do your job. I was wrong."

She frowned. Was this the same man who'd sent her careening onto her backside at the General Store fire? "And now you think I can?"

He shrugged. "Let's just say I admire your determination. You've stuck in there, and you deserve a shot at this job." With chagrin on his face, his wolf demeanor turned into whipped puppy. "I guess a guy could learn a few things from you if he paid attention."

"Thanks . . . ," she said slowly. "What made you change your mind?"

He looked past her into the darkened sanctuary. "It was something Dan said to me a few days back." His face twitched with the confession. "He called me up, told me to watch myself, that he'd been hearing rumors that I was trying to cause you trouble."

Strange behavior for a man who should be grateful that suspicion pointed to Mitch. She pushed the thought to the back of her brain as she eyed the door, wondering if her noodle legs would get her across the room in the event Mitch morphed back into his hairy former self.

"Truth is, I was trying to cause you problems. I heard the talk about arson, and I thought if I could whip up the idea that you were trouble for this town, then the city council would give you the boot."

"And you'd slide into my job."

He shrugged. "I've never worked for a woman before. I didn't think you had it in you. But then I saw you run into the fire after Bruce, and something else Dan said kinda hit me." His eyes were dark as night and piercing as they held hers. " 'The greatest love is shown when people lay down their lives for their friends.' Dan said it's a Bible verse. And when I remembered how you ran in after Bruce at the fire I realized you had something I didn't."

She swallowed.

"Love for your fellowman."

His words pinged in her hollow heart. She felt light-headed and wondered if she actually swayed. No, she didn't have love for her fellowmen. She had love for herself, love for Seth. But true love didn't fuel her motives.

Fear did. Fear that she'd never fill the gap Seth left. Fear that she wasn't worthy of his death. "Thank you," she mouthed and heard the words emerge strained.

The same verse had been spoken at Seth's graveside, and even then it had the power to shake her to her core. Seth had given his life for her.

She didn't deserve it. She knew she'd only gone to Colorado to strut her courage, to prove her heroism to him and to her father. And she'd ended up fighting for her life under a fire shelter, her brother's body given to save hers.

"So, I just wanted to . . . smooth things out between us." Mitch gave a wry smile.

Ellie tried to focus on him and not the indictment searing her soul. "Thanks, Mitch. I appreciate that. We're . . . uh . . . smooth." She nodded crisply, edging toward the door. "Why don't you come into the office tomorrow? We'll . . . talk. Okay?"

He frowned, then nodded. "Are you okay?"

"Yes." She grabbed the door handle and scurried down the steps, closing the door behind her. The fire engine had left, Guthrie along with it. She walked across the parking lot toward her Jeep, still dodging the sting of Mitch's words.

She heard the shuffle of feet against pavement a second before a gloved hand went around her mouth, mashing her lips into her teeth. *What — !* Her pulse rocketed as instinct kicked in. She clawed at the hand at her mouth, thrashed her legs, hoping for purchase.

Her assailant crushed her to his chest with his other arm. "Don't move."

Her pulse filled her ears, drowning out her scream, distorting the voice. He had her neck in a death clamp that should have buckled her knees, but he dragged her to the pickup. The tailgate hung open. "Climb in."

Shaking, she tried to turn, aiming to gouge out her captor's eyes, but he muscled her onto the covered truck bed without mercy. She kicked at the tailgate as it went up, then was locked from the outside. All light snuffed out.

"Help! Dan!" She banged on the cover, pain shooting down her arm. While she pounded, the ridges of the pickup bed dug into her shoulder blades. The engine started. *Please, no!* She gave the roof one last kick as the pickup roared, jerked. Her face slammed into the metal, and she felt heat gather in her nose. Tears welled as warm blood dribbled into her mouth.

Darkness pressed against her, filling her pores. The old air, redolent with dust and the cloying odor of cleaning supplies, made her gag. Her brain began to spin. She scrambled toward the tailgate, toward the pinpricks of shadow and pressed her mouth against the opening while the truck roared out of the parking lot and into her nightmares.

"Am I under arrest?" Dan sat in Sam's office, arms clamped over his chest. The hard planes of fluorescence flooding the chief's office and raining down over the wooden straight-back chairs and the wide, oak desk did nothing to soften Dan's anger. He felt stripped and beaten, and if Sam's pursed lips were any indication, the fun was just starting.

Sam sat back in his desk chair, a faux leather piece that had seen better years, and shrugged. "Ellie can hold you for twenty-four hours. The law gives her that right as an officer of the fire department. Let's wait until she gets here." Fatigue weighted his face. Dressed in his smudged suit coat and rumpled dress shirt, the chief looked like he wanted to line up behind Dan and wring Chief Karlson's pretty neck. "What does she have on you?"

Dan held up his hands, a gesture of defeat. "I have no idea. I guess she found the

Sterno canisters the hospitality committee left in the office and linked them to the source of the Simmons fire."

"Did you really say you were responsible?" Sam leaned forward, knitted his hands together. Concern furrowed his brow.

Dan scrubbed his face with his hands. "I really don't remember. My shoulder was dislocated, drugs fogged my brain. I could barely figure out my own name. Who knows what I said?"

He didn't add that the only thing he did remember, quite and painfully clearly, was announcing to Ellie that she was some sort of dream girl. Yes, definitely pain had warped his mind.

Unfortunately, she was exactly that. Without a doubt, Ellie Karlson was the dream woman who had finally set a match to his heart and started it aglow. Since she'd entered his life, like lightning in the atmosphere, she'd charged it, ignited emotions he'd only begun to explore.

Losing her felt like ripping out his lungs.

"Well, she seems to think you're guilty. Or at least that you know something about it."

"What do *you* think?" Dan tried not to let it matter, but he'd spent his life trying to make an impact on this town. This wasn't quite how he wanted to do it. He studied

Sam's face.

The guy smiled, and relief rushed through Dan, tingling every nerve. "We'll clear you, Pastor."

"Thanks, Sam. At least you're on my side."

"Oh, I think after the initial shock wears off, you'll find a mob down here, demanding your release. They'll probably tar and feather Ellie and run her out of town on a rail."

That image hurt Dan right in the center of his chest. "That's a little overboard, don't you think?"

"Well, you've touched a lot of lives here." Sam shook his head. "She can't expect to accuse you without a fight."

He didn't know whether to cry for joy or sorrow. "I've touched lives?"

Sam looked at him as if he'd just spoken Japanese. "Yes. Of course. In fact, Leo Simmons was in here two days before he died — checking in for his parole — and he said you'd talked him back onto the wagon."

"He did?" Dan's throat thickened. "I didn't know that."

Sam nodded. "Said Guthrie got him a job at Smoky Joe's. Night shift. He seemed in high spirits."

"He didn't commit suicide."

Sam frowned. "No. I don't think so. He didn't have any alcohol in his blood either, according to the ME report."

Dan hung his head in his hands. Leo had a job. A future. A family. "I don't get it. Who would want to kill Leo?"

Sam shook his head. "Who would want to set fire to the Garden?" He turned to his computer, began to type.

Dan thought back to the Garden fire. He'd been outside, walking the strawberry gardens with Joe, discussing funding for the next year. The wailing siren sent them back to the lodge in a panic. From there, he only remembered the chaos, Ruby screaming, a number of the patrons trying to gather the residents into a huddle.

Sam looked over at him. "According to the incident report Ellie filed, you and Joe and Guthrie were the first on the scene."

"Guthrie was part of the catering committee." Dan said it quietly, a cold realization running through his veins. "He works for Smoky Joe's."

"Yes," Sam agreed slowly as if evaluating Dan's state of mind.

"Listen," Dan said, hating that his next words would betray a confidence, "a couple months ago, someone at Smoky Joe's caught Bonnie in a romantic clench with one of her employees. She never told me who the man was, but she denied it, said it was one-sided and that nothing happened. Unfortunately, her marriage had been on a downward slide for months so Matt didn't buy her denials. She and Matt didn't show up for their last counseling appointment." Dan cupped his hands over his mouth, thinking. "What if Guthrie had an affair with Bonnie?"

Sam frowned. "Oh, c'mon. I highly doubt that. Guthrie wasn't —"

"Wait. What if it wasn't an affair? What if Leo caught Guthrie, um . . . getting too friendly with Bonnie? Guthrie loves his job. Next to firefighting, he spends all his time at Smoky Joe's, cooking barbeque and tending the bar. Maybe he thought he'd lose his job? Maybe he set the fire to frighten his brother-in-law into silence?"

Sam seemed to sift through his words, looking for evidence. "Guthrie is a church-going man. You know that."

Sam's words caught him in the chest. Dan shook his head. "You're right. I shouldn't do to Guthrie what Ellie's doing to me."

"But . . ." Sam turned, typed into his computer, and sat back, arms crossed. "Yep. I thought so. Guthrie had a string of arson charges in his teenage years. Burned his father's pickup, torched a field behind their house, and I caught him and two other boys burning a shack just up Highway 61."

"Was he ever punished?"

"No. We wrote it off as childhood pranks."

"But you kept a record of it."

"Incident reports. I keep all my files."

"Could he be up to his old tricks?" Dan asked, not wanting desperation to push him back toward accusation.

Sam turned back to the computer, running the mouse, clicking. His face tightened. "I forgot about this."

Dan's heart fell about thirty feet and landed hard. "What?"

"Guthrie had an assault charge when he was seventeen. Did some community service."

Dan wanted to dive over the table and strangle the chief. "Assault?"

"Yes. I remember now. He stalked a girl in his school. Said she'd agreed to go to prom with him, then stood him up. She claims he made it up. Anyway, he assaulted her right outside her house, nearly in full view of the neighborhood. Her father stopped him before she was seriously hurt. Let's see here." He moved his mouse, clicking open new files. "Emilee Kingsly. I think I have a picture."

"Emilee, Bonnie's sister? The one who died in an auto accident a few years ago?"

"Yeah. Real shame. Poor Mitch. I don't think he ever got over losing her. As I recall, they were a pretty hot item while she was in college." Sam reached over and pulled out a photo from his file. "Senior picture. A real cutie, huh?"

Dan stared at her photo, a sick feeling of familiarity rushing over him. Braids, freckles, a smile that could light up a room. "Yeah," he said slowly. "Sorta reminds me of Ellie."

"If I remember correctly, we had to take a restraining order out against Guthrie. Finally ended up admitting him to a psych ward in Duluth. I think he was even hospitalized down in Minneapolis for a time. Some sort of chemical imbalance."

Dan sat very, very still. "A chemical imbalance that is brought on by stress? loneliness? fear? Maybe exacerbated by grief?" His hands clenched into fists as he fought panic. "Would you say that Guthrie might direct his frustrations toward women who reject him?"

Sam frowned.

"As in a fire chief who he's had a crush on, who he sees kissing, say, the town pastor?"

Sam's expression became pained. "Or one that reminds him of the girl he could never have?"

Dan closed his eyes, seeing Guthrie's face when he'd barged into Ellie's office.

"We'll warn her as soon as she gets here," Sam said quietly.

"Which will be — ?" Dan said, his heart already out of the chair, out of the building, and down the road to the fire station. "Page her."

"It's too late."

Dan turned, stared. Horror had him by the throat.

Mitch braced his timber arms on the doorframe, as if holding himself up. He was breathing hard. "Someone took her."

Dan jumped to his feet. "Why didn't you go after her?"

Mitch's look could have blistered skin from ten feet away. "He took my truck."

22

Ellie awoke. At least she thought she'd awoken — it was difficult to discern consciousness when pitch darkness pressed her eyeballs, teasing her with bulky forms, shadows, then nothing. A cold so thick it filled her nose with icicles made her gasp, pulling at the tape over her mouth. She fought back nausea at a sweet, slightly cloying smell she couldn't place.

She must be on a cement floor. Pain speared through her hips, her shoulders and, combined with the chilly air, saturated every muscle in her body. When she tried to move her hands, she discovered bonds slashing through the skin of her wrists. Her legs were bound too, although the binds affixed over her pants proved less biting. She concentrated hard, moving her extremities, horrified to realize little feeling remained.

Where was she? As the first rush of panic settled into a bone-deep terror, she tried to quiet her pounding heart and listen. A low hum, perhaps a generator or a refrigerator, rumbled in the background. Her own breath sounded labored, thick. And the cold — so cold it invaded every pore like the spikes of a sixteenth-century iron maiden — pulled at her concentration, willing her to surrender to the moan roiling in the center of her body.

Mitch had gone to a lot of trouble to make sure she didn't escape.

Why hadn't she seen through Mitch's veneer, his "aw shucks" apology? Because she'd wanted to believe that he had done an about-face, that his chagrin and regret intoned authenticity. She wanted to be the one left standing when the smoke cleared.

Instead, he'd showed her again that she was not only easily duped but hadn't earned a morsel of respect. Tears wet her eyes, and she blinked them back. No, she would not cry.

She could get herself out of this. She just had to stay alert. Not panic.

Opening her mouth, she worked her tongue out between her teeth and lips, then licked the glue. Her tongue seized, recoiling against the taste, but she forced it out, moistening the tape until it eased from her lips. Her neck ached as she worked. Then while she rested, she twisted her hands, forcing her wrists apart until she whimpered.

Feeling light-headed, she leaned her head back, hoping that she wasn't lying on fleas or roaches. She felt them crawl up her body even as she told herself nothing multi-legged could live in this temperature. She shook away the creeps and fought another wave of tears.

Well, this confirmed one thing. Dan was innocent.

She closed her eyes, listening to his pleas echo through her thick head. How could she have accused him?

Because she was desperate, just like he'd said. Desperate to leave behind a legacy in Deep Haven. In life. Desperate to be worth the price her brother had paid for her life.

She lay on her side, her tears running like melting ice over her nose, into her ear, wetting her dirty hair. But she wasn't worth it. She'd leave no marks in the surface of the world when she left. She'd die in this damp, freezing . . . wherever she was, and not a soul would even blink when she didn't clock in at the firehouse in the morning. Or worse, they'd think she'd slunk out of town, showing herself to be the skunk she was for accusing the town good guy of being a criminal. Mitch would win. He'd slide into the position as fire chief — good riddance, Ellie — and life would resume without a hiccup in this town.

Until, of course, the day they found her rotted, skeletal remains. And even then they'd remember her as the scoundrel who'd tried to send the town pastor to the clink. The town outcast.

He had leprosy. The words flashed through her memory. She held her breath, searching her mental files. She could hear the voice and knew it wasn't one that she knew well. Someone had spoken those words recently, and even then they'd been embedded in her mind.

The missionary who had spoken in church a month prior. Of course. Even then his story had rocked her, left an impression on the soft tissue of her soul. "Let me tell you a story," he had said. He stood barely taller than the podium, work-worn hands gripping its sides. The morning breeze had mocked his attempts to disguise his slightly balding head and instead tossed his hair without compassion. But his bright eyes reached out, even from the distance of ten rows back, and caught Ellie around the heart. She'd sat next to Liza, who'd reached over once and touched her hand. She dredged up his words again, realizing now why they'd resonated.

"There once was a king named Uzziah. He was sixteen when he became king and Second Chronicles tells us he did right in the eyes of the Lord." He'd held the spine of his Bible in one hand; it flopped over his open palm. "Don't miss, folks, the way the Bible, when talking about the kings, always gives us a description of their relationship with God before it gives us a rundown of their successes or failures."

He went on, that thought hovering over the one-hundred-plus congregation. "Uzziah sought God . . . and as long as he sought God, God gave him success. Chapter 26 lists his feats. He defeated armies that came against him, increased the wealth of Judah, built towers, and increased his army. Then . . . he got proud.

"He stopped praying. Stopped seeking the Lord. The Bible says he became 'unfaithful.' His pride in his own accomplishments took ahold of him. Thinking he'd earned God's respect, God's attention, he marched right into the holy place to offer sacrifices, with about eighty horrified priests on his tail."

Ellie had grabbed her pew Bible and paged to the chapter, running her finger along the verse when he read, "And they said to him, 'Leave the sanctuary, for you have been unfaithful; and you will not be honored by the Lord God.'

"So, this man, who'd accomplished so much for God, had forgotten the secret of his success. Seeking God." The missionary set his Bible on the podium, then braced his hands on either side, leaning into his sermon and lowering his voice. "That moment, right in front of the priests, God afflicted him with leprosy. From that day forward, he had to live separately from his family. He forfeited his kingdom to his son to rule, and when he died, the people said only one thing about this king who had been great.

"He had leprosy."

Ellie had closed her Bible, and was smoothing her hand across it as his low, soft, even dangerous words burned her.

Even now, she remembered trembling.

Oh, Lord, how will I be remembered? As a leper? An outcast? Someone to run from?

She curled into a ball, drawing up her knees. A leper.

No, my child, you are not a leper. You are lost.

She felt, more than heard, the words, and a sob racked her.

But I've let my pride rule me, my desire to be someone special.

You already are. You are Mine. The greatest love is shown when people lay down their lives for their friends. I've already proven My love for you in the sacrifice of My beloved Son. Now embrace it and know Me. It is My greatness and My grace that make you special. Because I, the Almighty God, chose you to be Mine.

Ellie stilled, letting that truth settle into her bones.

Abide in Me, and you will find peace. You will find hope. You will find purpose.

Liza's words, so gently spoken, in the Deep Haven park, drifted through her mind like a fragrance. *The more we work for Him, the more we seek Him. The circle of joy.*

She'd been running in circles most of her life, one step behind joy. Because she hadn't stopped to abide. To let His love settle in, fuel her steps. It wasn't that her job wasn't important; she simply hadn't let God make it meaningful.

Because she'd refused to believe she was important to Him. She'd been trying to get His attention, but she already — *always* — had it.

Ellie had God's attention in a sweltering fire shelter, and she had it while freezing on a cold cement floor. She had it sitting on the shore of Lake Superior with Dan or

400

alone while she searched a smoke-filled building. She had it whether she had logged miles for the gospel and saved hundreds of lives, or if she simply wiped toddlers' noses and did mounds of laundry.

She had God's attention because she was His child.

Ellie closed her eyes. *Oh, Lord, I want my life to make a difference, but I'm not sure where to start.*

Me. Start with Me.

Alone, shivering, dirty, and frightened, Ellie bowed to the command, tears flooding her eyes. *Yes, Lord. Forgive me for trying to go it alone. For not believing in Your love for me. Help me see my worth in Your eyes. Help me not to base it on my accomplishments but on my relationship with You. As Your child.*

His child. His beloved.

As she lay there, bound and broken, she felt the first wisps of that truth, that *immensity.* Getting a tight grasp on it would change everything, just like Dan's friend Katie had said.

Warmth, radiating from the inside of her body, swept through her veins, her pores, her soul, making her tremble. Oh yes, His child. Nothing more. Nothing less. All the days of her life. However long it might be.

A time frame, she thought as she lay there,

breathing in and out under a supernatural calm, which might have an ending sooner than she wanted. Not only could she not feel her feet, but fatigue seemed like a sweet, enticing blanket against the cold, and her breathing required new effort, heavy as it was to draw into her lungs.

She closed her eyes and in the back of her mind decided that the new redolence filtering into her dark coffin smelled faintly of smoke.

Dan raced Mitch and Sam to the parking lot of the city municipal building. The night had turned black, the wispy clouds that remained of the day's deluge pushed north, and a new storm front headed in from the west, drawing a shadow over the stars, the moon.

Dan stopped, stood still, adrenaline burning through him, helplessness raging in his veins. Rounding on Mitch, ten steps behind him, he shot him a silent plea.

"I don't know, Preach. It was dark. I think he wore a mask. All I saw was him throwing her into the back of my pickup. I missed him by twenty feet." Mitch was still breathing hard, and the man looked genuinely stricken.

Sam opened his car door. "I put out an

APB for her, and I'll have a cruiser run through the neighborhoods."

Dan slid into the front seat. "Where are we going?"

"I don't know." Sam shoved his key into the ignition. "I thought we'd start with the firehouse."

The door to the fire station was open, a yawn of darkness where the engine took up daily residence. "Where's the pumper?" Mitch asked in a voice that matched Dan's horror. "I didn't hear a siren or a call."

"Is it still at the church?"

Mitch shook his head. "I thought Guthrie brought it back to the house."

"Guthrie," Dan growled. "What about Smoky Joe's?"

Sam radioed in their destination, while Dan braced his feet against the floorboard. Perhaps Sam had done time as a state trooper. He zipped up the highway at a speed that shed tears.

They saw the blaze a block away. A glow of flickering light against the haze of night. Dan's mouth opened, and out of him came a noise that sounded painfully like a groan.

Sam grabbed his radio. "Structure fire. Smoky Joe's. Highway 61. We need all crews." He faced Dan, a hollow, pained look as he finished. "The engine is already here."

Dan was out of the car before Sam stopped, a step in front of Mitch, who caught his arm. "You can't go in there."

The restaurant, a stand-alone wooden building a stone's throw out of town, billowed out ugly black smoke like a coal furnace. Flames licked out of the back windows; smoke tumbled out of the front door.

"It looks like a grease fire from the color of the smoke, lots of fuel, burning fast." Mitch had turned into a captain. He gripped Dan by the shoulder, half dragging him to the engine.

"Ellie!" Dan ripped out of Mitch's grasp, ran for the house.

Mitch had to tackle him. Dan landed, chin in the rutted weeds. It peeled a layer of skin.

"It's too hot, man! Wait for your gear!"

Dan twisted and shrugged the man off, eyes tearing against the smoke that scraped the air. "What if Ellie's in there?"

Mitch pulled him back to the engine. "Help me get out the hose."

Dan's hands shook as he unlatched the door, unhooked the hoses. Ellie couldn't survive that inferno. But maybe . . . okay, so maybe she wasn't in there. Maybe it was a coincidence.

"There's my truck," Mitch growled under

his breath and nodded toward the back.

Dan tightened his jaw, feeling like he might lose his supper, and rushed to the truck. It was parked behind the building, the tailgate still ajar. "Ellie!"

Dan heard movement and whipped around the truck.

Guthrie. The man sat, knees up, curled into a ball, hands over his helmet. He wore his turnout gear and air pack.

When he looked at Dan, his face wasn't his own. Wild fear ravaged his eyes, whitened his color.

Dan stood in paralyzed shock a second before he snapped. He seized Guthrie by the collar, yanking him to his feet, not caring that he had a reputation or that this man was a member of his flock. Not caring that Guthrie obviously hovered on the raw edge of hysteria. "Where is she?" he yelled.

The intensity must have rattled Guthrie, for the man's eyes focused, darkened. Then his mouth opened in a howl that sounded more like a wounded animal's than a human's.

"Where, Guthrie?" Dan said, trying to gentle his voice. It wasn't easy with a thousand gallons of adrenaline surging through him. He took off Guthrie's helmet, started to wrestle him out of his coat. "I'll go get her; just tell me where."

Guthrie blinked at him, then nodded. "The meat cooler. I . . . I didn't want to hurt her." He shrank to his knees, his hands over his face, sobs now racking him so violently that Dan had to fight them to get off the jacket. "I just wanted to rescue her. Prove to her that I could be . . ."

Dan stared at him, on the brink of ripping the words right out of his throat.

Guthrie looked up. "I just wanted her to love *me*." His eyes glazed. "Why can't she love me?"

He shook out of Dan's grip, backing away, his eyes widening. "But she loves *you*. I heard her calling out for you when I threw her in the truck." When his face twisted, some sort of mania-induced hope filled his face, his voice. "You'll rescue her, right? You'll do it."

Dan dropped to his knees. "I need the boots."

Guthrie worked them off, as if eager now to assist. He stripped out of the bunker pants and Dan put them on, snapped the suspenders up, and dived into the boots. The SCBA gear under his arm, he hurried toward the engine.

Guthrie grabbed him by the arm and Dan whirled, not sure if the man was trying to stop him. Guthrie shoved the helmet onto his head. "Be careful," he said, his eyes strangely bright.

Dan nodded, not sure exactly what to say.

Mitch had already unfurled the hose. John Benson had arrived, and one look at him told Dan that John knew the stakes. He was latching his coat, pulling on his gloves. Dan pulled on his mask and hood as the fire roared behind them, now sending a plume of sparks into the sky. "Guthrie stashed her in the meat locker."

"What?" Mitch's face darkened. "I just ordered the electricity shut off. She'll asphyxiate in there without the recirculating oxygen."

The picture of Ellie, white-faced in a death pallor, gasping for her last, poisoned breath filled his brain with icy pain. "I'm going in after her."

"No. We need two men on the hose," Mitch barked. "We have a better chance of saving her if we don't lose you too. We need to do this right, how she taught us."

Dan glared at him, then closed his eyes. *Oh, God, please help me!* He could run in, his fears unbridled, and leave behind common sense, or he could listen to his captain and hope they beat a path to the kitchen door. Either way, it would be in God's hands. Frustration felt like a living beast crawling up his stomach. He tightened Guthrie's helmet onto his head. "Okay. Let's go."

Dan tucked himself behind John as they sprinted toward the building with the limp hose. "She's in the meat locker! Near the back," Dan hollered, adrenaline garbling his voice through the mask amplifier. If he wanted John to understand him, he'd have to stay calm. He swallowed and repeated his words.

At the entrance John nodded and turned on the nozzle. The spray hit the flames with a serpent's hiss, loud and long and agonized. Steam buffeted Dan's mask while he wrestled the hose forward. They stepped into the building, staying low, spraying near the base, just as Ellie had drilled into them. Two steps. The blackness felt alive, moving in shadows. Dan made out nothing, not even John's form in front of him. He only knew the rush of the water, the steam, the pulsating hose in his hands.

And then hands behind him moved him aside. "It's Ernie. Go." When Ernie stepped up into his place, Dan dropped to the floor. Ellie would skin him alive for plowing into a fire without a buddy, but he'd apologize later. He reached out, knocking over what he surmised was a chair. He felt like a snail, slow, encumbered, blind as he crawled through the restaurant, the smoke mocking the efforts of his feeble flashlight. The heat pressed him down onto the floor, and dread seeped into his soul.

How would she survive this?

His head bumped hard into a wall, and as he felt it, he placed himself at the bar. Working his way along it, he hesitated at the lip. Through the darkness he made out orange-and-yellow flames, beckoning, outlining the kitchen door.

And just beyond, the meat locker.

"I need water!" he yelled, then realized he was wasting his breath. The fire devoured his words.

Gathering his feet, he tucked his light into his pocket and scrambled toward the flames, then dived.

He hit the door of the meat locker, fought for the handle, wrenched it open, and threw himself inside, closing the door behind him as the fire surged toward the new oxygen supply.

The cold breath fogged his mask, and the blackness felt as surreal and teasing as the smoke. He reached for his flashlight, flicked it on.

He gritted his teeth against the sudden

lurching of his heart when he saw Ellie, eyes closed, curled into a ball in the center of the floor.

23

Ellie roused to hands on her shoulders. Her eyes felt frozen; her throat burned with every breath. She had tried to fight the wave of sleep, vaguely aware of voices in her mind screaming at her to stay awake. But she no longer felt the pain spiking through her joints, the cold felt less brutal, and her mind — oh, she'd found sweet oblivion remembering —

"Ellie!"

When she heard the mumbled voice, tears flooded her eyes. She fought to open them as someone ripped at her bonds, growling in frustration. She conjured up a thought through her foggy mind — her wrists had to be bleeding because she'd spent the better part of the last twenty minutes rubbing them raw. Or maybe it had been longer than that.

Suddenly the tape snapped. She cried out while it tore from her wrists, a sudden flash of pain after so much numbness. She hunched over, breathing hard as she brought her hands around.

"Hang in there, honey," the fireman said.

Her heart jumped into her throat, pricking new tears. *Dan?*

He rolled the tape down her legs, off her feet as she awoke every muscle and lifted her head to look.

Yes, Dan, and he looked as if someone had bludgeoned him. Pale, eyes red, even through his mask. She pulled him down next to her. "You found me."

He dumped his helmet, ripped off the hook, and levered his mask from his head. "Where are you hurt?"

He moved his mask to her mouth, and sweet, compressed air rushed over her. Despite the coolness, it felt like fire on her frozen throat. She shook her head in answer.

He lay down next to her. "The kitchen is on fire. We're trapped. We'll have to wait until they find us." Taking off his jacket, he draped it over them, cocooning them in instant warmth, his flashlight lighting one side of his face. "I'm sorry I didn't find you sooner."

She scrabbled to focus, fight the press of sleep. "I can't believe you came in after me." Her voice sounded drowsy. But one thought centered her. He had tracked her down and risked his life to save her in the face of her betrayal. The realization left her weak. She didn't deserve this man. She wiggled away from the mask. "Breathe."

He obeyed, drinking in air, then covered her face again with his mask. "Of course I'm going to come after you. I love you. Don't you get it?"

She felt a sob build and pushed it back. "I want to. I do. But why?" Her voice was muffled against the mask.

"Because you're you," he said softly, as if they were sitting on the beach instead of huddling under his coat, buddy breathing. "Because God knew I needed someone who makes me feel, makes me want to embrace the day. You set my life on fire, Ellie."

"Is that good?" She pushed the mask toward him and watched him breathe, his eyes locked on hers. She dug her hand into his suspender, drawing him toward her.

"Very good," he said, his voice thick with emotion.

"Oh, Dan, I'm sorry I suspected you. What was I thinking?" She hiccupped back a sob. "I'm an idiot. I should never have suspected you."

He moved the mask from his face toward hers. "I forgive you. We'll talk about it later.

That, and why you seem to try so hard to keep me out of your life."

"No." She pulled the mask away, aware now that his face was only inches from hers. She could feel his five-o'clock shadow, feel his warm breath on her skin. His eyes held hers with such compassion she just wanted to burrow into his arms and hide from reality — the air heavy and filled with poison and a fire blocking their road to freedom.

A good fire chief would think of a way to escape.

Only she didn't want to be a fire chief right now. She wanted to be a terrified and wounded woman. She wanted to be protected, rescued, and cherished. She wanted to be the woman Dan needed, the woman she saw reflected in his eyes. "Dan, I'm not going to keep you out of my life. I'm ready to hang up my helmet. I'll do this on your terms."

Dan returned the mask to her face, forcing her to breathe. "That's just the fear talking. I know —"

She shook her head. "You don't know. I'm tired. Tired of trying to be enough for myself, for everyone else. I want to rest." She closed her eyes, her words settling deep. *I just want to abide. To be.*

"I'm not going to let you give up."

414

A *whoosh,* then water lashed them, drenching them. When Ellie jerked, Dan's arm tightened around her. Pinpricks of pain started at her legs, worked their way up her spine. She felt the temperature in the room immediately warm as the heat from the kitchen fire invaded the room. "Where am I?"

"In the fridge."

"The fridge? As in, a side of beef?"

He nodded. "It's better than being barbequed, don't you think?"

"Immensely." She smiled at the relief that washed over Dan's face. "Let me warm up and then we'll talk about my future as a fire chief."

The firemen turned the room into a cave of steam. Water dripped from the walls, the sides of beef, the wire shelves. Dan held Ellie under his coat until the deluge stopped. When John lifted Dan's coat, the fireman resembled some sort of outer-space alien in his mask amidst a fog of cooled smoke. "You guys okay?"

Ellie coughed through the mask Dan held to her face. "Yeah. Thanks."

Dan climbed to his knees, then lifted Ellie into his arms. To his complete shock, she looped one arm around his neck and pressed the mask back to his face. "Get me out of here."

"Aye, aye, Chief," Dan said, grinning.

John draped the coat over her, and she tucked her head under it as Dan picked his way out of the building. On a second hose, Simon and Doug battled a wall of flame still fighting for life on the far side of the kitchen. The smoke cover had lessened. Dan scanned the charred ceiling and a few burned tables before he stumbled out. The ratio of damage to smoke made him wonder if most of the damage was confined to the kitchen.

The rescue truck bathed the restaurant in halogen light. A crowd stood behind three parked police cruisers. An extra water truck had arrived, now pumping water into the hose that snaked around the back. Two other hoses ran from the engine, which sucked water from a nearby water main. Craig manned the gauge on the pumper. Mitch, now in his turnouts, came to relieve Dan of his burden, but Dan shook his head.

Ellie recoiled into the jacket and frowned at Mitch. "I thought . . ."

Mitch drew back, and Dan thought he saw hurt flicker across Mitch's expression.

"Mitch saw you being kidnapped, honey," Dan said softly, not quite sure why Ellie wore a pale look of confusion. "He ran to the police station — probably saved your life."

Ellie blinked at him, then stretched out her arm from under the jacket, touching Mitch's coat. "Thanks, Mitch."

Dan looked at the two of them, at something passing between them, feeling unease coil in his stomach. Did they — ?

And then Ellie wrapped her arms around Dan's neck. "My feet are starting to come alive, and they hurt," she whispered. "Can you hang on to me just a bit longer?"

He met her eyes, filled with a new texture that he hoped was trust, and nodded. Oh yeah, he could hold her into the next century if she wanted. Especially the way she was curled into his chest for the entire population of Deep Haven to see. He tightened his grip and carried her to the rescue unit. Dan sat on the bumper, put Ellie in his lap.

Steve Lund had arrived with his ambulance and hustled over a stretcher. "Hey, Preach, can I check her over?"

Dan grinned over the top of Ellie's head. "Only if you give her back."

Ellie had her hand in Dan's suspender. "No. He can check me right here."

Dan raised an eyebrow at Steve, who

frowned.

"Whatever," he stammered. He knelt before them and checked her pulse, her blood pressure. "I want to get some oxygen in you. Clear out your lungs."

Reluctantly, Ellie sat up, and Dan helped her over to the stretcher. She sat on it, his turnout coat around her shoulders, her huge eyes pinned to his as Steve put a mask over her face. She pulled it away. "Don't go far. I want to finish our talk."

Okay, so who was this woman? Had he rescued the right girl? What had Guthrie done with the "don't help me, I can do it myself" spitfire he'd come to know . . . and love? But he liked this version too — sooty, her hair in mud-caked tangles, nestled in his coat, eyes glued to him as if he were some sort of movie hero. Yeah, he'd take occasional appearances of this Ellie Karlson without argument.

Somehow he tore his eyes from hers, away from the weird sensation that something spectacular had happened in that locker, and watched the fire. Two men from the St. Francis Township crew were on ladders, cutting holes in the roof. The flames had vanished; only charcoal gray smoke plumed out of the roof. Dan turned, looking for Sam. He spotted him posed next to his car, talking to Mayor Romey Phillips. Something about Sam's dark expression hit Dan funny.

He crouched and arranged his coat tighter around Ellie's shoulders. "I'll be right back."

The night felt moist and heavy as he walked toward the duo. He was drenched in sweat and reeked of smoke. If someone stood too close to him, they were liable to need smelling salts. He looked about the furthest thing from pastoral, but he felt, in his soul, that someone needed protecting.

"I'm just saying that maybe this wouldn't have happened if it hadn't been a woman." Romey's voice sounded tired.

"What wouldn't have happened?" Dan asked too brusquely to be considered polite. He could almost see the mayor flinch.

"How ya doing, Dan?" Sam asked. He clapped him on the shoulder. "How's Ellie?"

"Alive. Brave." Dan crossed his arms. "What are you saying, Mayor?"

Romey lifted his chin as if resenting the fact that Dan towered over him. "I found us a new chief. He's from Iowa but has about ten years' experience. He's ready to start on Monday. Permanent."

Dan never felt like slugging someone so many times in one day. "What?" He shook his head. "What about Ellie? She's done her job."

Romey smiled, utilizing his PR skills, something Dan had obviously abandoned. "She has, yes. But you have to admit that her presence here has caused an unfortunate . . . situation."

"You can't blame her for another man's obsession. In fact —" Dan ran his hand through his hair — "I don't think you can even blame Guthrie. My gut tells me that his sister's death has knocked him more off balance than we imagined."

The mayor nodded, genuine empathy in his eyes. "I agree, Pastor. It's just that Ellie . . . well, I think the men would react better to working under a man."

Dan clenched his jaw and stared at Romey. "That's probably the most chauvinistic —"

"— and true statement I've heard in almost three months." Ellie limped up next to Dan. "They would. Having a woman at the helm breeds all sorts of problems."

"Even if she is able?" Dan asked curtly. He cupped his hand under Ellie's elbow to support her.

Ellie smiled, and when she looked up at Dan, he saw gratitude, even humor in her eyes. "Yes." Then, taking a deep breath, her smile faded. "Mayor, I've appreciated this job. It's been an . . . adventure." She held out her hand. "But I don't think Deep Haven is ready for a woman fire chief yet. And I'm not ready to be her, even if Deep Haven was ready."

"Ellie —"

Ellie shook Romey's hand. "Thank you for the opportunity. I'll clear my things out tomorrow, right after I finish the paperwork on tonight's events."

She left Sam, Romey, and Dan standing openmouthed as she limped back to her stretcher.

"What did you say to her?" Sam asked.

Dan shook his head, completely baffled. "Nothing. I . . . why is she doing this?"

Romey's eyes sparked with admiration. "Maybe she cares more about this town than she does about herself."

Dan turned and stalked back to her. No. This was *not* right. Ellie deserved this job. She'd fought prejudice, long hours, and an arsonist for her life. He wouldn't let her quit.

She sat on the stretcher, holding the oxygen mask to her mouth. "Hey," she said, pulling the mask away. "It's the right thing, you know."

"No, I don't know." Dan slid to his knees,

gripped her arms. "This job is your life. You can't quit."

"I can. I do." She grinned at him. He wanted to throttle her. "I don't need this job. In fact, I don't even want this job anymore."

Okay, now really, he was going to have to shake the truth out of Guthrie. Where was the real Ellie?

She touched his face, her fingers light and soft and sending flames through him. "I realized while I was trapped that I've been working my entire life trying to find the one thing I already had."

He frowned.

"God's love."

He had no words when he opened his mouth. Only confusion.

"Seth used to say to me, 'God is enough.' It drove me crazy. I never got it. Seth was my parents' golden child. He was going to follow in Dad's footsteps. Be a fire —"

"Chief." Dan cupped her face. "And when he died, you thought you had to take his place. Earn your right to live."

She smiled, a wobbly admission. "Something like that. Only I never felt good enough. Never felt like I'd done enough or said the right things."

He nodded, his throat thick, understanding better than she could ever comprehend.

"But I realized that God isn't looking for my outstanding deeds. He just wants me to realize His love for me. To embrace it. To find purpose in it."

"John 15. Have you been listening to my sermons?"

"I have. And they finally sunk in. Along with Seth's words: 'God is enough.' The last time he said them to me, we were fighting about my working on the hotshot crew. I'd been there about a month, and the fires were getting worse. We'd already had one crew nearly lose their lives. We were sitting together on a rocky outcropping, overlooking the fire camp three days before his death. He had a far-off look and told me, 'God is enough, Ellie. He has to be. In this life, there is no other answer.'

"You know, I never knew how much I idolized Seth until I realized I'd never find another hero. . . ." She dug both hands into Dan's shirt, pulling him close. "Until, of course, I came to Deep Haven."

Then she leaned forward and kissed him, her lips moist, tender; and he felt in her touch the honesty of her words. She pulled away but kept her face close. "God is enough and so are you, Dan. I love you."

He wanted to swing her up in his arms

and dance. No, fly. "You do?"

"Yeah." She rubbed his cheek. "Probably since the day you landed at my feet."

He pushed her grimy hair from her face, drew her into his arms. "Do you remember what I said to you?"

When she smiled, his heart leaped to attention. "Uh-huh. But you can remind me."

"I asked you if you were a dream. My dream. And you are. Marry me, Jammie Girl."

She looked beautiful in a blush. "I'm not sure I'll be much good at the pastor's-wife thing."

"I think you'll be a regular fireball."

She wrinkled her nose at him, and he kissed her again, this time taking his time, not caring that most of his congregation watched from the sidelines. This was his woman. His fire chief. His perfect match. "Is that a yes?"

"And a promise." Her radiant eyes twinkled with mischief.

He laughed, amazed that every moment with her seemed better than the last. "Listen, if you change your mind about the firefighting thing —"

She raised her eyebrows, teasing. "Over your dead body?"

He laughed. "No. I'm right behind you.

I'm just wondering if I can call you Chief at home too."

"You can call me anything you want, as long as you cook for me."

He chuckled, kissed her again. "Aye, aye, Chief."

She wove her fingers into his hair, her face shining through the grime. She'd never looked more breathtaking. "Well, now, Preach, that's the kind of response I've been waiting for." And when she kissed him, it confirmed what he'd known for nearly three months.

Ellie Karlson was the dream he'd been waiting for all his life.

EPILOGUE

Ellie leaned her forehead against the windowpane, watching snow peel from the leaden clouds. From the front window of Edith Draper's A-frame cabin, Ellie could see the residue of foam and debris washed onshore by Lake Superior's winter unrest. Crispness laced the air, as if winter in all her gusto waited to exhale.

For the first time in years, she anticipated the transition between fall and winter. It poured through her senses, and she knew it had nothing to do with the approaching holidays, the intoxicating smell of Thanksgiving turkey, or the fact that snow would soon cleanse the landscape and bedazzle the trees in brilliance.

No, the feeling that rushed through her in quiet moments over the past three weeks could be nothing but pure and untainted hope. The kind that comes with a keen knowledge of unfailing love.

God's unfailing love.

Love without rules, without expectations, without a list of qualifiers.

Warm hands slid over her shoulders, and she leaned back into Dan's embrace. He'd let his whiskers grow since Sunday, knowing she liked the scruffy look and now rubbed them against her cheek. "Dinner is nearly ready."

"Mmm," she responded, closing her eyes, relishing his nearness. Oh, how good God had been, giving her not only peace but this man with whom to share it. "Are Noah and Anne here yet?"

She'd met Dan's friends at their wedding almost a week ago. Noah Standing Bear looked like a pure bad boy, with his massive size, his shoulder-length black hair tied back in a ponytail, and eyes that seemed a thousand years wise. But when he'd swept his arms around his bride, Edith's niece Anne Lundstrom, the guy appeared downright princely. Beast into beauty.

And if that weren't enough to push tears into her eyes, Dan had grabbed her hand and squeezed.

Yes, hope had many different facets, and she loved every one of them.

"Pastor Dan!" Jeffrey Simmons ran up and flung his arms around Dan's legs. The boy's strength had returned with gusto and his emotional healing along with it under Joe and Mona's blanket of love. "Come and see the parade. They have a giant floating SpongeBob SquarePants!"

"Who?" Ellie asked when Dan bent down to swing the boy up into his arms. She could hear the laughter of Joe and Jordan in the other room, probably in a tangle of arms and legs as they watched the Macy's Thanksgiving Day Parade.

Dan angled for the den while Ellie made her way into the kitchen. Mona held Angelica on her hip while she stirred the gravy. A twenty-plus-pound, golden brown Butterball sat on the counter, calling to Ellie's stomach. Edith had tented a piece of tin foil over the top to hold in the heat. Still, Ellie longed to pick up a fork and dig out a piece of the oyster, the succulent part under the leg. She must have put on ten pounds the last few weeks, and this kind of offering wouldn't offer her waistline any mercy. Even though she wasn't pulling duty as the local fire chief, her job as deputy chief and investigator required that she at least *fit* into her uniform.

"Where's Edith?" Ellie asked.

"She went upstairs to phone Ed."

"Ed?" Ellie grabbed a pile of silverware

and began to set it on the table. "Have I met him?"

Mona laughed. "You'd know if you met Edith's son. He's legendary in Deep Haven. Was a real lady-killer."

"Sorta like Dan, huh?"

Mona raised one groomed eyebrow. "You're not serious, are you?"

She could never figure out why everyone in town acted like she'd thawed the ice man or something. Dan had always been . . . well, more than sufficiently warm and friendly with her. "Um, well . . ."

Mona laughed and tickled Angelica, who burst out in a grin. "It's probably a good thing Auntie Ellie doesn't get it, don't you think, Angie? We wouldn't want her to know that she has Pastor Dan under a spell, do we?"

Ellie frowned but couldn't help a giggle. If anyone felt under a spell, it was she, especially with the diamond sparkling on her finger and the way her parents embraced Dan like the son they'd always wanted. Yes, she'd entered some sort of fairy tale. "So, is Ed in town?"

Mona shook her head and continued stirring the gravy. "No. He lives up north, out in the bush somewhere. I think he's a missionary." Angelica reached for the spoon and nearly dumped the pot. "Oh!"

"I'll take her." Ellie reached for the little girl, but Angelica clamped her flabby legs around Mona's waist. Mona offered a silent apology.

Ellie waved it off. "I love stirring, I think," she said as she took the whisk from Mona.

"Just make sure to get out all the lumps." Mona moved away and hitched Angelica up on her hip. "I don't think Ed has been home for years. He left with some sort of dark secret that I can't seem to pull out of Edith. Once I overheard her and Ernie Wilkes talking about him at a picnic, but the second I walked up, they switched topics faster than the weather. I always felt like I'd intruded."

"I have a feeling there are quite a few secrets in Deep Haven," Ellie said, thinking about Guthrie and the fact he'd kept his mental illness hidden for over a decade. She and Dan visited him at the Hennepin County Medical Center locked ward on the morning before the wedding. Not only had his depression lessened because of the medication, but it looked like the county would weigh his illness into the murder charges. Ellie hoped that he'd be able to live in a facility that might attend to his needs. After she'd heard his confession and his motives, it scared her how much she related to Guthrie's need to be loved and accepted.

And it hadn't helped matters any that she did, indeed, bear an uncanny resemblance to the lady Guthrie had loved. Poor guy just wanted to be a hero . . . to matter to someone. He did matter — to God. And in cultivating her new habit of spending time with God every morning, she'd added Guthrie's salvation and healing to her daily list of prayer requests.

"I'm here!" Fingers of cold whooshed in around Liza as she stomped into the warm kitchen. Snowflakes dotted her dark hair, and she looked like a Siberian ski bunny in her faux leopard-skin jacket and black bell-bottom stretch pants. She held out a box. "My contribution to T-Day dinner."

While Liza shucked off her jacket, Ellie opened the box. It looked like lumpy oat-meal. However, as the tantalizing aroma of cinnamon and nutmeg escaped from the box, she decided she might be game to try it.

"Apple crisp. It's a Beaumont specialty." Liza plucked it out of Ellie's hands and pulled the pie plate out of the box. "It's good with peaches and pears too."

"Wow, she's an artist *and* a chef," Ellie said. She glanced at her own paltry attempts

431

to help. "I think I killed the gravy." She poked at a dumpling-sized lump. "Sorry."

Liza gave her a hug and turned off the heat under the pot. "Don't worry. No one cares. It's the company that counts."

Edith thumped down the stairs. "I just saw Anne and Noah drive up." She glowed like a kid at Christmas.

Thirty minutes later, they joined hands around the table, Ellie trying not to glance at the lumpy gravy and eyeing instead a choice piece of dark turkey meat on the platter. On one side of her, Dan held her hand, his thumb playing with the solitaire diamond ring he'd given her. On the other side, Liza was making goofy faces at Angelica on Mona's lap, whose grin seemed to light up the table. Across from her, Joe and Mona locked hands with Jeffrey and Jordan, and the smile on their faces swelled a lump in Ellie's throat.

Edith cleared her throat, looking at her guests and smiling at her husband, a quiet man who seemed to enjoy letting Edith have her yenta moment. "I'm so glad all of you have joined us for this day of thanksgiving," she said. "Will you pray for our meal, Dan?"

Dan nodded. His gaze went around the table, stopped at Ellie. She tingled to her toes at his smile. "Before I pray, I want to answer a question that Joe asked me a few months ago." He looked at Joe, who wore a frown. "What exactly does God require of us? Especially those who live surrounded by friends or family? By churches full of the healthy, as well as the hurting?"

Dan took a deep breath. He lifted Ellie's hand and kissed it. "I think the answer is in John 15:17: 'Love each other.' Love that is authentic. Love that erases condemnation. Love that means laying down your life for another. And then we will bear fruit. Fruit that will last to eternity."

Amen, Ellie thought as she bent her head in prayer.

A NOTE FROM THE AUTHOR

In my author's note in *Tying the Knot,* I wrote of my journey to understanding the depth of God's grace and how embracing that gave me the courage to surrender my future to God, including committing to return to the mission field in Russia, if He chose. Indeed, on New Year's Eve 2002 we decided to return, and by the time March rolled around, I had filled containers with supplies and even felt an excitement building for the next term. I knew in my heart that God had good things planned.

I just didn't expect how He would accomplish them.

Over our plans to return hovered the increasing threat of changing visa laws, continued violence, and our children's emotional needs for security. We knew that life might be difficult, but we clung with tenacity to our plans. Even when missionaries began to be ousted from the country, we gritted our teeth and said, "We will return!"

Perhaps that is why it felt like a knife to the chest when God said no. He slammed one door after another to our return and miraculously opened the door to a new chapter of our lives in northern Minnesota, in a tiny town where we'd always dreamed of living. We stumbled toward this new opportunity like confused children, looking back over our shoulders asking, "Are You sure?" But God put peace in our hearts, confirming His plans. More than that, He gave us a place to live where we could dig roots, heal, and recharge. He sent us to our very own Deep Haven.

However, it was in this peaceful place that questions began to simmer in my soul. I'd been a missionary, either in training or on the field, for fifteen years. My life plans had been to be a career missionary. Now what? Did my fifteen years of sacrifice etch any foothold in the kingdom of God? Did I still matter to God if I didn't live my life on the cutting edge of evangelism, my life poured out for that one purpose?

Again, God spoke to me through writing. *Yes,* He said. *You matter. Your life matters, your sacrifices matter, your dreams matter. Because you are My beloved child. And your dreams of making a difference in your world will be accomplished through Me, as you abide, one day at a time, in My love. For apart from Me you can do nothing.*

Like Ellie, I've surrendered loved ones and precious moments for the sake of a goal. Like Dan, I've looked back, wondering if I made an impact, wrestling with past choices or how I could have served better. And through writing *The Perfect Match,* God showed me that only by turning my eyes on Him and letting Him feed me is there any hope of bearing fruit.

I hope this thought encourages you. Life with Christ bears fruit, whether you serve in full-time missions proclaiming the gospel overseas or full-time missions wiping runny toddler noses in the middle of Iowa. And this fruit, my friends, is eternal.

Thank you for reading *The Perfect Match.* I'm blessed that you would spend time in Deep Haven with me. May you find the joy and hope of abiding in Christ, and may the truth of His love for you radically impact your life.

In His Grace,
Susan May Warren

ABOUT THE AUTHOR

Susan May Warren recently returned home after serving for eight years with her husband and four children as missionaries in Khabarovsk, Far East Russia. Now writing full-time as her husband runs a lodge on Lake Superior in northern Minnesota, she and her family enjoy hiking and canoeing and being involved in their local church.

Susan holds a BA in mass communications from the University of Minnesota and is a multipublished author of novellas and novels with Tyndale, including *Happily Ever After*, the American Christian Romance Writers' 2003 Book of the Year and a 2003 Christy Award finalist. Other books in the series include *Tying the Knot* and *The Perfect Match*, the 2004 American Christian Fiction Writers' Book of the Year. *Flee the Night, Escape to Morning*, and *Expect the Sunrise* comprise her romantic-adventure, search-and-rescue series.

Finding Stefanie is the sequel to *Reclaiming Nick* and *Taming Rafe* and the third book in Susan's new romantic series.

Susan invites you to visit her Web site at **www.susanmaywarren.com**.

She also welcomes letters by e-mail at **susan@susanmaywarren.com**.

The employees of Thorndike Press hope you have enjoyed this Large Print book. All our Thorndike, Wheeler, and Kennebec Large Print titles are designed for easy reading, and all our books are made to last. Other Thorndike Press Large Print books are available at your library, through selected bookstores, or directly from us.

For information about titles, please call:
  (800) 223-1244

or visit our Web site at:
  http://gale.cengage.com/thorndike

To share your comments, please write:
  Publisher
  Thorndike Press
  10 Water St., Suite 310
  Waterville, ME 04901